MISSING

CATHERINE LEE

For more information about the author, including other books in the series, please go to http://catherineleeauthor.com

Edited by Phoenix Editing, http://phoenixeditingandproofreading.com

Cover designed by the most fabulous Bill Duncan xx

For those who survive every day, and those who don't.

1

———

Bonnie Hunter slid in behind the wheel of her Jeep Wrangler and pulled away from the curb. It was another cold winter's day and she briefly considered stopping for coffee. A stack of paperwork awaited, and she was in no hurry to get to Headquarters. But Senior Sergeant Carmel Johnson had texted twice, asking when she'd be in. Plus, Bonnie had already had one coffee to warm up this morning after her ocean swim. She should at least wait until ten before her second.

Choosing her favourite Aussie Pub Rock Anthems playlist, Bonnie cranked the volume and settled in for the hour-long drive to work. She was three songs in and getting right into the groove when an incoming call stopped the music. It was Johnson.

"Where are you?"

"I'm on my way. About forty minutes out."

"No, I mean specifically. Where are you?"

"Oh. Just past Chatswood. You got something?"

"Domestic in progress. Macquarie Park. Can you attend?"

Bonnie pulled over and flicked the screen on her dash to navigation mode. "Give me the address." She entered the data as

Johnson spoke, the familiar mix of tension and dread already building in the pit of her stomach. "I'm eight minutes away," she said as she got back on the road. "What details do we have?"

"Husband, wife, two kids. Been going on since last night; he's threatening to kill them all. Unconfirmed reports of a firearm."

Bonnie overtook a small SUV and put her foot down. "Shit, Carm. Why are we just getting the call now?"

Johnson's voice remained even. "Uniforms attended after reports from neighbours last night. At that time, the wife said it was all under control. No sign of a firearm. Nothing they could do. Escalated a couple of hours ago when one of the neighbours says he heard a gunshot and screaming."

"What are their names?" Bonnie asked.

"Bessell family. Wife's name is Rhonda, husband Ian. Kids are Jayden, ten, and Ellie, seven. I've got McLeish on the way as well, but he's still twenty minutes out."

Bonnie resisted the urge to sigh. McLeish was not the partner she needed on this one. Not that anyone else in the Child Abuse and Sex Crimes Squad was lighting the world on fire at the moment. Good detectives were thin on the ground across the board.

"What do you want me to do, Sarge?"

"I want you to shut it down, Bonnie. Domestic violence is up fifty percent since the bloody pandemic. We can't lose another family."

Bonnie sensed the weariness in her boss's voice. They were all tired; the pandemic had taken so much more than lives over the past two years. It was the main reason for the shortage of staff right across the force, not just detectives. But even worse, Carmel was right. Lockdowns and frazzled tempers had meant a sharp increase in the already appalling domestic abuse figures.

"I hear you," Bonnie said. "I'm close. Three minutes. Tell McLeish to step on it."

She ended the call and concentrated on the drive through suburban streets. It looked like so many of the neighbourhoods she'd visited too often over the last couple of years – nice-looking houses in nice-looking streets hiding actions and words and people that were far from nice.

The Bessell's house was no different, except for the three police vehicles and two ambulances blocking the street on either side. Bonnie quickly parked the Jeep and made her way to the most senior-looking officer among them.

"Detective Sergeant Bonnie Hunter."

"Grimes," the sergeant said with a nod. "Welcome to the party."

Bonnie wasn't sure whether the guy was going for a *Die Hard* reference or he was just an insensitive prick, but she chose to ignore it either way.

"Reports of a firearm. Is that confirmed?"

"Affirmative. One of my guys went up to the door, saw it in the suspect's hand. Suspect pointed it right at him and threatened to shoot. That's when I called for backup. You a hostage negotiator?"

"No. What does he want?"

Grimes shrugged. "He's not made any demands, besides yelling at us to 'piss off and leave me and my family alone'. I asked for a hostage negotiator."

"Well until they arrive you got me. I understand the first callout was through the night. That your team?"

"Yeah. Neighbours reported a disturbance, yelling, screaming, the usual." Grimes pointed to a couple of uniforms standing by one of the patrol cars. "Gibbs and Khan responded, the wife said everything was fine. Misunderstanding, neighbours overreacting, that sort of thing. My guys sighted the wife and both kids, no-one was hurt. Nothing more they could do."

"What time was that?" Bonnie asked.

"One-fifteen am."

"And the two kids were out of bed at that time? A ten-year-old and a seven-year-old?"

Another shrug. "Not against the law."

"Should have rung alarm bells though, shouldn't it?"

Grimes shifted his considerable weight from one foot to the other. "Look, Detective..."

"Hunter."

"Right, Hunter. You know how it is. We're called out to domestics like this one every single damn day. We spend half our shift dealing with wife-beaters only to have the wife wipe the blood off her face and tell us she's not going to press charges, not going to leave. She's going to stay and let him do it again, even though she thinks he won't do it again. But of course, he *will* do it again, and we'll go back out there, and we'll waste our time all over again. So, if my guys didn't hear any alarm bells last night when they attended this address, I'm going to say there was nothing they could do."

Bonnie felt his frustration. She did know how it was, and he went up a notch in her estimation for backing his team. A tiny notch, but still. He was just trying to get through it, like they all were. But right now, Rhonda Bessell and her kids needed help that had already failed them once today. Bonnie wasn't going to let this family down again.

"Is there any history with this couple?" she asked Sergeant Grimes.

He shook his head. "Never been called here before. Doesn't mean he hasn't—"

"I know," Bonnie replied, all too familiar with patterns of domestic abuse. "Do we know what kicked him off?"

"Accused the wife of having an affair, according to Gibbs and Khan."

"Is she?"

"No idea, Detective. There a hostage negotiator on the way?"

"No idea, Sergeant. My partner is though. McLeish."

"He any good in these situations?"

Bonnie stared at him, ignoring the implication. "No better than me. When he gets here, tell him where I am."

"And where's that?"

She looked up at the house, at the closed front door.

"In there."

2

Bonnie approached the front of the house slowly, hands in the air. It was a tidy house, paint fresh, garden free of weeds, lawn maintained. Someone cared for this house, cared about neighbourhood appearances.

Her gaze flicked between the door and the windows, looking for any sign of movement. She noticed the curtain of the window to the left of the door twitch a fraction. She held her arms higher and spoke in a loud, clear voice.

"Mr Bessell. Ian. My name is Bonnie. Can I talk to you for a minute please?"

"I've told you people to fuck off already. Why is no-one listening to me?"

"It's not that simple, Ian. We need to make sure you and your family are safe."

"Of course we're safe. I'm in charge here. No-one touches my family but me."

Bonnie stopped at the bottom of the three steps leading up to the front door. "That's my reason for concern, Ian. You shouldn't be touching your family either. I think you know that."

Silence.

"Ian, we're not going away. I need you to open the door."

Nothing.

"Ian, we've ascertained that you have a firearm in there. I need to see that your wife and children are safe, then we can work this thing out, whatever it is, and you can go back to being a family. Sound good?"

Bonnie waited, her arms getting heavy as she continued to hold them aloft. She needed to demonstrate she was no threat to this man, no matter how badly she wanted to hurt him right now.

The door opened a crack and a tall man with a drawn face peered out. He cast his dark eyes over the scene on his front lawn. Police, ambos, the whole street blocked off.

Bonnie saw her chance. "I can make all this go away, Ian. I just need you to let me in so we can talk. Can you do that?"

He opened the door a fraction wider, lifted his chin. "Leave your gun outside."

"I can't do that. But I can leave it in the holster, and I'll have my hands away from my firearm the whole time. As long as you do the same. Sound fair?"

He thought about it for a moment, then opened the door wider, stepping behind it to protect himself from any trigger-happy cops in the street with half a shot. Bonnie could see the young girl now, crying in the corner of the living room. The sight gave her strength.

"Well come on, then," Ian barked.

Bonnie kept her hands up and slipped past him into the house without a backwards glance to her colleagues.

As her eyes adjusted to the change in lighting, Bonnie could now see that Ellie was sitting on the couch with her mother and brother. Rhonda was between the children, whispering to them while Ian's attention was on getting Bonnie through the door. Jayden was stoic, his face set, eyes projecting nothing but hatred for his father. Ellie was listening to her mother and trying her best to stop crying.

Bonnie took in as much as she could in those momentary glances at the three hostages. Rhonda was bruised and had patches of dried blood on her face and arms, as well as a nasty gash above her eye that was still bleeding. In spite of her injuries, she appeared conscious and calm. The children were outwardly unharmed.

"See?" Ian spat, waving the gun at his family like a pointing stick. "They're fine. We're all fine. There's no need for you lot to get involved in our business."

Bonnie spoke calmly. "I'm going to need you to put the gun down, Ian."

"Nope. You've got yours, and I've got mine. That was the deal."

"Mine is in my holster, and I'm not touching it. That was the deal. You can keep yours close while we talk, but that's not going to happen until you put it down."

They eyed each other for a long minute. Bonnie had managed to take a couple of steps toward the hostages, but she was nowhere near close enough to put herself between them and Ian. She needed to calm him down.

There were two armchairs in the room, one either end of the couch. "What about you take a seat in that chair," she said, "and I'll sit here in this one. You can put your gun on the coffee table, right where you can reach it. Then we can start talking."

Ian kept his eyes on her as he lowered himself into the chair. He scowled at his family before finally putting the gun on the table, but he kept himself straight-backed and on alert rather than relaxing into the seat.

"Great," said Bonnie as she slowly sat. "Now, I'll start by

asking you all some questions." Ian didn't stop her, so Bonnie turned toward the boy. "You're Jayden, is that right?"

"Yeah."

"How old are you, Jayden?"

"Ten."

"And Ellie, how old are you?"

Ellie buried her head behind her mother's arm.

"She's seven," said Jayden. "Why does it matter how old we are?"

"I'm just trying to get to know you better, that's all. My name is Bonnie."

"How old are you?" Jayden asked with just a hint of a smile, knowing he'd never get away with asking an adult their age under normal circumstances.

Bonnie smiled back. "I'm thirty-four, and right now I have to tell you I'm feeling every one of those years."

"Have we finished the getting-to-know-you bullshit yet?" said Ian.

"Ian, I wonder if this is a conversation that's better had between just the three of us. You, me, and Rhonda can sort this out. How about we leave the children out of it?"

"They're not going anywhere. They're part of this family. We sort our shit out together. As a *family*."

"Okay," said Bonnie. It had been worth a try. She caught Rhonda's eye briefly, tried to convey a message of calm control. *We've got this.* Then she turned back to the husband. "Ian, I understand the police were first called to your home in the early hours of this morning. Can you tell me what that was about?"

"Bloody neighbours not minding their own business, that's what. Couples aren't allowed to argue anymore without you lot sticking your noses in?"

His inflection made it sound like a question, but it wasn't one Bonnie was about to answer.

Ian pointed a menacing finger at his wife. "She's been fucking that dickhead across the street behind my back."

Rhonda obviously knew better than to react, instead pulling her children in a fraction tighter.

Bonnie thought quickly, trying to find the best way to ask the question. She settled on the direct approach. "Rhonda, is this true? Have you been seeing someone else?"

Rhonda shook her head. "We're just… friends."

"Bullshit," said Ian. He leaned closer to the gun. "I've seen the way he looks at you. Do you think I'm an idiot? Is that what you think, you stupid bitch?"

"No-one thinks you're an idiot, Ian," said Bonnie, and she meant it. He was a thug, sure. A selfish, violent arsehole who cared about no-one but himself. But he wasn't an idiot. Bonnie had seen too many of these men in her time. They weren't to be underestimated, especially not when within reach of a deadly weapon. She chose her next words carefully. "Why don't we give Rhonda the chance to explain, calmly, how you may have accidentally gotten the wrong idea about the man across the street?"

"Bitch! Are you calling me a liar?"

"No," Bonnie replied, her voice flat and even, eyes on the children, willing them to keep calm. "That's not what I said. This could all be a simple misunderstanding. Rhonda?"

"Dale is a single father," Rhonda began, looking at Bonnie rather than Ian. "He has a daughter Ellie's age, and they play together. That's all."

"That sounds innocent enough," said Bonnie. She had exactly zero experience at hostage negotiation, but she figured at least while they were talking no-one was getting hurt.

Ian shook his head. "What about the other day when I came home and he was here? Sitting in my living room, drinking coffee from my cup. With my wife! I don't have to stand for that."

"The girls were playing upstairs," said Rhonda, still talking to Bonnie. "Dale is raising Brooke on his own. His wife died last year, and he's struggling. He needed to talk. He needed someone to listen."

"He *needed*," Ian sneered. "Dale this, Dale that. It's pathetic." He pointed an accusing finger at his wife. "Do you think I can't see what's going on?"

Rhonda slowly wiped blood from the corner of her eye, and it was all Bonnie could do to stay calm. This man had beaten his wife, held his family hostage for over twelve hours, threatened to kill them all, and he was throwing a tantrum because she had the audacity to be caring towards another human being?

"Daddy, please stop yelling." Bonnie's heart broke as she watched Ellie come out from her hiding place behind her mother's arm. "Brooke's dad needs help with her hair. He doesn't know how to do a braid. Mum showed him."

"Shut up, Ellie," said Jayden. The look he gave his sister said it all. These kids had witnessed their father's rage before. Jayden knew when to be quiet, but Ellie still thought she could help. Bonnie had to get them out of harm's way.

"Ian, I don't think we can resolve this with Jayden and Ellie here. They're tired and hungry, and they probably need to go to the toilet, too. Is that right, kids?" They both nodded, and Ellie shrunk back behind her mother. "My partner is outside," Bonnie continued. "How about you let the kids go and hang out with him while we finish off in here?"

Ian looked at the gun, then at Rhonda and the kids. Bonnie knew she could draw her weapon quickly, but she wasn't sure she'd be quick enough to save all of them if he went for it.

He didn't.

"Go," he said with a flick of his head toward the door.

The children hesitated, as if they weren't sure whether to believe him. Bonnie carefully stood and took their hands, then led them to the front door and out to safety. Ellie ran straight

down the porch steps toward McLeish, but Jayden stopped and
swivelled back to the house. In an instant, Bonnie realised her
mistake. She'd turned her back on Ian, Rhonda, and the gun.

Bonnie and Jayden both stared into the living room, where
Ian now held the gun to Rhonda's head.

3

"No!" Jayden yelled.

Bonnie caught him before he could run back into the house. "Jayden, you need to go."

"Mum!"

"I've got your mum." Bonnie pushed him toward the steps, but the boy was surprisingly strong for a ten-year-old.

"Mum!" he yelled again.

"Go, Jayden," said Rhonda, her head pushed sideways by the force of the gun pressed to her temple. "Do as you're told, son."

Ian dragged Rhonda backwards into the kitchen, and Bonnie gestured to McLeish to take Jayden. "Get him out of here!" she yelled, handing the struggling boy to her partner.

"Mum!" Jayden screamed. "Get off me! Get your fucken hands off me. Mum! Mum!"

Bonnie went back inside the house, pulling her Glock from its holster as she followed Ian and Rhonda before coming up against the closed kitchen door. She heard the sound of furniture being dragged.

"Ian, what are you doing? We had a deal." She tried the door, but it would only open a couple of centimetres before it jammed.

He'd barricaded them in.

"You can fuck off with your deal, bitch. You women are all the same. Calling me a liar. You need to learn some respect."

"Respect? Are you serious?" Bonnie couldn't help herself. "You've got a gun to your wife's head, mate. You want respect, you need to earn it."

"Please, both of you, just stop," said Rhonda. "I'm tired. I'm sick and tired of it all."

"Well maybe I'll just put you out of your misery then, eh?" said Ian. Bonnie heard more dragging sounds, a chair this time. "Should I do that? Shoot you like the dog you are?"

"I can't let you do that, Ian," said Bonnie. She tried the door again, but whatever he'd put in front of it was too heavy. "I think you need to calm down, mate," Bonnie continued. "No-one needs to get hurt here. We were having a nice, calm discussion. Why don't you let me in there and we can pick up where we left off?"

"Why don't you take your bitch-cop attitude and fuck off out of my house?"

Damn it. How could she have let this happen? Never take your eyes off a suspect with a gun. Never. But the kids... there was no time for that now. She had to get Rhonda out of there safely. She had to get this door open.

McLeish appeared at her side. "Kids are safe with uniforms," he said before she could tell him to be quiet.

"Who the fuck is that?" yelled Ian.

Bonnie shook her head at McLeish. "My partner," she called through the crack in the door. "He just came to tell me your kids are safe. He's leaving now."

McLeish gave her a 'no fucking way' look and opened his mouth to speak, but she gestured for him to shut up. The last thing they needed was for Bessell to think the place was about to be swarming with cops. She needed to calm him down, not fire him up.

"Go see if you can find a window to the kitchen," Bonnie whispered. "I need to see what's going on in there. Don't let him see you."

McLeish nodded his understanding and backed away.

"Ian, it's just the three of us here now. You, me, and Rhonda. We can still talk this through. I can still make all the people outside go away. But you have to let me in. Can you do that?"

There was silence for a long moment, then Rhonda spoke.

"Are Jayden and Ellie really safe?"

"Yes, Rhonda. They're outside with my colleagues, waiting for you."

"Tell them I love them."

"You can tell them yourself. Both of you. Both of you can tell them as soon as we sort this out. As soon as you're all together again."

Bonnie heard whispering but couldn't make out what was being said. Then the sound of the chair scraping on the floor.

"Rhonda?" Bonnie called. "Ian?" She pushed on the door again, managed to get it open another half a centimetre. It was enough to peek inside. "Rhonda, no!"

A shot rang out, and everything happened quickly after that. Bonnie was suddenly surrounded by men and women in uniform, and the door was finally forced open just as the second shot went off.

Bonnie rushed into the kitchen. She circled the table, which had been pushed back by the tide of cops, to where Ian and Rhonda both lay on the floor. Ian was dead – mouth agape, dark, hollow eyes staring at the ceiling. Blood seeped from his chest across the linoleum floor.

Rhonda was alive, but the wound to her head was

catastrophic. Bonnie took the gun from the woman's hand and moved it out of reach. Rhonda was trying to say something. Bonnie crouched down close and strained to hear over the commotion in the room.

"Is... he..."

Bonnie took Rhonda's hand and nodded. "He's dead."

"Jayden... Ellie... never... safe..."

Bonnie understood. "They're safe now, Rhonda." She raised a hand and stroked the woman's blood-soaked hair. "They'll grow up and be strong, caring people. They'll have children and grandchildren, and long, happy lives. You saved them, Rhonda. But why didn't you save yourself?"

"They deserve... more."

"You're their mother. They need—" Bonnie stopped talking, realising it was no use. Rhonda was gone. She'd killed her husband to protect her children, then killed herself. Why? To avoid prison? Perhaps they'd never know. All Bonnie knew right now was she had to go outside and tell two kids both their parents were dead.

Why the hell did she do this job?

4

Bonnie had been punishing her punching bag for almost an hour when the doorbell rang. She ignored it; turned up the music instead. The bell rang again. Whoever it was, they were persistent. Too bad, she wasn't in the mood. There was a bottle of tequila on the kitchen bench waiting for her to reach physical exhaustion. After a morning swim, a 10k run on the beach, and now the afternoon boxing session, she was almost ready for her sweet, sweet, reward.

She heard the gate at the side of the house open. Ballsy. There were only two people familiar enough with her and her house to make the trek down the side, and her friend Jess was currently on holiday in Thailand. That left one possibility, and Bonnie wasn't sure she was up for a lecture today.

"Go home, Coop," she yelled, slamming the punching bag with a particularly hard left jab.

"Oh, come on, I can't drink this at home." Detective Inspector Charlie Cooper tapped on the glass with his own bottle of tequila. "I got the good stuff, too."

Bonnie smiled when she saw he was holding up her

favourite brand rather than the cheap shit he usually brought round. At least that message was finally getting through.

"Sure, you can," Bonnie replied. "Those kids must be old enough to pour it for you by now."

"I will not take part in the corruption of minors, Detective Hunter. And they're not that old. Michael is only eleven. The girls miss you, by the way."

"I saw them last month."

"Which is a long time when you're four. They've been practicing a dance routine they want to show you. It's pretty bloody cute. Except they're annoying Patrick with the music. Seriously, Bonnie, open the door. It's cold out here."

Bonnie caught hold of the punching bag and regarded him for a second. Cooper was one of the few people she trusted in this world, partly because he'd been through a bigger shit-storm than anyone else she knew, and she'd been right there with him when it all came to a head. It had hit him pretty hard, and his Homicide team had been decimated, but he'd bounced back with the help of his family and a few solid mates. Bonnie liked to count herself in that number. She pulled off one glove, turned the music down, and unlocked the back door.

"Finally," he said, then took in her sweaty appearance and the punching bag. "You about done with this shit? I need a drink." He walked through to the kitchen without waiting for a response.

Bonnie pulled off the other glove and threw them both in the tub she kept in the corner for all her sporting gear. Edna's house – her house, now – was old, but the layout suited her perfectly. It was a long, narrow home, living room at the front, kitchen and bathroom at the rear, and a couple of bedrooms off the hallway that ran the length of the house. Bonnie had kept it exactly as Edna had left it for many years, but after tripping over her gear one too many times she'd finally caved and added the sunroom. It wasn't much more than an enclosed verandah, really, but it was perfect for her assorted workout equipment. It was also right next to the bathroom – handy for hitting the showers once the sweating was done.

"Make yourself at home," she called out as she closed the bathroom door.

"Always do," came the reply.

Ten minutes later and freshly showered, Bonnie joined Cooper at the kitchen table.

"Cheers," she said, picking up the shot Cooper had poured for her and downing it. "Wow, fresh limes, too. You've gone all out."

"I heard you had a rough day yesterday."

"Nope. Not ready to talk about it yet." Bonnie sucked on a lime wedge and poured another round. "How's Patrick going? You said the girls' music was annoying him." Patrick was Cooper and Liz's second son, born with profound hearing loss. Complications had meant he couldn't get fitted for a cochlear implant until recently, just after his ninth birthday. Bonnie could only imagine how hard it must be to go from a silent world to one that involved all the noises of an older brother and twin four-year-old sisters.

Cooper nodded as he accepted the second shot of tequila. "We tell them to keep it down, but they don't really understand. Poor Pat goes from wide-eyed wonder to all-encompassing rage in seconds."

"Does he use the ear-muff things they gave him at the hospital?"

"Yeah, they help. He's getting better every day. Ultimately, it's a good thing, Liz and I know that. Just an adjustment period. For all of us." Cooper leaned over in his seat and opened the fridge door, got himself out a beer. "You want one?"

Bonnie drank her second tequila shot. "Of my beers? Sure."

They sipped in silence for a few minutes before Cooper finally spoke. "You couldn't have—"

"Don't, Coop. Don't tell me I couldn't have saved that woman. I took my eyes off an armed suspect."

"To get the kids to safety. Anyone would have done the same. *I* would have done the same."

Bonnie shook her head and stared down at her beer. "Why? Why'd she kill herself? He had a gun to her head and, somehow, she managed to turn it around. I heard her whisper something to him. I don't know what she said, but it worked. She got the gun off him. She got the gun and she shot him. Killed him to protect her kids. So, why'd she then have to kill herself, Coop?"

"I don't know. She say anything to you before she died?"

Bonnie took a swig from her bottle. "She said they deserved better. The kids. I don't get that. Who better than their own mother?"

"Seriously? You of all people—"

She shook her head. "We're not talking about me and my fucked-up childhood, Coop. We're talking about a woman with a clearly abusive husband. She loved her kids so much she was willing to commit murder to protect them."

"Yes, but what would have happened next? I spoke to Carmel Johnson at length this afternoon, Bon. She told me what went down yesterday morning, what your team has found since. It's likely Rhonda Bessell had been subjected to years of violence and coercive control at the hands of her husband. She'd probably been thinking about this for a long time. What she'd do if she ever got the chance."

"And you reckon taking her own life was part of the plan?"

"I don't know. We'll never know for sure. But she would have thought about what would happen next. She'd have known she'd be arrested, taken from her kids for a start. She'd be charged with murder, probably kept on remand until the trial, where the family would have to relive the whole nightmare. You know what cases like this are like, they feel like they never end."

"Yes, but they *do* end, Coop. People get through this stuff, they move on with their lives."

Cooper finished his beer. "I know that, and you know that. But when you're in it... you've got to realise that Rhonda would have lived her life one day to the next. She survived, and she kept her children safe, one day at a time. When you've been in something like that for so long, it can be hard to see the end point."

"So, she took the easy way out?"

"Nothing about this was easy, Bon."

Bonnie sighed. "I know. I just wish... shit. I wish men weren't arseholes."

"We're not all like that. Hey, I spoke to Carmel about something else today."

"No." Bonnie pointed her empty beer bottle at the fridge.

"You don't even know what I'm going to say."

"Yes, I do. You're going to ask me to come work for Homicide. You ask me the same thing every time I see you, Coop. The answer's been no every time."

Cooper leaned over and opened the fridge again, extracted two more beers. "Yeah, but this time is different. Carmel wants you to take a break from Sex Crimes, and I need help. It'd only be temporary. I've got a couple of good kids now, but they need leadership."

"I'm not leadership material."

"Well, it's about time you stepped up and became leadership material, Sergeant Hunter."

"Fuck you."

Cooper feigned shock. "I'm a happily married man."

Bonnie laughed and pulled the tequila bottle closer. Cooper and Carmel were right about one thing, she needed a break from Sex Crimes. But right now, all that consisted of was getting very, very, drunk.

5

The next morning dawned clear and almost bright, so Bonnie decided to skip her morning swim and go for a run instead. She got dressed and pulled her shoes on quietly. Bonnie and Cooper had continued drinking into the night, and he'd crashed in her spare room. It was a Sunday and she wasn't sure if he was supposed to work today, but he was a big boy and could take care of his own shit. No need to wake him, though.

As she pounded down the footpath toward the beach and her favourite running route, Bonnie thought about Cooper's request. He'd let it drop after a couple more tequilas last night, knowing that pushing her was exactly the wrong way to get her on board. The idea of working with the Homicide Squad again had always been a non-starter for her – too many painful memories – but she couldn't ignore Cooper forever. He had a point, too. The squad was completely different, hardly any of the original team remained.

On the plus side, if she moved over, she would no longer have to deal with the incompetence of some of her current co-workers. McLeish instantly sprang to mind. On the other hand, though, there'd be new co-workers, and the law of averages said at least one or two of them would be fuck-ups.

Working for Cooper would be a plus, definitely. They'd had their differences in the past, but they'd had different agendas back then. Bonnie had been hunting a rapist-turned-killer, while Cooper had been trying to weed out a rat in his ranks. Working together they'd make a formidable team.

Bonnie slowed her pace along the esplanade as she dodged the dog-walkers and pram-pushers. Manly was a popular place on a sunny weekend morning, even at this early hour. She thought of Edna, how much her old friend used to love walking down here. The woman who took her in all those years ago still held a massive place in Bonnie's heart, even though she'd been gone for well over a decade.

By the time Bonnie returned to the house, Cooper was showered and dressed in his usual work attire. Like her, and most cops whose jurisdiction covered the entire state, he kept a bag of clothes and essentials in his car.

"You sleep okay?" she asked as she poured herself a glass of water at the sink.

"As well as any other night I've helped polish off a bottle of tequila." He rubbed a hand through his short hair. "Damn, Bonnie, how can you put that much booze away and go for a run like it's nothing?"

Bonnie shrugged. "Physical stuff I'm good at. You want some eggs?"

"No time. We've got a case. Call came in while you were out."

"We? I'm taking a break, remember. And it's Sunday. The Swans are playing this afternoon. Only case I'll be working on is the rest of that case of beer."

"You're taking a break from Sex Crimes. This is a potential homicide."

"Coop..."

Cooper held up a hand to stop her. "Nope, not listening. I've got a missing woman. I have to drive to the Southern Highlands, and I've got a massive hangover thanks to you. The least you can do is drive me down there. Besides, Carmel doesn't want you left alone."

"Seriously? I'm a big girl."

"I know that," Cooper said as he fished around in Bonnie's fridge. "But you lost a victim two days ago, Bonnie. We all need a helping hand sometimes."

"What I need is to relax at home and watch the game." She crossed her arms defiantly. Cooper closed the fridge and turned to face her. "Okay. I'll let Carmel know. She said she'll send McLeish to babysit you."

"She wouldn't."

"I don't think she was joking. What happened to the rest of the pizza from last night?"

Bonnie opened the lid of the garbage bin and pointed.

Cooper looked crestfallen. "You threw it out? Seriously?"

"We left it out on the bench all night. You can't eat that."

"Maybe *you* can't. I've got a cast-iron stomach." He stared into the garbage bin, and for a moment Bonnie thought he was actually going to reach in there and pull out a slice.

"There's some cereal in the cupboard and milk in the fridge. Help yourself while I shower."

"So, you're coming?"

"Well, I'm sure as shit not staying here with McLeish." She headed for the bathroom, then turned back to face him. "I'll drive you down there, but I'm not getting involved, Coop. Homicide isn't for me."

Cooper smiled. "We'll see."

6

December 2016

"What time does Shahid get off work?" Max asked again, checking his watch.

"Ten," Juliet told him for the third time that night. "The restaurant is just around the corner, so he'll be here soon."

"You could go get us another round while you're waiting," said Tess, shaking her empty glass in front of Max.

"Not for me," said Gwen. "I've had enough."

Max rolled his eyes at Juliet, turning away so Gwen and Tess couldn't see. He was home from uni for Christmas; it'd been months since they'd seen him but the look that passed between him and Juliet said nothing had changed. Tess was still the party girl, Gwen the swot who took her studies way too seriously.

"What are you having, Jules?" Max asked as he stood.

"I'll have another vodka, thanks." She gave him a conspiratorial wink as he peeled his lanky frame out of his chair and headed to the bar. Juliet missed her best friend so much when he was in Canberra, but it was where he was supposed to be.

Studying political science down amongst the heart of that world was exactly where Max belonged, and from the way he lit up when he spoke of it, he was loving every minute.

"You know this is the pub where Princess Mary met her prince, right?" Gwen was full of this kind of information – some of it useful, most of it not. Juliet had no idea how she kept as much stuff in her mind as she did. Gwen was constantly telling them how much reading she had to do for uni, grossing them out with all the anatomy stuff. She was going to make a brilliant doctor one day but Juliet reckoned she'd be a high risk for boring her patients to death before any real health issues took them out.

"Speaking of princes," said Tess, nodding toward the front door. Juliet and Gwen both followed her gaze to see a group of men saunter in. One in particular caught Juliet's eye – great body, sharp clothes, dark hair, and that air of confidence she loved in a man. He said something to one of his friends, then suddenly looked right at her.

"Nope," said Max, placing the drinks on the table and re-taking his seat.

"What do you mean, 'nope'?" Juliet asked, tearing her eyes away from the guy.

"I mean nope, he's not for you. Too full of himself."

"I think he's gorgeous," said Tess.

"Exactly," said Max. "And he knows it. Look at him, swanning about the place as if he owns it. At least half the women in the room are gawking at him, and he's loving every minute of it."

"Half the women in the room can eat their hearts out," said Gwen. "Looks like he's zeroed in on our Juliet. He's coming over."

"Oh, shit." Juliet picked up her drink and took a big gulp.

"Maybe he's your prince charming," whispered Tess.

"Makes a change from Romeo," Juliet muttered into her drink as the guy reached their table.

"Well, here I am," said Prince Charming with a grin. "What are your other two wishes?"

Max nearly spat his beer as the girls laughed.

"That's terrible," said Juliet. "It ever actually work on a girl?"

He shrugged. "It made you smile. I'm Sam."

"Juliet," she replied, quickly adding her usual disclaimer. "Not fond of Shakespeare jokes."

"Noted," said Sam. "Can I buy you and your friends a drink?"

"We're pretty sorted, thanks, mate," said Max.

Sam ignored Max, kept staring at Juliet.

She raised her glass. "I've just got one, thank you."

"I'll take a pinot noir," said Gwen.

"I thought you'd had enough?" Max asked.

Gwen shrugged. "It's a woman's prerogative to change her mind."

"One pinot noir, coming right up," said Sam. "Don't go anywhere," he added, lightly touching Juliet's arm.

"What did you do that for?" Max asked Gwen once Sam was out of earshot.

"He's hot, and Juliet could do with a bit of hotness in her life."

Juliet was uncomfortable being the centre of attention. "I'm quite capable of getting my own hotness, thank you very much."

"I know," said Gwen. "But it's fun to flirt."

Tess laughed. "You only flirt when it's not going to go anywhere."

"No, I don't."

"Yeah, you do. Sam is clearly interested in Juliet, so you flirting with him is safe. That guy last week was gay. Again, safe."

Gwen pulled a face and turned to Juliet. "Is she for real?"

Juliet loved Gwen and Tess, but they did her head in with

their bickering sometimes. They'd both had just enough to drink for things to turn ugly, and that was the last thing Juliet needed right now. She broke the tension with a laugh. "Tess has a point. But I don't think there's anything wrong with safe flirting. It's good practice for when someone really interesting comes along."

"Exactly," said Gwen. "I'm practising for my own prince. Oh, here comes yours, back with my wine."

Sam handed Gwen her drink, and she thanked him profusely until Tess pulled her away.

"Finally!" said Max as he spotted Shahid. He stood and walked away from their table.

"Who's that?" asked Sam.

"Our friend Shahid," said Juliet, waving. "He just got off work. Max has been away at uni, hasn't seen him for months. This is the first night we've all been together since my birthday back in June." She half thought Sam might take the hint and leave the group alone, although she wasn't exactly sure she wanted him to. She'd missed Max terribly, but something about this confident stranger made her want him to stay.

"Oh. Looks like they have some catching up to do," said Sam. "Good, gives me a chance to get to know you." He settled himself in the chair Max had vacated. "So, Juliet who was born in June and doesn't like Shakespeare, what else is there behind that gorgeous smile?"

7

"You ever been to Bundanoon?" Cooper asked as Bonnie navigated her way through the northern suburbs and into the Harbour Tunnel. She usually preferred to take the bridge, but the tunnel made it easier to get to the M5 motorway.

"Not specifically, but I'm familiar with the Southern Highlands. I read an article recently about how many Sydneysiders are retiring down there."

"It's not just retirees. Tree-changers, too. Now that half the workforce is used to working from home."

"I guess," said Bonnie. She'd been to the area a few times for cases, but never really explored it. "There's a fair bit of National Park land, right?"

Cooper nodded. "Bundanoon is right on the western border of Morton National Park."

"That a possibility for your missing person?"

"Too early to tell." He opened his laptop and balanced it on his knees. "I hate this thing."

Bonnie glanced over and ascertained that 'this thing' was the trackpad, and Cooper was almost useless at using it in place of a mouse. He struggled for a few minutes, opening and closing emails and documents, before finally launching into the details of the case. "Right. The missing woman is Juliet Keller, age twenty-five. Staying at the family holiday house for the weekend with her husband, Sam Keller, thirty. Apparently, it was his birthday and they were hosting a small dinner party last night to celebrate."

"Who else was there?"

Cooper checked his screen. "Two couples, but Juliet disappeared before they arrived." He went on to explain that Juliet had gone to the local store for a last-minute grocery item just before five pm, and never returned.

"What time did the friends arrive?" Bonnie asked.

"Not sure. That's something we'll need to ascertain. The husband and his mates – Jonathan Walsh and Oliver Pearce – went looking for Juliet around seven pm last night. They found the car parked outside the grocery store, locked. Sam rang Juliet's phone, and they located it in the grass a few metres from the car. The keys were with the phone."

"What about a purse?"

Cooper shook his head. "None mentioned."

That didn't necessarily mean anything. Purses and wallets had become almost redundant these days; so many people just paid for things with their phones. They'd have to check with the husband whether Juliet carried one.

Bonnie pictured a car parked outside a grocery store in a small country town. "So, she got out of the car, locked it, then... were the phone and keys in the grass *between* the car and the store, or the opposite direction?"

"Yeah, I had the same question," said Cooper. "Don't know yet."

"Right, we'll – *you'll* – need to find that out." Bonnie reminded herself not to get involved. She was the driver here, nothing more. Still, it was intriguing. "Did she make it into the grocery store?"

"No-one remembers seeing her," Cooper answered. "The owner closed up herself yesterday, said she had no customers after four-forty pm. Remembered seeing the car parked there when she drove out to go home, but didn't see who left it there."

Bonnie sighed. She was going to need to talk this through. "So, we have a husband and wife at their country holiday house. It's the husband's birthday. She's making dinner for friends – two couples – who are due to arrive soon, realises she needs something last minute, runs out to the grocery store before it closes. She takes his car, her car?"

"It's registered in his name."

"Right. If they've come from Sydney for the weekend then they probably only brought one car. So, she drives his car to the store, parks outside, exits the vehicle, locks the vehicle, but before she can enter the store something happens and she disappears, leaving her phone and the car keys in the grass metres from the vehicle."

"That's what we know at this point," said Cooper.

"The usual canvassing taking place? CCTV?"

"Yeah. Nothing so far." Cooper explained that the grocery store was in the town's main street, but it was a few hundred metres away from the main business area. It was closer to houses than other businesses, not that any of the businesses they'd checked so far had cameras. It was a quiet country town.

"What does your gut tell you, Coop?"

"I tend not to ask too much of my gut these days," he replied, eyebrows raised.

Bonnie couldn't argue with that, not after all he'd been through. "Fair enough. What do we know about the Kellers?"

"Sam Keller is a lawyer with a big city firm. Juliet's not listed as employed. No kids. They live in an apartment in the city. Pretty pricey building."

A young couple with an expensive city apartment and a country house. Bonnie was starting to build a picture. "Family money?"

Cooper nodded. "On his side. Parents are loaded. The house in Bundanoon is theirs, apparently. Been in the family a couple of generations." He pecked at the keyboard some more. "I'm going to have to answer some of these emails."

"Right." They drove in relative silence while Cooper worked, pausing every now and then to express his displeasure with typing on the go. Bonnie ignored him and thought about the case. As much as she didn't want to get involved, she could already feel herself getting sucked in.

On the face of it, Juliet's disappearance had all the hallmarks of an abduction. The woman had vanished while out in public going about her business. The phone and car keys discarded nearby indicated she had not left of her own accord.

Juliet was twenty-five years old, and while Bonnie hadn't seen a picture yet, if the young woman was married to a wealthy lawyer, chances were she was attractive. Were they looking at a sexual predator? Someone who took her by surprise as she exited the vehicle? Or was this about the money?

Cooper swore at his laptop and closed the lid.

Bonnie smiled. "I take it there's been no ransom demand?"

Cooper shook his head. "Not at this stage. We're keeping tabs on the husband's phone. Apparently, he's not best pleased about that."

Bonnie stared at Cooper. "Why not? What's his story?"

"I want to wait to form an opinion on that when we interview him ourselves. Can you watch where you're going, please?"

She rolled her eyes but turned them back to the road. Her

mind was suddenly racing. "You said they were staying at the holiday house for the weekend. When did they get there?"

"Hang on." Cooper opened his laptop again and navigated for a few moments. "Here it is. According to the initial interview conducted by uniforms, Sam said he and Juliet drove down from Sydney after he finished work Friday night."

"Did they go anywhere? Friday night or Saturday?"

Cooper scanned the record of interview. "Doesn't say."

"But no-one saw her arrive at the grocery store. And the friends arrived at the house *after* she went missing. They never saw her?"

"No." Cooper frowned. "Don't go jumping to conclusions, Bon. We haven't interviewed the guy yet."

"Well, I'd make that priority number one if I were you. Get his story, Coop, then we'll see if we can break it. You know how this goes as well as I do." A familiar feeling was starting to rise in the pit of Bonnie's stomach, and it had nothing to do with last night's tequila. "If no-one saw Juliet Keller in Bundanoon this weekend..."

"Yeah," Cooper agreed with a sigh. "We need to look very closely at the husband."

8

April 2017

Juliet had just finished hanging the last of the new season stock on the racks when Sam arrived, yet another beautiful bouquet of flowers in hand.

"Hey, gorgeous!" He literally swept her off her feet.

"Sam! Put me down, we have customers."

He obliged, but not before spinning her around in a full circle. Juliet couldn't decide whether she was thrilled or mortified. She'd completely fallen for this man, but her place of work was important to her. Besides, she didn't know how much longer Maria would put up with Sam's antics.

He'd become a regular fixture at the store on Saturday afternoons, picking her up after her shift and whisking her off to fancy restaurants across the city. In the four months since he'd blown off his work Christmas party the night they'd met, Sam and Juliet had spent every moment they could together.

"Samuel," Maria said with a curt nod, but the smile at the corner of her lips let Juliet know things were okay.

"Maria, looking as stunning as ever." Sam thrust the flowers in her direction. "These are for you. Any chance I could pinch Juliet a bit early today? I've got big plans."

"Sam, I've still got twenty minutes left of my shift," Juliet protested. She loved him, but she loved her work, too. In her second year of design college, she had already built up quite a portfolio of work. Ultimately, she wanted to design her own range of workout wear.

Maria waved a hand at them. "Go on, you two lovebirds. It's quiet here. I can finish up."

Sam kissed Maria on the cheek, then pulled Juliet away before she could argue.

"Where are we going tonight?" Juliet asked as they walked to his BMW. She'd given up driving her own car to work on Saturdays. After having to leave the old Corolla in the shopping centre carpark a few times she'd finally learned that Sam liked to play knight in shining armour and he wasn't used to taking no for an answer.

"It's a surprise," he said, opening the car door for her.

Juliet settled into the passenger seat, happy, but also a little put off. Sam was usually pleased to see her, so that wasn't unusual, but today he seemed even more upbeat. The flowers and kiss for Maria were new. She got the feeling he was planning something, and that maybe Maria had been in on it.

"You know I'm not a big fan of surprises, babe," she said as he drove out of the shopping centre carpark.

Sam smiled. "Nonsense. You're going to love this one." He looked her up and down. "I'll take you home to change."

"What's wrong with what I'm wearing?" She'd bought a new dress at lunchtime and slipped into it just before he'd arrived at the store. If she was honest, she was a little disappointed he hadn't noticed.

"Oh, nothing," he backtracked. "But I got you something real nice." He tossed his head toward the backseat. Juliet turned and saw a bag from Zimmermann, one of her favourite fashion stores in Sydney.

"Oh, my goodness, Sam!" She reached for the bag and pulled it into her lap. Inside was the most gorgeous button-down mini dress she'd ever seen. Floral print linen, with a mandarin collar, fitted bodice, and a relaxed mini skirt. The blouson sleeves had elasticated cuffs, and the dress was finished off with a fabric-covered buckle belt. It was simply stunning.

"Do you like it?" he asked, head swivelling between Juliet and the road.

"I love it! But it must have cost a fortune, Sam. You really shouldn't—"

He cut her off with a wave of his hand. "Stop it, Jules. I've told you before, I love spoiling you. You're worth every penny."

He *had* told her that. So many times. But it still felt strange for someone to buy her a piece of clothing that cost more than twice her week's wage. Sam came from a different world.

Sam pulled the car into her street, frowning when he reached her house and there was nowhere to park. Juliet's parents were home, their cars in their usual spots in the large driveway. Juliet's Corolla was parked on the grass, looking lonely and unloved – she couldn't remember the last time she'd washed it. Sam usually parked behind her parents' cars, but today that space was taken by her brother's big four-wheel drive. Nick was a frequent visitor to the house – he and their father worked together – but he didn't usually come over on Saturdays. Unless... yes! The screen door opened and Nick's wife appeared, the baby squirming in her arms.

"Ooh, Renee's here with Luke! I love nephew-cuddles!" Juliet jumped from the car, Zimmermann bag in tow, and was halfway to the house when she realised Sam hadn't followed. "Aren't you coming?" she called back to him.

He shook his head.

"What's wrong?" she asked, walking back and leaning into him through the car window.

"I've got a bit of a headache, babe. Not really up for the baby stuff."

"Oh, please? I haven't seen them for a week, look how much Luke has grown! Come on, Sam, just five minutes. Nick will be pleased to see you."

Sam shook his head, narrowed his eyes. "We're running late, babe. I've got a big evening planned for us. Can't you just go inside and get changed? It'll be quicker if I wait here. I'll take you to see your nephew tomorrow if you like. Maybe we can offer to babysit."

Juliet was disappointed, but Sam was right. If they both went in the house her mother would insist on them having a drink at the very least, and it'd be an hour before they could extract themselves. It was a decent drive from Castle Hill to the city, and the idea of a proper visit with Luke tomorrow *was* appealing.

"Okay." She gave him a kiss through the window before turning for the house. "I'll try not to get caught up in the baby stuff."

It was dark by the time they got to the city. Juliet loved Sydney at night – the lights, the people, the potential. Sam usually parked underneath the building where he worked, as it was pretty central and he knew all the good restaurants within walking distance. They headed in that direction but before they got to the usual entrance, Sam drove into the underground carpark of a different building.

"Where are we going?" Juliet asked, thrown by the change in routine.

"It's all part of the surprise. You'll see." Sam pulled into a numbered parking space and killed the engine. "Come on."

Juliet thought it might be one of those office buildings with a restaurant on the top, but when they got in the elevator Sam pressed the button for the fourteenth floor.

"You look beautiful," he said as they rode up.

"It's a gorgeous dress, and it fits perfectly. Thanks, babe. You know me so well." They reached the fourteenth floor and when the doors slid open, Juliet realised they were in a residential apartment building rather than an office tower. "What is this—"

"Shh," Sam cut her off. "You really aren't very good at surprises, are you?"

"Sorry," she said with a smile.

Sam took her hand and led her down the hall, stopping at the door of apartment 1407. Juliet desperately wanted to ask who lived here but didn't want to get shushed again. She expected Sam to knock, but instead he reached in his pocket and pulled out a key.

He turned to her and smiled, then unlocked the door. "Welcome," he said, pushing the door open to reveal a stunning apartment with views of the city.

Juliet's jaw dropped. "Oh, my goodness, it's amazing!" The apartment was unfurnished, a gorgeous canvas waiting to be filled. She couldn't help herself. "Sam, whose place is this?"

He walked over to the floor-to-ceiling windows, unable to hide his grin. "Mine," he said, taking her in his arms. "My parents bought it. It's supposed to be my twenty-fifth birthday present, but when I told them what I wanted to do, they gave it to me early."

She was struggling to take it all in. The kitchen, living room, the views, it was all beautiful. Then what he'd said finally registered. "Wait, what did you want to do?"

Sam pulled her down the hall and opened a door. It was a bedroom – empty of furniture, but filled with pillows, blankets, and rose petals. There were three candles by the window, which

Sam lit before taking Juliet by the hands and bringing her into the centre of the room.

He kissed her, deeply and passionately. "I've wanted to do this since the moment I saw you," he said, lowering himself onto one knee. "Juliet Evelyn Wilson, will you marry me?"

9

"That's it there," said Cooper, pointing to the third driveway on the left.

"Got it," said Bonnie. All they could see from the street were high hedges and fences, so Bonnie turned into the drive and followed its slow curve until the house came into view. Well, house was a bit of an understatement. It was more of an estate. "Just how much money do these people have?"

Cooper leaned forward to get a better view. "Yeah. If this is the holiday house, what must they live in?"

There were two patrol cars off to the left, so Bonnie parked next to them. "I've heard of places like this. They have full-time gardeners. *With* assistants. It's next-level money."

"Good point," said Cooper. "Place like this would have help. Maybe one of them saw something."

"Or at least saw Juliet this weekend," Bonnie suggested as they climbed out of the car. "Or not, as the case may be."

There were a couple of uniforms standing around outside near the patrol cars. Cooper strode over to them and exchanged a few words. Bonnie left him to it. She was the driver, heading straight back to Sydney as soon as she could disentangle herself. If she was lucky, she might still get back in time to catch the second half of the Swans game.

The door to the house opened and a tall, thin man in his late-twenties or early-thirties stepped out. "Hi, I'm Jonathan Walsh," he said, holding out a hand to shake.

Bonnie raised hers in greeting instead. "Detective Sergeant Bonnie Hunter," she said. "Prefer to stay contactless these days, if you don't mind." The no-touching thing was one of the few aspects of the pandemic Bonnie planned to keep hold of for as long as possible.

"Understood." Jonathan glanced up as Cooper left the uniforms in the drive and joined them. He introduced himself, and Jonathan didn't try shaking this time. "Sam and the others are inside, please follow me."

He led them through an entranceway larger than Bonnie's entire living room and kitchen combined, down a hall lined with paintings that probably each cost more than her yearly salary, and out into a sunroom with views of the immaculately maintained garden. There were two other men and a woman waiting in the sunroom, and Bonnie could hear noise coming from the nearby kitchen. There was also a uniformed officer in the corner of the room, engrossed in his phone. He looked up when Bonnie and Cooper arrived, and Cooper acknowledged him with a nod.

Sam Keller was almost exactly as Bonnie had pictured him. Not overly tall but solidly built, he obviously maintained himself with some sort of lifting regime. He was handsome and well-groomed – perhaps a bit too well-groomed for a man who should have been up all night worrying about his missing wife.

The other male friend, Sam's work colleague, Oliver Pearce, or 'Ollie', was equally good looking and well-groomed. His girl-friend, Amanda Wells, popped her head out of the kitchen briefly for the introductions. Bonnie got the feeling the woman was trying to stay busy. Heather Walsh, Jonathan's wife, rose from her perch on the edge of a lounge chair and extended a hand, causing Bonnie to go through the whole contactless routine again.

"Oh, sorry," said Heather. "I must admit we've moved on from that pandemic business. We've all had it in our family; no-one got very sick. Can't see what all the fuss was about, to be honest."

Bonnie wanted to educate the woman on just how big a toll COVID-19 had taken on the world, let alone their own society, but she held her tongue. There was a time and a place, and this wasn't it. She turned her attention to Sam, who was flanked by his mates and looking ready to unleash a tirade on Cooper.

"About time you lot made a decent showing of it," Sam said, arms folded, biceps bulging. It was winter, but the guy was dressed in smart casual slacks and a polo shirt that was obviously chosen to show off his physique. He cast a disdainful glance at the uniformed officer in the corner of the room, who now looked equal parts bored and pissed off.

Cooper took control. "Mr Keller, is there somewhere we can talk privately? I've been apprised of your wife's disappearance but I'd like to hear what happened directly from you, please."

Sam ignored the request. "What are you doing to find my wife?"

"I can assure you we are doing everything we can," Cooper replied, "but we need to speak with you to ascertain the details of what happened last night."

"She's been out there all night! Where are the search parties?" Sam pointed to the officer. "You've got him in the corner there playing on his phone, more standing around outside. They're doing nothing! What are you actually doing to find my Juliet?"

Bonnie made a point of staring at the officer's phone until he rolled his eyes and slipped it into his pocket.

Cooper remained calm. "Mr Keller, if we could speak in private, please?"

Sam sighed, then nodded and led the way through the kitchen. Bonnie glanced at Cooper, his slight head tilt indicating he wanted her to join them. They followed Sam to an office where he sat behind a desk bigger than most dining tables, and pointed them to two chairs on the other side.

"Thank you," said Cooper once they were seated. "Now, Mr Keller, Sam, can I call you Sam?"

Sam shrugged. "Whatever."

"Sam, please take us through what happened this weekend. From the beginning."

"My wife went to the grocery store—"

Bonnie held up a hand to stop him. "From the beginning," she said. "You and Juliet live in the city. When did you come down here?"

Sam stared at Bonnie for a long moment before turning back to Cooper. "We drove down after I finished work on Friday night. Jules had already packed the car so we could get away quickly."

"Did you stop anywhere on the way?" Bonnie asked.

Sam dragged his eyes to look at her. "No. Oh, well, once we got to Bundanoon, we stopped in town to pick up a pizza for dinner. I'd called ahead to order it while we were driving."

"You called ahead? Or did Juliet?" asked Cooper.

"I did."

"Which one of you was driving?" asked Bonnie.

"I was. Jules doesn't like to drive much. She goes shopping, stuff like that. But she doesn't like doing the drive down here. She prefers to be chauffeured." He said this with a smirk, as if proud of himself for taking such good care of his wife. Bonnie's creep-o-meter went up a notch.

"If you were driving, wouldn't it have been easier for Juliet to call in the pizza order?" she asked.

"What? Why does it matter which one of us called for pizza on Friday night? Juliet went missing on Saturday night, twenty-four hours after that. I have hands-free in my car, if that's what you're worried about."

"Some of our questions might seem irrelevant," Cooper explained, "but we need to get a full picture of what happened in the days surrounding Juliet's disappearance. Please, just bear with us."

"Fine," said Sam. "I called because Juliet had a headache; she didn't want to talk to anyone. Benny at the pizza place is a mate, we get dinner from there practically every time we come down. We get the same order – large Benny's Special and a garlic bread if you must know – so it's not like I had to look at a menu or anything. Is that good enough for you?"

Cooper nodded. "And you didn't stop anywhere else on the way?"

Sam gave it some thought. "We might have stopped so Juliet could take a... so she could go to the toilet. I can't quite remember."

"It was only two nights ago," said Bonnie. "You sure you can't remember?"

"We come down here a lot. The drive is the same, they all tend to blend together. Again, does it really matter whether we stopped for a piss-break the night before—"

"Okay, let's move on," said Cooper.

"Actually, Sam, do you mind if I leave you with Detective Cooper while I take a look around? You have a lovely house."

Sam waved her off. "Yeah, whatever. I have nothing to hide."

I'll be the judge of that, thought Bonnie as she left Cooper to finish the initial questioning. In just twenty minutes Sam Keller had ticked at least three boxes on Bonnie's mental domestic abuse checklist. She found herself hoping Juliet had seen a way out and taken it.

Because the alternative didn't bear thinking about.

June 2017

"Oh, my goodness, would you look at this place!"

"I know! What a view. Wow. Our girl really did meet her prince at that pub!"

Juliet watched on, grinning, as Tess and Gwen ran around the apartment, opening doors, touching all the furniture, and squealing like schoolgirls.

"Good call getting them to come over before all the guests arrive," said Sam, taking a sip of his beer.

Juliet smiled at her fiancé. "Yeah. They'll settle down soon, I promise." She leaned against the kitchen bench, earning a hard stare from one of the caterers who was busy setting out plates. "How long have we got?" she asked Sam.

"Just under an hour. Shouldn't you be getting ready?"

She shrugged, nodded at her friends. "Give them another minute or two, then we'll all get dressed. Thank you, Sam."

"What for?"

"All this. Having my twenty-first in your beautiful apartment. I know it's a big deal for you. My friends aren't..." she lowered her voice as Tess ran by. "They aren't quite as sophisticated as yours."

Sam pulled her in for a hug. "Stop it. I love your friends. And your family, too. They are coming, right?"

Juliet nodded. "Nick and Renee are bringing Mum and Dad. They got a babysitter." It was one of the two disappointments she'd come to terms with about this party. Sam hadn't wanted kids to come, which made sense because the apartment really wasn't set up for it, but it meant her little nephew wasn't going to be there.

The other thing missing was Max. Her best friend couldn't make it up from Canberra. Some group assignment thing he absolutely had to work on all weekend. Whatever.

"Hey," said Sam, taking her into his arms. "I know it sucks Max isn't going to be here."

Juliet marvelled at how Sam could read her mind. She tried to shake her disappointment off; she could catch up with Max anytime. Sam had gone to a lot of trouble to put on this party for her. Besides, she was twenty-one and engaged to be married. Time to grow up.

"It's okay." Juliet surveyed the party preparations and plastered on a smile. "His loss."

"Yeah, definitely," said Sam. "But maybe we can take a drive down that way soon? Catch up with Max, visit a couple of wineries. Would you like that?"

"I'd love it!"

Sam grinned and gave her a kiss, before pushing her gently in the direction of his bedroom.

"I don't think we have time," she whispered.

"I mean go and get ready, silly. And take those giggling girls with you."

"Oh, right." She kissed him back, then managed to pull Tess

and Gwen away from the views of the city long enough to get ready for the party.

The night was fantastic. Sam's friend, Heather, who was married to his best friend, Jonathan, had recommended a party planner she'd used for their engagement party. Juliet had no idea party planning was even a real job. She knew they had wedding planners, but weddings are big events. Imagine spending your days planning people's engagement parties and twenty-firsts? Juliet had to hand it to her, though. This party planner was very good at her job.

The place looked amazing, stylishly decorated with flowers and balloons in a red and black theme. They weren't Juliet's favourite colours, if she was honest, but Sam had said how striking they'd look against the apartment furnishings and the backdrop of city lights. As usual, he'd been right.

The food was magnificent, and very fancy. It was all finger food, brought around on trays by waiters in tuxedos. And the champagne – proper French stuff – kept flowing as well. It was truly a twenty-first any girl would dream about.

Nick and Renee made their way over. "Hey, Jules," said Nick, half a crab cake in one hand, beer in the other. "When's the real food coming out?"

"That is real food," said Juliet.

"Ignore him," said Renee. "I told him to eat a sandwich on the way in. This place is amazing, Juliet. These people..." Juliet followed her gaze to where her mum and dad were seated on the lounge with Yvonne and Richard, Sam's parents. Her mum was chatting away to Yvonne in her usual big-arm-gesturing way, while her dad was awkwardly trying to balance a napkin of food on his knee and eat it without spilling his drink or copping one of his wife's flailing arms. Juliet couldn't tell whether Yvonne and Richard were mesmerised or bored stiff.

"Yeah, I know. It's a bit fancier than we're used to, hey?" She tried to play it down, but Juliet was starting to feel like there was a massive divide across the room, and she was caught in the chasm down the middle. She'd never had a problem fitting into Sam's world up until now. She liked his friends; once you looked past the money, they were quite nice people. And his parents – well, Juliet was getting used to them. Sam loved her and she loved him, and that was the important thing.

"Listen, Jules, I think we're going to have to take off," said Nick.

"Oh, but we haven't cut the cake yet," she replied. He couldn't take her parents home before the cake. How would that look?

"We can stay another half an hour," said Renee.

"But the babysitter costs—"

"It's your sister's twenty-first, Nick," Renee cut him off. "We can stay another half an hour."

Nick shoved the rest of the crab cake in his mouth and grabbed another from a passing waiter. He wandered off, mumbling something about getting McDonalds on the way home.

"Ignore him, he's a big boofhead," said Renee.

"Yeah, but he's also right. It's a long drive home, and you have to be getting back to Luke. I'll go and chase up the cake."

"Jules." Renee caught her arm as she turned. "You're happy with this guy, right?"

"Why does everyone keep asking me that? What's wrong with Sam?"

"Nothing," she answered quickly. "It's just... it's really fast, that's all. You only met him six months ago, and now you're engaged, and he's throwing you this fancy party. You're still only twenty-one, Juliet. Nick's just worried you're rushing into this too fast. So am I."

Juliet crossed her arms. "How old were the two of you when

you got married?"

"That's... yeah, fair point. We were twenty-two. But we'd known each other for years. I was literally the girl next door. Nick and I were always going to get married."

Juliet was sick of hearing this. Yes, she and Sam had only met six months ago, but when it was just the two of them, it felt like she'd known him her whole life. He made her feel special. Made her feel like a princess. People needed to back off and let them be.

She turned away from Renee. "I'll go and see about that cake."

Juliet hadn't made it to the kitchen when she felt a tap on her shoulder. Renee was persistent, but why did she have to choose now? Juliet got ready to tell her to back off, but it wasn't Renee behind her.

"Max! What are you doing here?"

He picked her up and twirled her around. "Did you really think I'd miss my Juliet's twenty-first birthday? Seriously, Jules, do you know me at all?"

She wriggled out of his arms and slapped him playfully on the shoulder. "Why are you so late then? It's almost ten o'clock."

"Ah, yeah. I really did have a group assignment to work on this weekend. But I made them all work for eight hours straight today. We got it done, then I jumped in the car and came here. Which reminds me, you got any food? I'm starving."

"Glad you could make it." Sam appeared at Juliet's side. He shook hands with Max then slid an arm around her waist.

"Wouldn't miss it," said Max, his voice an octave deeper.

Juliet left them to chat while she made Max up a plate of food and checked with the caterers about the cake. By the time she returned, Sam was back over in the corner talking with his mates and there was definite tension in the air.

"What now?" Juliet asked, handing Max the food. The two of

them had only been together a handful of times, but she knew they didn't get on. Evidently that hadn't changed.

Max shrugged. "Same old same old. Forget it, Jules. It's your birthday, and I've had a long drive."

Before Juliet had a chance to answer the lights went out, and Gwen and Tess were either side of her. "Come on, birthday girl," said Tess. "It's cake time!"

11

Bonnie could hear the house guests talking quietly in the sunroom. She decided to leave them for the moment and check out the rest of the country mansion uninterrupted. After a few minutes searching through multiple living, dining, and entertaining spaces, she finally found the bedrooms.

The first two were obviously guest rooms, each large enough for a king-sized bed and with their own en-suite bathrooms. A quick scan of personal belongings revealed these were the two rooms allocated to Jonathan and Heather, and Ollie and Amanda. Bonnie moved on.

The third and fourth doors were also guest rooms, currently unoccupied. The door at the end of the hall opened onto the master suite, and Bonnie nodded to herself. The house was owned by Sam's parents, so this must be their room, but of course Sam would set himself and Juliet up in here when he was using the house with his friends. It was all about appearance and pecking order in the world of money.

Bonnie entered the room and took a moment to survey her surroundings. It was neat and tidy, no clothing or belongings strewn across the room as there would be if it were her pitching up somewhere for a couple of nights. The only thing out of place was the unmade bed – presumably that was Juliet's morning task.

Satisfied there were no obvious signs of a struggle or foul-play, Bonnie looked over the couple's personal items. She found the usual collection of clothes, toiletries, make-up, and accessories. Sam had a designer shaving kit in the bathroom, and almost as many grooming products as his wife. Bonnie found nothing to suggest either of them had packed for anything other than a typical weekend away.

She left the master suite and went to explore the kitchen. Amanda had given up on whatever she'd been doing there, so Bonnie had the kitchen to herself. Again, things seemed consistent with a weekend away.

"Do you need help with anything, Detective?"

Bonnie looked up to see Amanda standing in the doorway between the sunroom and the kitchen. "No," she replied, not feeling the need to elaborate.

"Oh." Amanda seemed unsure what to do or say. "Um... is it okay if I put the kettle on? I could really use a cup of tea."

"Sounds like a great idea," said Bonnie. She watched as Amanda moved about the kitchen, having obviously familiarised herself with the place earlier. She seemed younger than the others, and less self-assured. Bonnie got a second cup out of the cupboard and placed it next to the one Amanda was preparing for herself. "Do you mind?" she said with a half-smile.

"Of course. Sugar and milk?"

"Actually, is there any green tea? I could do with a bit of detoxing."

Amanda searched cupboards and drawers and came up with the goods. She placed the green tea bag in the cup just as the kettle boiled.

"Have you known Juliet long?" Bonnie asked as Amanda poured.

"Oh, no. I've never met her, actually. I only just met the others last night. Ollie and I haven't been dating long. I wasn't sure about coming here, to be honest. But it was important to Ollie, being Sam's birthday, so..." Amanda handed Bonnie her tea.

"This must be very strange for you, then," said Bonnie.

"Totally. Do you know when we'll be able to leave? Oh, sorry, that sounded so disrespectful. But... I don't know, it's a weird vibe here. Do you have any idea what happened to her? Juliet?"

"It's very early in the investigation. We need to consider all possibilities. Actually, you might be able to help with that. You got here yesterday evening, right?"

"Yes, shortly after five." Amanda finished making her cup of tea as she spoke. "Ollie played rugby in the morning, and by the time he got home and showered it was past one o'clock. We left Sydney and had a late lunch in one of the towns on the way. Bowral, I think it was. And we had a peek through the shops there, too. Ollie was a bit pissed off, actually, because he wanted to get to the house and relax but Sam had said not to arrive before five. I didn't mind, the shops were cute and to be honest, I was in no rush to get here."

"No, I can understand that. Spending a weekend with strangers is a big ask. You must really like Ollie." Bonnie leaned against the bench and sipped her tea, just two women having a casual chat.

Amanda relaxed a little. "He's lovely. And it's not that big an age difference, five years. The same as Sam and Juliet, apparently. That's what Ollie says. I was looking forward to meeting her. Ollie told me she's into fashion, which is totally my thing too."

I bet. Bonnie then inwardly chastised herself for jumping to conclusions. Amanda was sweet. "Hey, do you have any idea why Sam told Ollie you guys shouldn't arrive before five yesterday? Seems weird, given he and Juliet got here Friday night."

Amanda shrugged. "I don't know. You'd have to ask the boys. Sam knew Ollie was playing rugby. Sam's on the team as well, but he wasn't playing yesterday. I suppose because he was coming here. Again, you'd have to ask him."

"Ask who what?" Ollie joined them in the kitchen, putting an end to Bonnie's casual questioning approach. He was closely followed by Jonathan and Heather.

Amanda slipped her hand into Ollie's. "Detective..."

"Hunter," Bonnie filled in.

"Right, yes. Detective Hunter was just asking why Sam didn't play in the game yesterday. Oh, and why we weren't supposed to get here until five o'clock."

Heather stepped forward. "It was my understanding the timing was Juliet's request," she said. "Yesterday was Sam's birthday, and she wanted them to spend the day together. Plus, she needed to prepare for the dinner party."

"Really?" said Bonnie. "There were only six of you. How much prep time would she need?"

Heather sighed, and Bonnie realised she didn't understand these people at all. "Juliet was using us as a trial run for the family's annual Christmas in July," Heather explained. "Yvonne – that's Sam's mother – had entrusted a significant part of the meal to her for the first time, and Juliet was nervous about getting it right. So, this was her practice run."

"I didn't know that," said Jonathan.

Heather glared at him. "You didn't need to know."

Jonathan held up his hands and backed away.

"So, you two were also instructed to arrive after five o'clock?" Bonnie asked.

"Yeah," said Jonathan. "Sam said Jules wanted them to have

some alone time. That's why he didn't play yesterday. Well, that's what he told us. He told coach he'd pulled a hammy at the gym, which could have been true too. I reckon he just wanted a weekend off."

"We've been pretty slammed at the office for a while now," said Ollie. "Sam and I are with the same firm," he added. "We were both keen for a break. Didn't see this happening, though. You guys have any idea yet what happened to Jules?"

"They haven't a clue."

Bonnie turned to find Sam in the doorway, Cooper behind him.

Sam looked Bonnie in the eye, finally speaking directly to her. "My wife has been missing for almost a full day, and you cops know nothing. I've told you everything I know multiple times, so can you please stop questioning my friends and get out there and find her?"

Cooper stepped forward, saving Bonnie from answering. Or perhaps because he could see her seething inside and didn't want to risk her answering. Good call.

"Thank you all for your time," he said, then to Sam, "we'll be in touch."

12

June 2017

Juliet's family and Sam's parents left the party after the speeches and cake, and Sam and his friends moved the couches aside so the remaining guests could dance. Juliet had a few more champagnes, her anxiety over the divide between her world and Sam's forgotten, and it truly was one of the most special nights of her life. She said as much to her friends as they chatted into the early hours, the guests long-gone and the spare mattress on the floor in the living room between the couches giving them all teenage slumber party vibes.

"You're so lucky," said Tess. "I still can't believe this place. When are you going to move in? Officially, like."

"After the wedding," Juliet replied. "Sam's parents are old-fashioned."

"What's it got to do with Sam's parents?" asked Gwen.

"They pretty much own him, from what I can tell," said Max, not looking up from his phone. "I'm ordering food. Who wants?"

"They do not own him," said Juliet. "And keep your voice

down." Sam had gone to bed hours earlier as he had a rugby game in the morning. He hadn't been too happy about Max and the girls staying over, but Juliet had promised they wouldn't keep him awake. She couldn't make them pay for a hotel room in the city.

"What are you getting?" Gwen asked Max. "Burgers? I'll take a cheeseburger."

"Done," said Max. "Tess, you want anything?"

"Who's going to deliver at this time of night?" Tess asked. She twirled her finger in the throw rug Juliet had found for her. Sam didn't have a lot of spare bedding, but they'd turned the heating up after all the guests left and the room was nice and toasty. A couple of throws and the couch pillows would do for extra warmth.

"It's the city," Max answered. "Plenty of places deliver twenty-four seven."

"Oh. I don't want a burger. I'd have some fries, though. Thanks."

"Fries, got it. Jules?"

"No thanks. There's food in the kitchen, you know. The caterers put all the leftovers in the fridge."

Tess screwed up her nose. "No offence, but that was all a bit fancy for me. So, you're moving in after the wedding. That's only a couple of months away, right?"

"Three. It's in September," said Juliet, trying to ignore the fancy food comment. It had seemed perfectly acceptable when Tess was hoeing in a few hours ago.

"What's the address of this place?" Max asked, looking up at Juliet. She reeled it off.

"Look at you," said Gwen. "Already so at home. I can't believe you're going to live here. It's such a gorgeous place."

"It's a bit 'bachelor pad', though, isn't it?" said Max as he entered the details in his phone.

Juliet laughed. "Sam's allowed to have his bachelor stage. I'll add some feminine touches once I move in."

They chatted for a while about the type of feminine touches Juliet might add, and Gwen and Tess had a few suggestions. Max stayed quiet, except to give updates on when the food was due to arrive. Juliet asked him to go downstairs to meet the delivery driver so they wouldn't buzz and wake Sam. He grumbled but did as she asked. She gave him the keycard she used when she was here to let himself back in.

"So how long is your commute going to be?" asked Tess as she plucked fries from their container and ate them one by one.

"Shouldn't be too bad," said Gwen. "She'll be going against the traffic. Most people live in the suburbs and commute to the city. Jules will be going the other way." She took a bite of her cheeseburger. "Oh, this is so good. Why is everything better in the city?"

"It has nothing to do with the city," said Max. "It's all about reading the reviews. This place had the best. You're welcome." He bit into his own burger, and a clump of sauce-covered lettuce squeezed out onto the mattress.

"Be careful," said Juliet, getting up to find a cloth.

"Sorry," said Max. "So, your commute?"

Juliet wet the cloth and wiped up the mess, giving them all plates to prevent any further spillage. "Actually, Sam thinks I should quit my job once we're married."

"What?"

"Seriously?"

They all stopped eating and stared at her.

"But you love that job," said Tess. "You've been working for Maria since you were fifteen."

"Yes, but times change. It won't be practical to live here and drive out to Castle Hill every day. Sam says I can get a job in the city instead. There are so many clothing stores here, it shouldn't be a problem."

"I guess that's true," said Tess with a shrug.

They resumed eating, but Juliet could tell the mood had shifted. Max's face darkened as he stared at her before silently going back to his food.

Gwen came straight out with it. "We're not going to see you once you get married, are we?"

"What? That's nonsense."

"No, it's not," she argued. "You already spend your weekends here. We used to go out together every Saturday night, but now you're here and Max is in Canberra, even Shahid is working most of the time. It's just me and Tess left." She reached out to Tess. "No offence."

Tess's back straightened. "None taken."

"You guys, don't be ridiculous. Well, yeah, I'll be married so I'll be here with Sam most of the time, but I'll come back and we can go out together sometimes. And you can come here, too. We'll get a proper bed for the spare room, and we can have nights out in the city. You can crash here whenever you want."

Gwen pulled a face. "Your new husband might not like that idea."

Juliet couldn't win. The problem was, they were right. Things were definitely going to change when she and Sam were married. She couldn't wait to be Mrs Keller, but she didn't want to lose her friends in the process.

"Come on guys, let's cut Jules some slack," said Max. "We all have to grow up sometime." He popped the last of his burger into his mouth and stood, holding out a hand to collect the empty plates from the others.

Juliet followed him into the kitchen. "That was unexpected," she said, taking the plates from him and placing them in the dishwasher.

"What?"

"You, sticking up for me. You hate Sam." She folded her arms and leaned against the sink. She'd wanted to have this conversation with Max for months but had never had the courage. The champagne and the party had made her bold.

"Hate's a strong word, Jules."

She stared at him.

"All right, I'll admit I don't like the guy. He's not right for you."

"Why not? What's wrong with him?"

"I just..." Max stepped forward, took Juliet's hands in his. "I don't trust him, that's all. This place, those people tonight, it's all so fake. It was supposed to be your big day, but it felt like he was showing you off rather than making you feel special."

Juliet didn't know what to do with any of this. Was Max jealous? He'd never been like this about any of the boyfriends she'd had in the past. They'd been friends since primary school, but there'd never been anything romantic between them. She'd thought that was the way it would always be.

"Sam makes me feels special every day," Juliet argued. "He's going to be my husband."

Max dropped her hands, stepped back. "You're right. I don't know, maybe I got the wrong impression because I was so late."

"Maybe you did," she agreed. "Look, Max, I love you. You're my best friend. But I'm going to marry Sam. Please, can you try to get along with him? I really need my best friend to like my husband. I don't know if I can survive this world without you."

He nodded, then grinned and lifted her in one of his big bear hugs. "Of course, I can. Anything for you, Jules." He put her down and turned her around, guiding her by the shoulders past the living room where Gwen and Tess were settling in amongst the blankets, and giving her a gentle shove toward the bedroom.

"It's really late. Go on, go sleep with your fiancé," he whispered. "We'll see you in the morning."

"Goodnight," Juliet said to all of them before heading down the hall to Sam's bedroom. She was glad she and Max had finally talked. Maybe he and Sam could spend some time together tomorrow, start to get to know each other. Sam might even agree to take Max to his rugby game. She decided to ask him first thing in the morning.

But as she turned to close the bedroom door behind her, she caught a glimpse of Max's face. She was kidding herself. Hate might be a strong word, but it was the right one. Max hated Sam, and if she was completely honest with herself, she had to admit something else, too.

Sam hated Max right back.

13

"The guy checks all the boxes, Coop," Bonnie said as they walked to the car.

"What boxes?"

"I have a mental checklist for domestic abuse. There's an actual one, but I've built up my own over the years. This guy..." Bonnie paused as they got in the car.

"Give me some examples," asked Cooper. He'd climbed in the driver's side this time.

"Well, he's got a bad temper, for a start. Deflecting blame – 'why aren't you out there searching for her', instead of asking us what he can do to help. And he's the textbook definition of white male privilege. He sees women as inferior."

Cooper paused, keys halfway to the ignition. He turned to face Bonnie. "How do you figure that?"

"Did you notice how he didn't want to talk to me? Kept addressing you, even when I asked the questions."

"Yeah, I did see that."

"That's half the reason I left the room, much as I hate that kind of behaviour."

Cooper nodded. "You thought I'd get more out of him

alone." He started the car and turned it around rather than reversing out of the driveway.

"So, did you?"

"Not really. Usual denials, nothing helpful. He stuck pretty close to his story."

"A bit too close?"

"Maybe. But let's keep our minds open for now, huh?"

Bonnie nodded. "You ask him whether she carried a purse?"

"Apparently she did, but Sam said she left it at the house last night and just took a twenty to the store."

"Sounds plausible."

The cold wasn't keeping the tourists away, Bonnie noted, as they drove through town. It had to be less than twelve degrees, but people were still out in their designer winter coats and boots. At least it wasn't raining.

"That's popular," said Cooper as they drove past the local school grounds. There was a weekend market on, and Bonnie could see stalls full of brightly coloured knitwear and home-made cakes and bread. There was also a coffee cart.

"Ooh, can we stop for caffeine?"

Cooper kept driving. "Maybe later. I want to get to the scene before it's completely trampled by this lot." He opened his hands palm-up on top of the steering wheel in a 'what the' gesture as a tourist crossed the road right in front of them.

"You can arrest him for jaywalking, you know," said Bonnie with a smile.

Cooper ignored her. "How did you go talking to the other occupants of the house?"

Bonnie shrugged. "Kept getting interrupted. Amanda clearly isn't one of them. She said she's only recently started dating Ollie, hadn't met the others before last night. Meaning she never met Juliet at all. She said something about a weird vibe in the house, but I didn't get any more before her boyfriend and the other couple walked in."

"Jonathan and Heather. What did you make of them?"

"Bit of tension there, perhaps. Again, got interrupted. It's definitely a boys' club, though. I wouldn't be surprised if the three of them went to the same private school. They play rugby together." She shifted in her seat. "Did you find out whether there were any staff on site?"

Cooper shook his head. "Caretakers clear out before the family arrive, and the gardeners are scheduled through the week. To maintain privacy."

"Of course."

They arrived at the scene and Cooper parked outside the grocery store, then they crossed the road to where two cops were guarding a taped off area of grass. The car was no longer there; presumably taken away by forensics.

A sergeant in uniform approached them, nodded a greeting. "Levine," he said. "That's Senior Constable Curran. We were first on scene last night."

Curran waved from her position near the fence.

"Detective Inspector Cooper, Detective Sergeant Hunter," said Cooper. "You're local?"

Levine nodded. "We're only a small station. Called it in to Moss Vale soon as we knew we were dealing with a missing person; they sent a few more bodies our way." He pointed to the other side of the train tracks. "SES arrived first thing. Got a grid search going on over there."

Bonnie could see a few uniformed cops mixed in with the bright orange jumpsuits of State Emergency Service personnel walking slowly in the distance.

"We've already done all the area this side of the tracks," Levine continued, pointing. "Found nothing. Forensics finished up about half an hour ago, took the car back to Sydney with them."

"Good work," said Cooper. "Talk me through the initial call-out."

Levine stood like a soldier at ease – legs shoulder-width apart, arms folded despite the bulk of equipment strapped to his body and chest that made Bonnie thankful she was no longer in uniform.

"Call came in just before seven pm," he said. "Station isn't far from here, so we were on scene within ten minutes."

"Probably closer to five," added Curran as she walked over to join their huddle, hands shoved into her pockets.

"Yeah, probably," Levine agreed. "Saw two cars when we arrived. The black BMW X5 SUV was parked on the grass here." He pointed to the middle of the taped-off area. "And the Audi was pulled in behind it."

"Jonathan's car," said Bonnie.

Curran had her notebook out. "Jonathan Walsh," she read. "He and another guy, Oliver Pearce, were with the missing woman's husband, Sam Keller."

Levine nodded. "According to Keller, his wife Juliet had left their home—"

"Holiday home," Curran interrupted.

"Yes, thank you, holiday home, shortly before five pm in his vehicle to drive to this store." Levine pointed to the grocery store across the road, the Bundanoon IGA according to its signage. "When she hadn't returned by six pm, and wasn't answering her phone, the three men drove out here in Walsh's vehicle. They saw the parked BMW and pulled in behind it. They went across to the store, but by then it was closed."

Curran took up the story. "Keller said he called Juliet's mobile, and they heard it ringing. They followed the sound and found the phone in the grass." She stepped over to a spot roughly five metres from where the BMW had been parked, in the direction of the train tracks. Bonnie noted a stick had been inserted into the ground. "I put that there for you guys when Forensics took their markers away," said Curran, looking proud of herself.

"Thanks," said Bonnie.

"The men found both the phone and the car keys there," said Levine. "They said the car was locked. Husband unlocked it and looked inside, including the boot. No sign of Juliet. They looked around, went up and down the street, found nothing. That's when they called us."

"Who called?" asked Cooper.

"Walsh called triple-o," said Levine.

"Anything else you can tell us?" asked Cooper. "What was their state of mind?"

"Husband was quite agitated," said Curran. "Kept yelling at us to do something, get out there and find her. The mates tried to calm him down."

"Were they successful?" Bonnie asked.

Curran shrugged. "To a point. He settled while we asked questions, got the story. But then he wanted to take the car. Wasn't too happy when we told him it had to stay put for forensics."

"Was even less happy we wouldn't let him keep his wife's phone," Levine added.

"Oh yeah?" said Bonnie. That was interesting.

"Yeah. They took off in Walsh's car not long after that. Said they were going to look for her themselves. I tried to tell them to go home – back to their holiday house," he corrected himself with a sideways glance at his partner, "but Keller was pretty riled up. I believe they trawled the streets for a few hours before giving up and leaving it to us."

"What else can you tell us?" Cooper asked.

Levine detailed the rest of the investigation so far for them but basically, they'd found nothing. Canvassing of local houses and businesses had come up empty; no-one had seen Juliet arrive outside the grocery store yesterday afternoon. Which was not unusual, given that it was the middle of winter and already getting dark at that time of day. The store owner had been interviewed; she'd closed up herself yesterday. She'd only had two customers after four pm, both of whom were locals she knew. She didn't recognise Juliet's picture.

"That's about the size of it," Levine finished. "Although there are still a few dog-walkers we're yet to talk to."

"Dog-walkers around here are creatures of habit," Curran explained. "They tend to have their favourite routes and follow them day after day. We'll come back down here later this afternoon, around the time Juliet went missing, see if any of them are here. We could get lucky."

"Good thinking," said Cooper, handing them each a card. "We'll stick around a bit longer, run through some possible scenarios." He tilted his head at the squads conducting the grid search. "Keep us informed."

"Will do." Levine hooked his thumbs into his belt and walked off. Curran turned to follow.

Bonnie caught her lightly by the sleeve. "One more question. Where's the best coffee in town?"

B onnie stood in line at the cafe Curran had pointed out, while Cooper went to speak to the owner of the grocery store. She was just emerging with two steaming takeaway cups and a bag of pastries when he came sauntering down the path.

"Anything?" she asked, handing him his coffee and offering the greasy bag.

Cooper shook his head and reached into the bag. "Just as Levine said. She didn't see Juliet but did remember seeing the car there when she drove out after closing up. Thanks for this."

"What time was that?"

"About five-twenty," Cooper said, spraying sugary pastry crumbs over the pavement. "Oh wow, this is good."

Bonnie took a bite of her own and concurred. "They call them morning buns. Cross between a croissant and a cinnamon scroll, I think. So, we're looking at a thirty-five to forty-minute window where Juliet has disappeared?"

"Uh-huh."

Bonnie glanced down the street. "There's Benny's," she said, pointing out the pizza restaurant Sam claimed they'd stopped at on Friday night. "It's not open yet but it looks like someone's in there. Shall we go have a chat?"

"Lead on," said Cooper, popping the last of the morning bun into his mouth. He stared at the cafe as they passed, and Bonnie knew he was contemplating getting another one. She quickened her step so she wouldn't be tempted herself.

They finished their coffees and disposed of the rubbish before Cooper knocked on the door of the pizza restaurant. He held up his badge when someone approached, and the door was duly opened.

"Can I help you?" The man was medium height, middle-aged, and balding, with the physique of someone who spent long hours on his feet. He wiped his hands on a tea towel slung over his shoulder.

"Are you Benny?" Cooper asked.

"Yeah, this is my place." Benny gestured to the crime scene across the road. "I wasn't at work last night, but my staff said there was something going on out there. Don and Leonie came in asking about a missing woman."

Cooper cocked his head. "Don and Leonie?"

"Sorry. Officers Levine and Curran. Did they find her?"

"No," said Bonnie. "We wanted to ask you a few more questions if you don't mind. Can we come in?"

"Oh yeah, sure." Benny stepped aside and pointed to a table in the window. "Take a seat. You want anything? Coffee? We're still setting up, but the machine's on."

"We just had one, thanks," said Cooper as they settled at the table. "Do you know Sam and Juliet Keller?"

Benny nodded. "The Kellers own a house out on Spruce Drive. Sam's been coming here since he was a kid. Oh, shit – is it Juliet that's gone missing?"

"Yes," said Bonnie. "Sam mentioned that they picked up a

pizza on their way to the house on Friday night. Were you here then?"

"Yeah. I was out the back when he came in, but I saw him through there." Benny pointed to the window through to the kitchen. It was large enough that Bonnie could see two staff members in there chopping ingredients and making dough.

"He was by himself?" Cooper asked.

Benny nodded again. "Sometimes they eat in, but more often they just pick up on a Friday night. I only saw Sam, and just briefly. It was pretty busy."

"You didn't happen to see Juliet waiting in the car?" Bonnie asked.

"No, but I wasn't looking. Like I said, we were busy."

"What's your opinion of the Kellers?" asked Bonnie. She felt Cooper stir slightly next to her, but he didn't say anything.

"I don't know. They seem nice enough, I suppose. His parents are a bit stuck up, but they don't come in here. I see them around town occasionally."

"But you're more familiar with Sam Keller," said Cooper.

"Well, he comes in here more often. Usually Friday nights, if they're in town."

"Would you classify him as a mate?" Bonnie asked.

Benny shook his head. "I wouldn't, no. Look, I've nothing against the guy. He's a decent spender. Always tips my staff pretty well. Makes a show of it of course, like he's a big man. But that's just how these rich city-types are. My team pocket the cash and ignore the attitude."

Cooper and Bonnie asked a few more questions of Benny and his staff, and besides adding to the picture of Sam Keller as a rich twat that had already formed in Bonnie's mind, they learned nothing new. They thanked the team for their time, promised to get a pizza if they were still in town by dinner time, and left the restaurant.

"So, what are the possibilities?" Cooper asked as they walked back to the spot where the Keller's car had been parked.

"The car was locked, according to Sam and his mates. And the keys and her phone were over here." Bonnie stood by the stick Curran had used as a makeshift marker.

"That's away from the store," said Cooper. "Which means she parked, got out, locked the car, then something happened to take her in the opposite direction than she intended."

"Maybe she saw something over here, or heard something that made her come this way," suggested Bonnie.

"Maybe," said Cooper. "Or maybe someone disabled her as soon as she locked the car and dragged her over there."

Bonnie studied the grass around her. It was ankle height and had plenty of footprints from being trampled by all and sundry, but there were no discernible drag marks. "I don't think so, Coop. There's nothing over here. Not enough cover for a sex offender to get his shit done without being seen, and the fence and train tracks prohibit her being dragged too much farther."

"So, you think she was disabled close to the car, and the keys and phone were ditched over there? Maybe someone threw them?"

"Seems more likely to me," said Bonnie.

Cooper's head swivelled a few times between the car location, the stick marker, and the fence before he nodded. "Agreed. All right, so someone waits for her to get out of her car and lock it, then approaches from behind and disables her before she can cross the road to the store?"

"He could have called out," said Bonnie. "Got her talking – asked directions, the time, whatever – while he got close enough to attack."

"And once he disabled her and got her into his vehicle, the National Park is only a few kilometres away. Not far to go to find somewhere secluded."

Bonnie looked up and down the street. "Pretty bold move. I know it was close to dark, but still. It's the main street of town, the grocery store is right there and the pizza place is in view as well. Risky place to attempt an unplanned abduction."

"True. What's the next possibility?" Cooper asked, although Bonnie figured he knew damn well what she was going to say.

"She was never here."

Cooper nodded. "Talk me through your theory."

"Keller's story is they leave Sydney Friday night, drive here, maybe stop for a toilet break, maybe not, and call for a pizza – he makes the call – while they're driving. They pick up the pizza – he goes in alone, which we've confirmed with Benny – then go to the house, where they stay until Juliet supposedly goes out for a last-minute dinner party ingredient some twenty-four hours later. He say what that was, by the way?"

"Said he didn't know," Cooper answered.

"Course he didn't," said Bonnie. "Juliet takes the car and goes out. She leaves before the guests arrive, so up to this point no-one has seen her in town. Then no-one sees her here, either. We only have Sam's word she was in Bundanoon at all. Hell, do we know if she even left Sydney? When was the last confirmed sighting from someone other than her husband?"

"That is something we'll need to check out. But go on. How did the car get here if Juliet didn't drive it?"

"Sam," said Bonnie. "He does something to Juliet, either back in Sydney or on the way down here, then realises he's going to be the number one suspect. He knows his friends are due to arrive Saturday at five – hang on, he *told* them not to arrive *before* five – maybe he planned this whole thing?"

"Let's come back to that one," said Cooper. "Stay with your theory."

"Right. So, he's got Friday night and all day Saturday to come up with his plan. He gets the pizza like they usually do, pretends

Juliet is in the car as normal. Goes to the house, unpacks, makes it all look like both of them are there. Then just before five he takes the car, leaves it outside the grocery store, throws the keys and Juliet's phone into the grass, and hot-foots it back to the house in time to receive his mates."

"Then he goes through the big panic routine when she doesn't return," Cooper added, "and because he doesn't have the car, he gets Jonathan to drive them out here."

"So Jonathan and Ollie can be there when they find the keys and phone, and witness his shock and pain when he realises his wife is missing," Bonnie finished.

"It's quite a theory," said Cooper. "Will take some proving."

Bonnie stared at him, answering his unasked question with a barely perceptible nod. She was in. "We'd better get started then."

15

September 2017

"Oh wow, this is amazing!" Juliet couldn't help herself, she raced around the honeymoon suite like a giddy child. "Are you sure we can only stay here tonight?" Sam grabbed her by the hips and pulled her close. "Baby, we've got a plane to catch tomorrow. But don't worry, the hotel in New Zealand is going to be even better than this one." He kissed her, and she couldn't believe how lucky she was to have married this man.

The day had been everything Juliet could have dreamt and more. Her parents refused to disclose how much they'd spent on the wedding, but Nick did let slip that they'd taken out a second mortgage on the house. She wished they hadn't done that. Sam's parents had offered a significant contribution, but her father kept saying no. He told anyone who would listen that he only had one daughter, and he was determined to give her the wedding she deserved. How could Juliet argue with that?

"Champagne?" She turned to find Sam holding a bottle.

"Actually, I think I've had enough," she said, suddenly very tired.

"Rubbish." He popped the cork. "It's your wedding night, my sweetheart." Sam poured a glass and pushed it into her hand. "And this is a two-hundred-dollar bottle of bubbles. It won't keep, you know."

"Then maybe you shouldn't have opened it." She took a sip. "Oh, it's so good, though."

"Exactly." He poured himself a glass, took a sip, then put it down and stripped off all his clothes. He winked at her, then ventured into the massive bathroom. Juliet followed and gasped at the size of the spa bath. It looked so inviting, full of steaming, bubbling water.

"Come on, wife," said Sam as he climbed in. "Don't make me bathe alone on our wedding night."

Juliet giggled. "Okay, husband." The water was the perfect temperature as she sank down into it beside her perfect man.

Later, when they were finally exhausted and cuddled up in bed, Juliet thanked Sam for a wonderful day.

"There's plenty more where that came from, my love," he said, holding her tight. "You're Mrs Sam Keller, now. Remember that, baby. We'll go places together. Starting tomorrow, with New Zealand!"

It wasn't quite her idea of the perfect honeymoon. If she was honest, she would rather lie on a beach somewhere for a week, drinking cocktails and swimming and working on her tan. The Gold Coast, maybe, or perhaps even a nice resort in Bali. But Sam wanted an adventure. He wanted to go jet-boating, and bungee jumping, white-water rafting, all that crazy stuff. He was so keen she hadn't had the heart to talk him out of it. And like he said, the wedding day had been all about the bride. It was only fair the groom got to do what he wanted for the honeymoon, wasn't it?

Sam kissed her, and Juliet drifted off to sleep, wrapped in a bubble of love, her mind full of happy memories of a perfect day.

It was some time in the early hours when Juliet woke. At first, she wasn't quite sure what she was seeing, but as her eyes adjusted to the dim light in the room, she recognised Sam in front of her face. Or, more accurately, Sam's erect penis.

"Sam, honey, what time is it?" She took in his naked form kneeling over her, gyrating above her breasts. He held the bottle of champagne in one hand, his penis in the other. When he saw she was awake he rubbed himself all over her chest.

"You like that, huh? You like being woken up like this, don't you? You're a horny bitch, aren't you? My wife is a horny bitch." Juliet was still sleepy, and not sure whether he was actually expecting an answer.

He continued touching her, grabbing her breasts, pushing his erection into her face. "See what I've got for you, wife?"

"Sam, what are you doing? I'm tired, baby. Can we just cuddle?"

He drank from the bottle then poured the rest of the champagne over her breasts, sliding his erection around in the sticky mess. "Oh, this isn't going to wait, baby. I need you. God, Juliet, you're so hot. My wife is so fucking hot." He threw the empty bottle into the corner of the room, smashing it against the wall, then reached between her legs. "Yeah, see?" he said, thrusting two fingers inside her. "You're so wet already. You love this."

Juliet was wide awake now. They'd made love twice that night, once in the spa bath and again when they went to bed. Sam, as always, had been so tender, so caring. This wasn't what she was used to.

"Sam." Juliet tried one more time, pushing him away. "Can we save it for the morning? I'm really tired..."

He reached for her hands, interlocking his fingers through

hers before pinning her arms to the bed. He stared into her eyes, and for a tiny second, she didn't recognise him. Then he smiled.

"Come on, baby. I'm so hot for you." Juliet struggled, but he held firm. "You're my wife now, Juliet. You don't get to say no." He leaned down and kissed her hard before entering her with a force he had never used before.

"Oh! Sam—"

"Shh, it's okay." He held his hand over her mouth as he moved inside her. "Oh baby, I can feel every part of you. I'm so hard right now. I love being your husband. You love it when I do it like this, don't you? You love it when I take charge. That's what husbands do, Juliet. This is what you wanted, right? A husband who takes charge? It turns you on, doesn't it? I turn you on. Oh fuck, yes, I turn you on. Oh baby, you're going to make the best wife. You're going to make me a very happy husband. Oh, Jules, Jules... fuck, yes, Jules..."

And then it was over.

Sam rolled off her and was snoring within seconds.

When Juliet climbed out of the bed, she saw spots of blood on the sheets. She pulled the doona up to cover it and stared at Sam's sleeping form, tried to ignore the throbbing between her legs.

Was that how married couples had sex?

Or had her husband just raped her on their wedding night?

16

"Okay, here we are, come and meet the team." Cooper was acting like he'd just hired Bonnie and she was stepping into the Homicide Squad office for the first time. It was both sweet and annoying.

"I've been here before, you know. I work in the same building."

"Yeah, righto." Cooper threw his keys into the bowl on his desk, ran a hand through his hair. "Let's get on with it, then. Briefing, now," he said to the spattering of his team still in the office late on a Sunday afternoon. He led the way to one of the meeting rooms lining the outside of the open-plan office.

Bonnie knew some of the faces. Detective Sergeant Lance 'Mars' Marsden nodded and smiled as he took a seat in the middle of the long meeting table and opened his laptop. Zach Ryan and Nora Reynolds, two of the best technical analysts on the force, quickly set up their equipment at the end of the table. Bonnie had witnessed Zach and Nora's brilliance first-hand when she'd joined Homicide for the Baby-Faced Killer case two years prior. She'd met Mars a few times, but never worked with him.

Two new faces completed the assembled team. Must be the good kids who needed leadership. Bonnie introduced herself.

"Oh wow," said the young guy. "You working with us now?"

The woman slapped him lightly on the arm. "Dude. Manners." She held out a hand for Bonnie to shake but didn't seem offended when Bonnie just waved back. "Detective Senior Constable Kate Riley. I'm the smart one. That's Anik. He has personal boundary issues."

"At least I don't have big head issues," said Anik. "Detective Senior Constable Anik Jhaveri, at your service, Sergeant Hunter."

"Call me Bonnie."

"If you're all done, can we get on with it, please?" said Cooper. He stood at the front of the room next to a whiteboard.

"Sure thing, boss... ah, sorry, Coop." By the look on Anik's face, it wasn't the first time he'd made that mistake.

Cooper ignored him. "You're all across the details of this case so far. Juliet Keller has now been missing for..." He checked his watch. "Just gone twenty-four hours. Possibly longer, if Bonnie's theory is correct, but we'll come to that."

Nora handed him a folder, which he opened. Top of the pile was a photograph of Juliet. Cooper taped it to the whiteboard.

"Juliet Keller is twenty-five years old, approximately one hundred and seventy centimetres tall, slight build, long blonde hair, blue eyes. Reported missing from Bundanoon, in the Southern Highlands, by her husband Sam Keller yesterday evening when she failed to return from a trip to the grocery store."

Anik raised his hand. "Why are we involved? Homicide, I mean. If she's just missing."

Kate rolled her eyes, which Cooper obviously noticed.

"It's not a stupid question," said Cooper. "The location of the car, car keys, and Juliet's phone indicate a strong likelihood of foul play. That means we need to act fast. So, let's run through the possible scenarios."

As they discussed the possibilities Bonnie and Cooper had already been through at the scene, Cooper wrote them up on the board. In the end there were three most likely scenarios: foul play – at the hands of either a stranger or someone known to the victim; she left of her own accord; or – and this was top of Bonnie's list – foul play at the hands of her husband at some point prior, and he'd set up the scene to make it look like she'd been abducted.

"Why wouldn't he have set it up to look like she'd run away?" asked Kate. "I mean, he's a criminal lawyer, right? He knows a possible abduction would bring a lot more attention to Juliet's disappearance than if she'd just run off."

"Doesn't have good optics for him," said Bonnie.

"Huh?" Anik looked confused.

"This guy is all about image," Bonnie explained. "The big-city lawyer job, the car, the flash apartment, the family holiday house, the good-looking wife. It's all 'look at me, I'm winning at life' kind of stuff. His wife running off tarnishes that image."

"But his wife being abducted lets him play the victim," Kate added, nodding her understanding.

"Exactly," said Bonnie. "Now he gets to front the media, plead for whoever has his wife – who he'll speak about as a possession, no doubt – to let her go, don't hurt her, I love her, etcetera. He'll be drowning in sympathy before the end of the six-o'clock news."

"Or the public will see right through him and be gunning for him," said Mars. "People aren't stupid, and most are aware of the statistics on women who go missing."

"Okay," said Cooper. "Let's keep all that in mind, but we have no proof yet that he's involved. Remember Jill Meagher, people. It's not always the husband."

True, thought Bonnie, but Juliet Keller's husband is nothing like Tom Meagher.

"I've done some preliminary background on the families," said Mars. "Sam comes from money, as you already know. His parents are Richard and Yvonne Keller. Big time property developers. No siblings.

"Juliet is the youngest child of Dominic and Ellen Wilson. He's an electrician with his own business. No occupation listed for Ellen. Juliet's older brother, Nick, works with Dominic. Nick is married to Renee, three young kids. They all live in Castle Hill."

"So how did the son of wealthy property developers come to marry the daughter of a middle to working-class tradie family?" asked Cooper.

"They met at the Ship Inn, according to their socials," said Kate. "Juliet's friends teased her about meeting her prince, just like Princess Mary. It certainly looks like it. All her posts changed from pictures of solo bush walks and girly nights out to loved-up couple shots practically overnight."

"What about his social media?" Bonnie asked.

"Doesn't have any, as far as I can find," said Kate. "Juliet's is actually 'Juliet Sam Keller', and all the posts since their wedding are 'we' and 'our'. She must have changed it when they married."

Bonnie wasn't at all convinced that Sam Keller had no social media accounts. "Keep looking for anything connected to him," she said. "If he has a Facebook or whatever account somewhere, I want to see what type of groups he's part of. There's some scary underground shit on social media."

"I can dig deeper on that," said Nora.

"Good," said Cooper. "What else?"

"I've pulled traffic cameras from the M5 motorway for Friday afternoon," said Nora. She hit a few keys and a picture came up on the screen in the corner of the room. "That's the Kellers' BMW. There are definitely two occupants at five forty-nine pm."

Bonnie squinted at the photo. The woman in the passenger seat looked like Juliet in that she had long blonde hair and was the right build, but no-one could definitively say that was her. She said as much to the team.

"Who else would it be?" asked Anik.

"A friend, maybe?" suggested Kate.

"Yes, but why?" asked Mars. "Unless it was a really elaborate plan to cover up a murder, and Sam Keller had another woman willing to help him by posing as Juliet to confuse the timeline. Is that what we're suggesting here?"

"I've seen worse," said Bonnie.

"Let's not focus on that as a top theory," said Cooper. "Bonnie's right, it is possible, but based on that picture it's more likely Juliet and Sam left Sydney together on Friday afternoon, like he said."

"Doesn't mean she made it all the way to Bundanoon," Bonnie pointed out.

"There are no more traffic cameras between this one and Bundanoon," said Nora. "I can check local businesses, see if there are any they may have driven past, but I'm not hopeful. The building where they live in Sydney will have cameras, though. I'll get what I can from those."

"Good," said Cooper. "We want to fill in as many blanks about this weekend as possible. Zach, what are you working on?"

"I've got Juliet's phone, but I'm still trying to get into it. Sam says he doesn't know Juliet's passcode, so it'll take me a couple more hours. I'm due an update from the guys working on the car soon, too."

"All right. That's good work, team." Cooper put the cap back on his whiteboard marker and threw it on the table. "Call it a day as soon as you can, all of you. We've a lot to do tomorrow."

"Speaking of," said Bonnie, raising her eyebrows at him.

"Right, assignments. Bon, you and Anik head out to Castle Hill first thing and interview Juliet's family. Mars and Kate can track down some of their friends. The locals in Bundanoon are still searching down there and canvassing the town. I'll get updates from them and keep you all posted."

"Should we be searching the National Park?" asked Anik.

Cooper shook his head. "Not yet. What would we be looking for? A body? A woman hiding? The park is a vast area, and Juliet went missing a couple of kilometres away. We need more information before we start looking in there."

"Fair enough." Anik followed the others out of the room, leaving Cooper and Bonnie behind.

"You really think he could be innocent?" Bonnie asked.

"It's possible," Cooper replied. "I know Sam Keller has set off your DV alarm bells, but you and I have been at this long enough to know that people aren't always what they seem."

She couldn't argue with that.

17

March 2018

"Can I help you, dear?" The sales assistant regarded Juliet with her best down-her-nose stare. Juliet smiled politely and shook her head.

"Just looking, thank you." She continued browsing the dress racks but couldn't see anything Sam would like her in. That was the way her day had gone, and she was over it.

As she walked out of the store – the fifth for the day with only one barely passable dress to show for it – Juliet wondered what Gwen and Tess would make of the obscene amount of money Sam gave her to spend on clothes. No... *required* her to spend on clothes. 'My wife will be the most beautiful woman in the room,' he was fond of saying, and lately she was starting to feel like it was a command rather than a compliment.

How ridiculous, Juliet chastised herself. Complaining about her husband giving her money. Tess would be horrified if she knew, Gwen would probably laugh. Juliet missed her friends. It must have been months since she'd seen them. Just before

Christmas, maybe? Yes, when Max had been home from uni again. Now it was the first of March already.

The afternoon was starting to cool, so Juliet pulled her cardigan out of her bag and stopped to put it on. She was outside East West Vintage, one of her favourite second-hand clothing stores, and they had the most gorgeous burgundy knit dress in the window. It looked about her size, and would be perfect for Sam's family's Christmas in July celebration later this year. She hesitated for a moment, looking around as if she were about to rob a bank, before darting inside.

"Hi, Juliet!" Samira, who could brighten anyone's day with two words and her infectious smile, was fast becoming one of Juliet's favourite people in the city.

"Hi, Samira. That dress in the window—"

"I knew you'd love it!" Samira interrupted, coming straight over and taking both Juliet's hands in her own. "It only arrived yesterday. Come on, let's get it down and get it on you immediately."

Samira's energy was hard to argue with, and before Juliet knew it the dress was off the display mannequin and hanging in the change room, ready for her to try on.

"I'll just see if there's anything else," Juliet said, the racks of colourful clothes joining forces with Samira to make her mood lift complete. She selected a few items, a couple of dresses plus a shirt she knew she could alter to meet Sam's approval, and locked herself in the changing cubicle.

Sam would die if he knew she shopped at a store like this. Which was completely ridiculous – vintage and recycled clothing was very much in fashion right now. So much better for the environment. She knew his friends were into that kind of thing – Heather and Jonathan were involved in at least three save the planet-type charities, and Juliet was sure Ollie's latest girlfriend was vegan. But

Sam insisted on Juliet buying the latest fashions from the top stores. He even went shopping with her a few times, pointing out the stores she should shop in and the dresses she should try on. She had to admit it felt nice to have a partner who *wanted* to shop with her, who cared so much about how she looked. It didn't last, of course. He was far too busy to take her shopping now.

The burgundy knit fit perfectly, and Juliet wondered if she could get away with passing it off as new. She decided she could, so she took it with the other items to the counter.

"Card or cash?" Samira asked, as she always did.

"Cash," Juliet replied, as she always did, fishing in her bag for her purse. Sam was a cash man. He enjoyed pulling out a big wad of notes and peeling them off to pay for things. If Juliet didn't know better, she'd swear he was a drug dealer or something in a former life. She hated carrying cash herself, it felt so unsafe, so she was always very careful where she opened her purse.

Juliet handed over the money, thanked Samira, and went on her way. Outside, the wind had picked up and a threatening black cloud hovered over the city. It was still about a twenty-minute walk to the apartment, and there was a café within sight which would be a perfect place to ride out the storm. She checked her watch. Sam would be finished work soon; better he didn't come home to an empty apartment. After a longing glance at the café, she braced herself against the gusting wind and headed for home.

She still had two blocks to walk when the rain came. A taxi approached and Juliet considered hailing it, but it seemed ridiculous to pay for a ride so close to home. She could see their building up ahead. She pulled her bags in closer as the cab drove past.

Inside the building, Juliet waved to the doorman as she headed to the elevator bank. She was dripping wet, but it didn't matter. A little water never hurt anyone, and she would get herself cleaned up before Sam arrived home. At least the bags seemed to have kept her purchases mostly dry.

As always, Juliet marvelled at the view as soon as she walked through the apartment door. She remembered the first time Sam had brought her here, his proposal, and how lucky she'd felt when she'd said yes. It was still like a dream sometimes – a fantasy, even. The girl from the suburbs falling for the rich guy and moving to the big city.

Juliet dumped her bags in the entrance and grabbed a towel from the hall closet to dry off. She pulled off her boots and put them neatly in their place, then picked up the bags and took them through into the bedroom. She removed her East West Vintage bargains from their plain brown bag and spread them out on the bed. The burgundy knit and the other dress were perfect, so she cut off the tags and left the dresses ready to parade when Sam got home. The shirt needed altering, so that would have to wait until she next visited her parents and could access the sewing machine she'd left behind in her old bedroom. She stashed the shirt in the bag she kept at the bottom of her side of the wardrobe for such purposes. She then changed out of her wet clothes and returned to the living room.

After making sure there was no mess on the floor from her walk in the rain, Juliet pulled her purse out of her handbag. She hadn't spent half of the clothing allowance Sam had given her last month, and with it now being the first day of the month again, he'd reach into his pocket sometime this evening and hand her another large pile of cash.

Juliet couldn't see the point in spending such outrageous amounts of money on clothes. She'd tried to argue the first few months, but Sam was insistent. 'It's just a drop in the ocean for me, babe,' he would say. 'You deserve nice things.'

So, she'd stopped arguing, and started spending. The shopping had been fun, there was no denying it. But after four months of filling her wardrobe with designer dresses and accessories, it had become all too much. Juliet just hadn't grown up with frivolous spending. She'd considered putting the excess money in the bank but now that they were married she and Sam had joint bank accounts. He'd ask why she was putting money in, and she just didn't want to go through the whole thing again.

Then last month she'd come across a lovely jewellery box with a false bottom in it – another great find in East West Vintage. It was the perfect solution. She could save some money for a rainy day, and not bother Sam with her old, thrifty ways.

Juliet opened the jewellery box and removed the few pieces she had in there. She took out the false bottom, then added this month's leftover cash to last month's. It was a decent-sized jewellery box, but still, it wasn't going to take much to fill it up at this rate. Then she'd have to find another safe place.

She laughed at herself. Was this really the biggest problem she had to contend with these days? Finding somewhere to hide excess cash? She replaced the contents of the jewellery box just as the apartment door opened. Quickly stashing the box back in its place, Juliet returned to the living room to welcome her husband home.

18

Bonnie pulled the goggles down over her eyes and plunged into the ocean. She'd gone with her full wetsuit; the cold of late autumn had really started to set in. Not that it deterred any of the hundreds of swimmers making the daily pilgrimage out to Shelley Beach this morning. Rain, hail, or shine, thirty degrees or less than ten, they were always out there.

She'd lived in Manly for years, but Bonnie had only started swimming with the group at this end of the beach in the last six months or so. For a long time, she'd preferred the solitude of the ocean at the other end of Manly Beach, and a quick dip and roll in the waves over the more formal trek out to Shelley and back. Maybe it was the loneliness of COVID isolation, maybe not, but one day she decided to see what all the fuss was about. She'd donned her swimming cap and goggles and taken to the ocean with the large group of morning swimmers, and by the time she'd reached the little sheltered beach at Shelley Bay, she was hooked.

Not that she'd made friends or anything like that. There were nods to familiar faces, a few words of encouragement here and there, pleasantries exchanged over coffee after the swim. There were definite groups, of course. In addition to the elite swimmers and hardened fitness fanatics, there were plenty for whom the social occasion was clearly more important than the exercise. But for Bonnie it was about solitude in a literal sea of people; camaraderie in a shared pursuit without actually having to share anything. It was as close as she dared get to a team sport.

As she swam, Bonnie thought about the upcoming interviews with Juliet Keller's family. The parents were notified last night by uniformed patrol officers that their daughter had been reported missing. If it were up to her, Bonnie would have made the trip out to Castle Hill last night herself. But Cooper was in charge of the investigation, and as much as Bonnie felt something terrible had happened to Juliet, as yet there was not a lot of evidence to suggest foul play.

Sam Keller had told Cooper that Juliet and her family weren't on good terms. There'd been a falling out, but Sam was vague on details. "I'm a busy man, Detective," he'd apparently said. "I don't have time to worry about my wife's squabbles with her brother."

Mars had managed to ascertain that Juliet's father, Dominic Wilson, was an electrician with his own business. 'Wilson & Son' had been named so since before Nick Wilson, Juliet's older brother, was born. Nick was destined to work in the family business, and according to Sam, Juliet felt that Nick had always been the favoured child. It led to sibling rivalry that came to a head shortly after Juliet married Sam, and they'd barely seen Juliet's family since. Or so Sam told it. Bonnie was very keen to get Nick and Dominic's sides of the story. Not to mention Juliet's mother, Ellen, and Nick's wife, Renee. Hopefully, the Wilson family could give Bonnie a better picture of the woman they were trying to find than Juliet's piece-of-work husband had managed.

Bonnie pulled herself through the water, arm over arm, poking her head up every five or six strokes to make sure she was still on course. It wasn't the roughest sea she'd swum in, but there was enough of a chop out there to keep the swimmers on their toes. At least concentrating on the surf helped her to block the smug face of Sam Keller from her mind.

When she made it back to shore, Bonnie decided not to hang around for coffee. The queue for the coffee window in the surf club building was long; the one for the cafe across the street even longer. Anik was picking her up at eight and it was past seven now, so a quick brew from her pod machine at home was going to have to do. She climbed the steps and found her stuff in amongst the strewn-out collection of towels and beach bags.

"Rough out there this morning." Bonnie turned to find a man in budgie smugglers grinning at her as he towelled off his hair.

"It's not so bad," Bonnie replied, picking up her own towel and unzipping the back of her wetsuit. She'd seen him here a few times, but only in the last month. "You new?"

"Moved in six months ago." He pointed in the direction of the apartment buildings overlooking the bay. "Saw the action from my place the first day, thought you all were crackers. Every morning, hundreds of sets of arms churning up the water out here. It's quite a sight from the fifth floor, let me tell you."

"I can imagine. What made you come out and give it a go?"

"Just that – hundreds of people. A few hardy souls I can ignore, but not this many. You can't all be nutcases. Turns out I was right."

Bonnie glanced at his skimpy attire. "Looks like you've settled in pretty quickly. It's only the hardy souls who dress like that this time of year."

The man shrugged as he wrapped his towel around his

waist. "I hate wetsuits. Feels too constricted." He held out a hand. "I'm Steve."

Bonnie gave her usual wave. "Bonnie. No offence, I tend to avoid unnecessary physical contact these days."

Steve turned his outstretched hand into a wave too. "Fair enough. No offence taken. Can I buy you a coffee, Bonnie?"

"Sorry, gotta be somewhere." Bonnie grabbed her bag and took a few steps away. "Another time, maybe. Nice to meet you, Steve."

"You too. Take care."

Back home, Bonnie quickly showered, changed, and scoffed down some coffee and toast. She was rinsing the dishes in the sink when Anik rang the doorbell.

"Nice place," he said when she opened the door. "You live here alone?"

"You always ask personal questions this early in the morning?"

Anik's hand flew to his chest. "Detective Hunter, I'm hurt." Then he grinned and stepped past her into the house. "Whoah, okay. So, it's nice on the outside." He waggled a finger over the living room. "What's going on in here? Or rather, what's not going on in here?"

Bonnie followed his gaze. "What's wrong with it?"

Anik picked up an ornament from the cabinet in the corner by the door and examined it. "Looks like you live with your grandma." He raised his eyes to meet hers. "Oh shit, sorry. *Do* you live with your grandma?"

Bonnie took the ornament – a small porcelain dog that had been one of Edna's favourites – from him and put it back in its place. "Long story, which I have no intention of telling you." She grabbed her bag, spun him around, and pushed him out the door. "Come on, we've got a long drive."

"Ooh, a woman of mystery. I like it." Anik unlocked the car, then Bonnie reached up and snatched the keys from his hand. He shrugged and changed direction to the passenger seat.

"You do realise I'm your superior officer, right?" Bonnie started the engine and manoeuvred the car from the tight space, secretly admiring Anik for his parking skills as well as his self-confidence.

"Yes, Detective Sergeant Hunter. Doesn't mean we can't be friends though. The world's an unfriendly enough place as it is. I reckon we could all use more friends. Even you. Or are you sorted in that department, what with your grandma and all?"

Bonnie smiled. It was impossible to be angry with Anik. She gave him a sideways glance. "Just Bonnie will do, Anik. Let's keep it informal."

"Good. I like that. So, Bonnie. What's the deal with Detective Cooper? How come no-one ever talks about—"

Bonnie's left hand flew off the steering wheel and stopped millimetres short of slapping Anik across the chest.

"Do not finish that sentence."

19

September 2018

"This is amazing," said Juliet, savouring another mouthful of the delicious food. It was taking every ounce of her effort not to scoff the entire contents of the plate immediately. They were at their new favourite city restaurant, and Juliet had been looking forward to the night for weeks.

"Nothing but the best for my wife on our first anniversary," said Sam, topping up her wine glass.

"Can you believe it's been a year already?"

"It's definitely flown," he replied. "The Reynolds account has seen to that, for one thing." He cut into his steak and piled a large bite with mashed potato.

"You have been very busy, darling," Juliet agreed. "Which is why... I haven't wanted to bring it up, but..."

Sam kept chewing as he looked up at her, knife and fork paused in mid-air.

Juliet took a deep breath, steeling herself to continue. "Remember my twenty-first birthday?"

"Sure," Sam nodded. "Great party. We know how to entertain, don't we?" He went back to his steak.

"Yes, it was a fantastic night. But that's not what I meant. When you gave me my present, we also spoke about my idea for a sports clothing line, remember? You said you'd help me get started with all the business stuff. I've got some really good ideas, and—" she stopped when she realised Sam had rested his knife and fork on the sides of his plate. He only did that when he was about to get serious.

"Jules, babe, I don't think it's the right time. I want to help you, but I'm just so busy at work."

"You don't need to do much," she said. "Just point me in the right direction. Or not even that – I'll make a start for myself and then I can ask you when I get stuck."

Sam tilted his head to the side and smiled. "Jules, you're so cute. Keep working on your designs, babe. I promise we'll get to it. Just not now, okay?" He picked up his cutlery and began eating again, signalling the end of the conversation.

But Juliet wasn't finished. "I found a business class I can study online, and—"

This time Sam's cutlery hit the plate with a crash that made Juliet jump and brought a few stares from diners at nearby tables. "I told you, not now." The words were hard, but then he softened. "Besides, there's something else we need to discuss tonight. You won't have time for business classes soon." He took both her hands in his. "Juliet, I think it's time you stopped taking the pill."

This was not how she'd expected the night to go.

"What? Sam... do you mean..." She could tell by the look on his face it was exactly what he meant. She shook her head. "I'm only twenty-two. I'm not ready to be a mother."

"But you're ready to be a businesswoman? Come on, Jules. I've got a great career; I make more than enough for us both. You don't need to work. You never need to work. You're the best wife on the planet, but I need more. I'm twenty-six. It's time you made me a father. You'll be a great mum. It's the next step for us, Jules." He sat back, rested an arm over the back of his chair. "You know I'm right."

Juliet stared down at her plate. Over half her risotto remained, but the lump now forming in her throat made it impossible to finish. She pushed the plate away.

It's funny the little things that set people off.

"What's the matter?" Sam lifted his chin to indicate her unfinished meal. "Isn't it good enough for you? Jesus, Jules. You know how hard I work. Every day, busting my gut, so you can have the good things. So we can eat at places like this. And what do you do?" He stared at her, waiting for an answer.

"I..."

"Seriously?" He was yelling now. "You don't appreciate anything I do for us." He threw his napkin onto his plate. People were staring now.

"I'm sorry, Sam," said Juliet. She needed to shut this down. "You're right, of course you're right. I'll go off the pill. We can start trying." She almost choked on the words. There was no way she was ready to be a mum. Or was she? She hadn't thought she was ready to be a wife, either. But she was handling that okay. Mostly. Except for moments like these.

She pulled the plate of risotto back toward her and forced herself to take a mouthful, as Sam regained control of his temper. The people around them went back to their own meals and their own conversations. Juliet smoothed her dress, tucked her hair behind her ear, and asked Sam about his day. He pushed his empty plate aside and cradled his wine glass in front of him, nodded, and started a story about a prank they'd played on one of the guys at work. By the time their dessert came, the Sam she loved was back, and Juliet had pushed thoughts of both fashion careers and babies to the back of her mind.

She was not expecting him to pick up where he left off when they returned to their apartment.

"How dare you," he growled as soon as the door was closed. "I can't believe you'd show me up like that. I take clients to that restaurant, Juliet. I can't show my face in there now. Why do you have to ruin everything for me?"

Juliet stood rooted to the spot as he paced the living room around her, fists clenched by his sides.

"I'm sorry," she said. "But it wasn't that bad, baby. People don't care about a little lovers' tiff."

He stopped in front of her. "Of course, people care. *I* care. No-one needs to know our business!"

"I'm sorry, Sam. You just... you took me by surprise, that's all. I'm not sure I'm ready for the baby thing."

Sam grabbed her by the arm and shoved her in the direction of the bedroom. "You're ready when I say you're ready," he yelled.

"Sam, honey..."

"Shut up!" He pushed her onto the bed then started rifling through her bedside drawers. "Where are they?"

"What?"

"Your pills! Where are they? Don't lie to me."

"Why would I... they're in the bathroom." Juliet tried to keep her voice calm. She knew what was coming. Maybe, if she could get him to turn the rage down a notch, perhaps it wouldn't be so bad.

Sam pulled open drawers and cabinets in the bathroom, throwing packets and personal items around until he finally found what he was after. He then proceeded to punch all the pills out of the blister packs and into the toilet, before flushing them away.

"There," he said, finally satisfied with himself. "Now we don't have to discuss it anymore."

"But—"

"Seriously, Juliet? You're seriously going to push me right now?"

Juliet shook her head. "No." She stood, caught a glimpse of herself in the bathroom mirror. The bruising on her arm was already starting to show. "I just... this wasn't what I had in mind for our anniversary, babe."

Sam's face was an inch from Juliet's. He stared at her for what felt like hours but was probably only a few seconds. This was the moment where it could go either way. Other times he'd lost his temper she'd been able to bring him back from the edge, back to her. Those times he became tender, loving. The man she first met, the man she married.

This was not one of those times.

As he slapped her across the face, pushed her back down onto the bed, and ripped off her clothes, Juliet's mind wandered back to their wedding night a year ago. The first night Sam had forced himself upon her. That night, and at moments like these in the year that followed, Juliet had reasoned she could stop him if she really wanted to. Now, though, as he held her down and thrust himself inside her, she realised how wrong she'd been.

How very wrong she'd been.

20

"What the... are you serious? You nearly hit me!"

"Oh, calm down." Bonnie had pulled her arm back and was concentrating on the traffic. "I didn't even get close. You flinched, though. Not really super-cop material."

Anik ran his hands down the front of his shirt, as if smoothing an invisible tie. "Don't change the subject. I've been with Homicide six months, and no-one ever talks about... that thing with Cooper. How come? You were there, right?"

Bonnie kept her eyes on the road as she slowly nodded. "I was with Sex Crimes at the time, but we had a crossover case. A rapist I'd been chasing for years escalated to murder. I teamed up with Charlie and his team in Homicide."

"You got that guy, didn't you?"

Bonnie nodded. "The case was solved. But things went... well, pear-shaped is an understatement. I'm sure you know the story. It was front page of every paper for weeks."

"Exactly. It's no secret what happened."

Bonnie could understand his frustration. "Look, it was a difficult thing for everyone to process. Homicide lost a lot of good people, for various reasons, and it took Cooper a long time to work through it. Charlie and I have our differences, but he's a good cop, and a good man. The Force was lucky not to lose him too."

The Vigilante Killer. That was the nickname, before they knew who it was. Cooper had suspected there was a vigilante operating in Sydney for a long time, long before Senior Sergeant Munro, or any of the leadership team for that matter, had believed him. When Bonnie joined forces with Homicide to catch her rapist-turned-murderer, she hadn't wanted to believe it either.

How wrong they all were.

Bonnie had done her best to lock the whole experience away in a deep corner of her mind. At first, she'd spent many nights trying to process what had happened, usually with a bottle of tequila, and she'd been a relative outsider at the time. She'd always come back to thanking her lucky stars she wasn't Charlie Cooper. How the man carried on after all that, she'd never know. But carry on he had, eventually making Inspector and replacing Munro in charge of Homicide, and Bonnie had the utmost respect for him. They'd become firm friends, and he hadn't stopped trying to convince her to join his team since.

"So, I'm just supposed to never talk about it? Act like it never happened?" Anik asked.

"Correct," said Bonnie. "It was over two years ago, Anik. Things have changed, steps put in place to make sure it never happens again. Homicide was dragged through the ringer. You'll win no friends bringing it up. And trust me, you never want to mention any of it – or the people involved – around Coop. Not unless you want to be chained to a desk doing paperwork for the next twenty years."

Anik stared out the side window as they headed over the Spit Bridge. It was a clear day, with just enough wind to ensure the clinking of halyards against sailboat masts rang out across the harbour. Bonnie changed the subject.

"Let's focus on the case in front of us. We need to get a picture of who Juliet was in order to find out what happened to her."

"Who she was... you really think he killed her, don't you?"

"Don't you? The stats on domestic homicide are horrific, Anik. One woman a week in Australia is killed by a current or former partner. One per week, murdered by the person who is supposed to care for them, protect them. Love them." Bonnie swerved to avoid a bus on Military Road before joining the line of traffic waiting to turn onto the Warringah Freeway.

"Well, yeah, it doesn't look good. But shouldn't we be assuming innocence until proven guilty, all that stuff?"

"That's for the lawyers," said Bonnie. "It's our job to find her and nail his arse."

Anik shrugged. "As you wish. Good thing we have Deadpool on the team."

"Huh?" Bonnie had no idea what he was talking about. "Deadpool?"

"Zach and Nora."

She shook her head. "Nup. You've lost me."

"Zach Ryan and Nora Reynolds. Ryan Reynolds, the actor. Deadpool. It's his most famous role."

"I know who Ryan Reynolds is. That's terrible."

Anik smiled. "No, it's genius. One of my many gifts. Zach thinks it's hilarious."

"And Nora?"

He shrugged. "She's coming around."

Bonnie shook her head. The light turned green and she turned, merging seamlessly into the flow of traffic on the freeway. According to the GPS, the trip from Manly to Castle Hill should take about forty-five minutes, and they'd already been on the road for fifteen. They needed to focus.

"We're interviewing Juliet's parents first, what do we know about them?"

Anik pulled out his notebook. "Dominic and Ellen Wilson. Fifty-eight and fifty-two years old, respectively. Dominic is an electrician, runs his own business with his son, Nick. No occupation listed for Ellen. They've lived in their current home for thirty years."

"Any record for either of them?"

"A few traffic infringements for the father. Lost his licence once. Nothing for the mother. Beyond that, they've never troubled us."

Bonnie pictured a typical couple living in suburbia, raising their two kids and being good citizens. Then their daughter married a jerk who probably killed her. She shook the thought from her head and listened to Anik.

"According to Sam, Juliet lived at home until she married him."

"When was that?"

"Their wedding?" Anik flicked a few pages in his notebook. "September 2017, so not quite five years ago."

"And when did they meet?"

"December 2016."

Bonnie did a quick calculation. Barely nine months from meeting to marriage, and Juliet must have been young. She would've been only nineteen or twenty when they met. "What's her date of birth?"

Anik checked. "June twelfth, nineteen ninety-six."

"So, she was twenty when they met, and barely twenty-one when they married. And he was what... twenty-five?"

"Turned thirty this weekend, so yeah. Twenty-five when they married. Even that's young. I'm twenty-six, and I wouldn't even consider marriage right now. Luckily, neither would my girlfriend."

Bonnie briefly thought about asking if he was sure about that but decided to save that rabbit hole for another day.

"Okay. We'll have a good chat with the parents about Juliet meeting Sam, the whirlwind romance, etcetera. What else... what can you tell me about the brother?"

More notebook pages flicked by. "Nick Wilson, twenty-eight. Married to Renee Wilson, twenty-seven. They live around the corner from Mum and Dad. Nick joined Dom in the family business straight out of school. Renee is a hairdresser, works in a salon at the shopping centre. They have three kids, two boys and a baby girl."

"Sounds like they have their hands full. Any records?"

"Nick has as many speeding fines as his father, apparently this family like to drive fast. There's a possession charge for Renee when she was seventeen, small amount of weed. Nothing major."

Bonnie couldn't hold a small juvenile offence like that against anyone, given the things she'd gotten up to in her own adolescence.

"Nick and Renee sound worlds apart from Juliet and Sam," said Anik. "Suburban tradie parents versus big city banker-wanker and his trophy wife. No wonder they don't get on."

"He's a lawyer, not a banker, but yeah." Bonnie checked the Castle Hill street signs against the GPS. Dominic and Ellen's house should be the next left. "Sam said Juliet had had a falling out with her family. According to him they hadn't spoken in more than a year."

"You reckon he was telling the truth?"

Bonnie located number sixteen Chalmers Way and pulled up out front. "Let's go find out."

21

September 2018

"You look nice," Sam said as Juliet fixed the scarf around her neck. She'd hoped the grey knit dress with the high collar would cover the bruising, but it didn't quite do the job.

"Mum's coming over for lunch," she replied, watching him as he finished dressing for work.

"Say hi to her for me. Where are you going? I've got back-to-back meetings today, but I might see if I can get away for a few minutes, come say hi."

"Actually, I thought we'd stay here," said Juliet. "I've got a new recipe I'd like to try out on her."

Sam paused, looked Juliet up and down. "You're a bit over-dressed for lunch at home, babe."

Juliet shrugged. "Nothing wrong with looking my best for family, right?"

He came close, gently brushed the side of her face. At least the redness from the slap had gone this morning.

"I'm sorry about last night," said Sam. "I shouldn't have hit you. I just... I get frustrated sometimes, Jules."

"It's over now," Juliet whispered. She never knew the right thing to say at times like these. Should she agree with him? *You're right, you shouldn't have hit me.* Would that make it better? Make him less likely to do it again? Probably not. Better to work on not frustrating him in the first place.

"I'm glad we've agreed to start trying," Sam said, pulling away from her and shrugging his suit jacket on. "You're going to be an amazing mother." He leant in and kissed her on the cheek before grabbing his wallet and phone. "I'll bring a bottle of wine home tonight," he said over his shoulder as he left the bedroom. "We can get some practice in. Bye, babe. Love you."

"Love you too," Juliet called, and then he was gone. She pulled the scarf away from her neck and examined the bruising from last night's 'practice'. How could he shrug what he did off as if it was the most normal thing in the world? *Was* it the most normal thing in the world?

Juliet had had boyfriends before Sam. She knew how young men acted around their mates, full of bravado and sexual innuendo. It had never translated to the bedroom before, though. Sam was the only guy who was that rough with her.

Was he really that rough? Maybe she was overreacting. She *did* bruise easily. Had done so ever since she was a kid. Looking at it now, the marks on her neck weren't that bad. A bit of creative makeup application and she could probably ditch the scarf. Juliet opened the drawer containing all her compacts and concealers and got to work.

By the time her mother arrived Juliet was in a much better headspace. She'd been through the morning's cleaning routine, making sure the apartment sparkled, and the coffee machine was warmed up and ready to go.

"Oh, that view gets me every time," said Ellen when Juliet opened the door.

"Hi, Mum. Here, give me your coat."

"Thank you, darling. I can't believe it's still so cold out there. It's supposed to be spring."

"Another couple of weeks will do it," said Juliet. "It always gets warmer as soon as daylight savings starts." She hung the coat on the coat rack and joined her mother in front of the window overlooking the city.

"You must spend hours here, watching the world go by," said Ellen. "I know I would."

"It's a top spot for people watching," Juliet agreed. "Coffee?"

"I'd love one. Almost two hours on the train to get here, you'd think we lived in a different state rather than the same city."

"You can drive, you know," said Juliet. "We have guest parking spots in the building."

"Oh, I couldn't drive in the city. Too much traffic, not to mention all the one-way streets. I'd get terribly lost. At least with the train I know my way. Plus, it gives me time to read. That Jane Harper is very clever, isn't she?"

Juliet laughed. She always enjoyed catching up with her mother, hearing stories from home. They chatted over their coffees, Ellen filling her in on the latest with Renee's pregnancy – her sister-in-law was six months along now, and over the morning sickness apparently, which Juliet was pleased to hear. She knew Renee had struggled this time around, the second pregnancy giving her a lot more trouble than Luke had.

"So, tell me," said Ellen. "How was your anniversary yesterday? Did you go out for dinner? Did that son-in-law of mine spoil you?"

Juliet's hand reached up to her neck, but she caught herself before she could give anything away. Ellen loved Sam, and Juliet didn't want to say anything that might tarnish their relationship. So, she told her mother what she wanted to hear.

"We did, and he did," she said. "I can't believe it's been a year already."

"I know." Ellen took hold of Juliet's hand. "My baby girl, you're so grown up. Next thing we know you'll be starting a family of your own."

All the tension and stress of last night came rushing back at Juliet, and this time she wasn't able to conceal her feelings from her mother.

"Oh, dear, what's wrong?" Ellen squeezed Juliet's hand tighter, and Juliet burst into tears.

"It's... Sam..."

"What? What's he done? Juliet, you can tell me."

"He... he wants us to start trying, Mum. Sam wants us to have a baby."

Ellen's shoulders dropped as she relaxed. "Oh, Juliet. You had me worried there for a minute. You're going to start a family? That's wonderful news."

"Is it?"

"Isn't it? What's wrong, honey?"

"I just don't think I'm ready." Juliet pulled her hand away, stood in front of the window. She looked down at all the people fourteen floors below, rushing about their days.

"Well, yes, you are still quite young," said Ellen. "But you've been married for a year, Juliet. You've got a wonderful husband, who loves you, and can obviously provide for you and a family. He has a good job, doesn't he? A career?"

Juliet turned back to her mother. "Yes, he does. But what about my career, Mum? I don't even have a job anymore. Every time I start looking, Sam comes up with a reason I shouldn't."

"Well maybe he doesn't want you to work, hun. Is that so bad? I know it's different these days, but I didn't work after I had you kids. Your father ran the business and that was enough for us. Looking after him and you and your brother, that was my job. There's nothing wrong with that."

"I know, Mum." The last thing Juliet wanted to do was offend her mother by criticising her life choices.

"You're a wife now, dear," her mother continued. "Marriage is a partnership. You can't just think of yourself anymore. You have to work together. If Sam's job is enough for you to live on, then I think you should see that as a bonus. Not many women these days have that luxury like I did, like you do now. Your job is to look after your husband, and your family."

Juliet didn't know what to say. Maybe her mother was right.

"How old were you when you got married, Mum?"

"I was twenty-two, like you are now. And I was pregnant with Nick a year later. There's a lot to be said for having your children young, Juliet. Look at me – I'm not even fifty yet, and both my children are out on their own with their own lives."

That was a good point. Maybe having a baby now wasn't such a bad idea. And it would be good for her children to be similar in age to their cousins. Sam was an only child, which meant Nick and Renee's kids were the only cousins her children would get. Luke was about to turn two, and their second child was well on the way.

And maybe giving Sam what he wanted would make my life a little easier, too.

"Maybe you're right," Juliet said to her mother. "And Sam is five years older than me. Maybe now is a good time to start trying."

"There you go," said Ellen, giving her daughter a hug. "My baby, all grown up."

Juliet smiled. "Speaking of grown up, I'd better get busy in the kitchen. Lunch is not going to make itself."

22

The Wilson's house looked like many of the others on the suburban street – neat and well-cared for, but a closer look revealed the effects of too many weekends of rest prioritised over home maintenance. Bonnie had once heard somewhere that tradespeople were the worst at finishing jobs around their own homes, and the pile of steel and corrugated iron in the corner of the Wilson's front yard seemed to back that sentiment.

The front door opened before Bonnie and Anik had made it onto the porch. An imposing, broad-shouldered man stood in the doorway, a much shorter woman at his shoulder.

"Dominic and Ellen Wilson?" Bonnie asked.

"That's us," said Dominic.

"Have you found her?" asked Ellen.

Bonnie introduced herself and Anik. "Can we talk inside?" she asked, without answering Ellen's question.

Ellen turned and walked down the hall, while Dominic stood aside and let the detectives pass. They followed Ellen through a tidy lounge room at the front of the house and emerged in the more lived-in open-plan area at the back. Ellen put the kettle on and started assembling mugs on the countertop.

"Please, have a seat," said Dominic, taking his place at the head of the table. Bonnie and Anik obliged. "What can you tell us?"

"We'd like to ask you a few questions—" Bonnie began before Dominic held up a hand.

"Yeah, I get that. And no disrespect, Detective, but we've been going out of our minds all night since your Detective Cooper called. He said our Juliet had been reported missing on Saturday night, and that you'd be here this morning to talk to us. But that's all he said – nothing about where she went missing from, the circumstances. We're in the dark."

"I understand," said Bonnie. "We'll provide you with as much information as we can. But first—"

"I've been calling her phone, but it's switched off. I went to their place in the city," Dominic interrupted, louder this time. "That bastard husband of hers either wasn't there or he wasn't answering. He's not answering his phone, either. What's he done to my daughter?"

"Don't be like that, Dom," said Ellen from the kitchen. "There must be an explanation. Juliet wouldn't just disappear. Let's all have a nice cup of tea, and let the detectives explain." She placed a tray of steaming mugs on the table and joined them.

"You're right, I'm sorry," said Dominic. He opened his hands to Bonnie. "Please, what can you tell us?"

"Like I said, we'll get to that," Bonnie said patiently. "But first I just need to ask a few questions." She pressed on before he could interrupt again. "When was the last time either of you saw your daughter?"

"November," said Ellen.

"As in six months ago?" asked Anik.

"Yes. I had lunch with her in the city just after lockdown ended."

"Why so long ago?" asked Bonnie. "Is that typical for your relationship?"

Ellen sighed. "It is these days. I used to go every month when she was first married. Sometimes we'd go out, other times I'd go to their apartment. Jules loves to cook, she was always trying out new recipes on me. But once COVID hit, and with the lockdowns, I don't know. It got hard."

"*He* made it hard," said Dominic.

"When was the last time you saw your daughter?" Bonnie asked him.

Dominic scratched his head. "I don't know exactly. The last time they came here for dinner, whenever that was." He looked to his wife. "A few months?"

"It was almost a year ago, Dom," said Ellen. "Juliet's birthday, June last year, right before the city went back into lockdown."

"Oh, that's right. Has it really been that long since we saw our baby girl?"

"Since *you* saw her," said Ellen, distributing the cups of tea. "Like I just said, I met her in the city in November. Help yourselves to milk and sugar."

"Thank you," said Bonnie. "Mr Wilson, why do you say *he* made it hard to see your daughter? I assume you're referring to her husband, Sam Keller."

"Yeah. Look, I thought he was a good guy at first. We all did. He doted on Juliet, bought her expensive presents, brought her to the hospital every day when I was in for my back surgery. Honestly, we thought she was so lucky to find him."

Ellen wrapped her hands around her mug. "When they were first married, they'd come here every Sunday for family lunch. Sam would always bring flowers for me and an expensive bottle of wine."

"Then things started to change," said Dominic.

"How?" asked Bonnie, although she was fairly sure she knew. This story was all too familiar.

"I don't know, exactly," said Dominic. "We just saw less and less of them. Juliet said Sam was busy at work, but pretty soon we got the feeling that was an excuse. Nicky always struggled with him, too."

"Nick is your son?" Bonnie clarified.

"Yes," said Dominic. "He and Sam don't get on."

"They're from different worlds," said Ellen.

"It's not just that," said Dom. "You don't know…"

"What don't I know?"

Dominic shrugged. "Some of the things Nick told me, things Sam would say to him when they were alone, it didn't sit right."

"What things?" Ellen pressed.

"I don't know," said Dominic, clearly frustrated. "I can't think of any examples off the top of my head." He looked at Bonnie. "You'll have to ask Nick – my son. But the bottom line is that slimy bastard drove a wedge between my daughter and her family, and if she's gone missing now…" Dominic's hands curled into fists.

Anik leaned forward in his seat. "Do you know if Sam was ever physically violent?"

Dominic took a deep breath, relaxed his hands. "I don't know for sure, but I suspected."

"You what?" Ellen twisted in her seat to face him.

Dominic ignored her, looked at Bonnie. He was on the verge of tears. "What has he done to my daughter?"

Bonnie explained what they knew so far – that Sam and Juliet had gone to Bundanoon for the weekend, she'd gone out for groceries and never returned, how Sam and his friends had found the car, the phone and car keys in the grass.

"This is all my fault," said Dominic, head in his hands.

"How so?" asked Bonnie.

When he looked up, Bonnie could see his tears had started falling. "I went around there one day, to their apartment. I had a meeting in the city, which is rare for me, and Jules hadn't visited for a few months. This was back before COVID or any of that. Anyway, I had some time, thought I'd surprise my little girl."

"You never told me about this," said Ellen.

Dominic shrugged, continued his story. "She had some bruises on her arms she said she got at the gym. They didn't look like anything you'd get at a gym to me, but when I pushed, she got angry. So, I let it go. The next time I saw her everything seemed fine. I should have..." Dominic started properly crying now, and Bonnie gave him a few moments. She sipped her tea and turned to Ellen.

"Do you have any recent photographs of Juliet?"

"I think so. I'll see what I can find." She gave her husband a puzzled look, then went off in search of a photo. Bonnie figured Dominic Wilson was not a man who cried very often, or at least not in front of his wife.

Bonnie gave him a moment, then broached the tricky subject. "Dominic – we heard that there may have been some tension between Juliet and you and your son. Over the business, perhaps?"

"He tell you that, did he?"

"Sam mentioned it, yes."

"It's bullshit." He held up his hands in apology. "Sorry, it's rubbish, I should say. We always treated our kids equal. Juliet could have done the trade and joined us if she'd wanted to, she knows that. She had no interest. I respected that, like I would have done if Nicky said he wasn't keen. But he was. That's just how it worked out."

Anik tilted his head. "Then why would Sam say Juliet felt left out?"

"Because he's a slimy prick who's very good at putting ideas into her head." Dominic took a large gulp of tea, and Bonnie could see he was doing his best to remain calm.

"I'm sorry we have to ask," she said.

Dominic nodded. "You're just doing your job." He ran a hand through his hair, then looked up at her. "You say she drove to the shop, got out of the car, and then something happened?"

"That's what the scene indicates at this stage, although we're not ruling anything out."

Dominic shook his head. "I've been to Bundanoon, Detective. Besides the weekend tourists, it's a very quiet place. And my Juliet is a smart woman. Always aware of her surroundings. I just can't see how someone could have taken her by surprise like that."

Neither could Bonnie, but she kept her own theory to herself. Dominic had already been to the city in search of Sam after finding out his daughter was missing, adding fuel to that fire was the last thing they needed.

"As I said, we're not ruling anything out." Bonnie stood, fished a card out of her pocket. "You have Detective Cooper's number, and here's mine. We'll keep you informed as best we can." The front door opened, and Bonnie looked up to see a younger version of Dominic followed by a woman with a baby barrelling down the hall.

"Nicky!" said Dominic. "You're supposed to be at the Macquarie site today."

"Screw that. Where's Jules? What's he done to her?" Nick's head swivelled from his father to Bonnie and Anik. The baby started crying.

"They haven't found her yet," said Dominic. "It's all right," he added, holding up his hands to placate his son. "They're doing everything they can. These are Detectives Hunter and... Jav... I'm sorry, I've forgotten..."

"Jhaveri," said Anik. "You are Nick and Renee Wilson, is that correct?"

"Yeah," said Nick. "What has that bastard done to my sister?"

"Nick! Language!" said Ellen as she returned to the room. She placed a couple of photos on the kitchen counter before taking the baby girl from her daughter-in-law's arms and bouncing her up and down. "There's no proof Sam had anything to do with this."

"Why do you always stick up for him, Mum?" said Nick.

"Why do you always think the worst of him?" Ellen countered. "He works hard, and he provides for your sister. Just because they live in a fancy apartment in the city—"

"It's got nothing to do with where they live!" Nick yelled.

The baby cried louder.

"Shh," said Ellen. "See what you're doing!"

"Enough," said Bonnie. She took the baby from Ellen and passed her to Anik, whose eyes became round as saucers, but to his credit he took the crying child to the other side of the room. "Now, let's all sit down and take a moment," Bonnie continued, pulling the chair she'd just vacated out from the table again.

When they were all seated, she passed over the still red-faced Nick and turned to his wife instead. "Renee – what can you tell me about Juliet and Sam?"

Renee's eyes narrowed. "I knew Sam was trouble the moment we met."

23

April 2019

"I'm sure he'll be home soon," said Juliet, glancing at the time again. Nick and Renee had been there for nearly two hours, and Sam was still yet to show. Juliet had called and texted him twice, but he wasn't answering. She didn't like to bother him more than that. He must be busy.

"It's okay," said Renee. "We're mostly here to see you, anyway." Josh started crying, so she leaned over the baby-carrier and put the dummy back in his little mouth.

"Aunty Jules!" said Luke, holding up a toy car for Juliet to examine for the twentieth time.

"I see it," said Juliet patiently. "Why don't you line all the cars up over there, and maybe Daddy will race them with you."

"Kay."

Luke got to work while Nick helped himself to another beer and gave Juliet death stares.

"Ignore him," said Renee. "While he's getting more sleep than me he doesn't get to be cross."

Juliet checked on dinner again. She'd turned the oven off,

but the lasagne had already been in there an hour too long. If Sam didn't hurry up it would be completely ruined.

"Maybe we should start without him," said Renee. "He's obviously been held up at work."

"Great idea," said Nick, standing next to Juliet in the kitchen. "I'm starving."

Juliet figured she had no choice. She had to feed her guests. If she dished up slowly enough, maybe Sam would make it home in time. She checked her phone again; still no response. Sighing, she turned to get plates out of the cupboard. She held a stack mid-air when she heard loud voices out in the hall. Was someone yelling?

The noise got closer until the front door opened and Sam came bustling in. His mate Ollie trailed behind, the two of them singing their hearts out.

"Am I ever gonna see your face again?"

"No way, get fucked, fuck off!"

"Sam!" Juliet yelled, horrified.

Sam turned to see her, then took in the room. He raised an eyebrow at her family.

"Oh shit, sorry," said Ollie to Juliet. He slapped Sam on the arm. "Dude, you didn't tell me you had company."

"I didn't know," said Sam. "Hi." He waved to Renee, nodded at Nick, then turned to Juliet. "Jules, what's going on?"

"What's going on? Nick and Renee are here for dinner. We scheduled this months ago, before Josh was even born."

"Why didn't you tell me?"

"I did tell you. And I reminded you at the beginning of the week."

Sam tilted his head to the side. "No, you didn't. It's Friday night, Jules. I would have remembered if you told me these guys were coming on Friday night."

"Dude, I'll head out," said Ollie.

"Nah, mate. Stay. There's plenty of beer in the fridge. Unless Nicky drank it all." Sam laughed as he closed the apartment door.

Nick rolled his eyes. "Wouldn't dream of it, mate." He took a few steps toward them and shook hands with Ollie. "Nick Wilson, Juliet's brother. My wife, Renee."

"Hi," said Ollie. "I remember you from the wedding. Oliver Pearce. Sam's best man. Sorry to crash your party."

Nick shrugged. "Not really a party, just catching up with my sister." He looked at his watch. "It's getting late," he said to Renee. "We'd better get the boys home."

"But what about dinner?" said Juliet. "You just said you were starving."

"Lost my appetite," Nick replied. He was over with Luke now, hustling the little boy to put his cars in the Disney backpack Juliet had bought him for his second birthday.

Renee joined Juliet in the kitchen as Sam and Ollie moved into the lounge, taking spots on the couch and putting their feet up on the coffee table.

"Don't worry about it," Renee said, her voice low. "It's been good to see you, Jules. Let's try again another time. You can come out to ours. You still haven't seen the extension, you know. Luke's moved into his new bedroom."

"I know, the photos look great. I can't wait to see it in person." Juliet glanced over at Sam. "I'm not sure when we'll be able to get out there..."

Renee squeezed her arm. "It's okay. We'll figure it out."

Nick appeared at her side, weighed down with both boys and assorted bags. He kissed his sister on the cheek. "See ya, Jules. Take care."

"See ya!" Sam called from the couch, one arm straight up in the air.

"Thanks for coming," Juliet said as she closed the door

behind them. She turned, leaned against the door, and stared at her husband joking with his mate. She was so angry.

"Seriously, Jules," said Sam. "You need to tell me when people are coming over."

"I did..." she stopped, realising now wasn't the time. Sam didn't like them to argue in front of company, and Ollie was still here. She returned to the kitchen and pulled the overcooked lasagne out of the oven.

"Get us a couple of beers while you're there, hun," Sam called. He put the television on and flicked around with the remote until he found some sport they could watch. Juliet did as Sam asked then considered dishing herself up some lasagne, but like her brother, she'd lost her appetite. She left Sam and Ollie laughing and yelling at the television and went to bed.

Sam climbed in beside her hours later, pulling her close and wrapping his arms around her.

"I'm sorry, babe," he said, kissing her softly on the cheek. "But I swear I didn't know they were coming. If I did, I wouldn't have gone for drinks after work."

Juliet had been thinking about it all night. She and Renee had made the date months ago, she remembered, when Renee was heavily pregnant and desperate for a night in the city. She just wanted one fancy drink in one fancy place; so, they'd arranged to have dinner at Sam and Juliet's, and then the girls would go out for one drink while the boys watched the kids. Juliet remembered thinking it would be good for Sam and Nick to spend some time alone together, even if it was only an hour.

She'd put the date in the calendar app she and Sam shared and told him about it at the time. Then she'd reminded him on Sunday. Sam was very organised; he liked to spend time on Sunday nights going through the week's appointments so he always had a clear picture of what was coming.

"It was in the calendar," Juliet said, turning to face him. "And I'm sure I reminded you on Sunday night."

Sam shook his head. "It's not in the calendar, babe. I just checked. And like I said before, I would have remembered if we had something scheduled for Friday night. I always grab a drink with the boys after work Friday night, you know that. So, I would have paid attention if you'd said anything about it." He pulled her in closer. "Is everything okay?" he asked. "Are you feeling okay?"

"What do you mean?"

"It's just... this is not the first time you've got things wrong lately, Jules. I'm starting to worry about your memory."

Juliet broke away from him and sat up in the bed. "What else have I got wrong?"

Sam sat up beside her, pulling the covers over them both. "Oh, nothing major," he said. "Just a few little things. You bought me the wrong shaving cream. And you forgot to pick up my dry cleaning a couple of weeks ago. Stuff like that." He took her hand. "Don't worry, it's not a problem. The dry cleaners called and I got it on my way home, and I can cope with the different shaving cream. But... it's not like you, Jules. Are you sure you're okay?"

Juliet shook her head. *Was* she forgetting things? She picked up her phone from the bedside table and scrolled to the calendar app. There was nothing listed for that night.

"I could have sworn I'd put it in here," she said, puzzled.

"It's okay," said Sam. He took the phone from her and put it away. "Your family will understand. You're under a lot of stress right now, babe. Hey, do you feel like trying again?"

"Now?" They'd been trying to get pregnant for months now, with no success. Was Sam right? Was the stress of it all affecting her memory?

He leaned in and kissed her, slipped the strap of her nightgown off her shoulder. "Sure, now," he said, planting tender kisses on her neck and chest. His finger gently circled her nipple. "Come on, babe. Forget about all that stuff. Let's make a baby."

Juliet softened and melted into her husband. "Okay," she said, and kissed him back. "Let's make a baby."

24

"Why do you say that?" Bonnie asked.

"I never trusted Sam," Renee replied. "I've seen his type before. All the love and attention stuff at the beginning of the relationship, then they slowly start manipulating you and pulling you away from your family."

"Sounds like you're speaking from experience," said Bonnie.

Renee shrugged. "Nick and I went to school together, but we weren't always together. There was a guy... doesn't matter. Point is, I saw through Sam from the beginning, and he knew it. He did his best to distance Juliet from us."

"How, exactly?" asked Bonnie.

"He moved her to the city, for a start."

"They got married," said Ellen, shaking her head and adding a 'tsk'. "The city is where Sam lives and works. Juliet was always going to move in there when they got married. That doesn't mean anything."

"It's still a long way from here," said Nick. "And the whole thing was very quick. They were married nine months after they met."

"He made her sell her car," said Renee. "Then he made it

difficult for her to use his to drive out here. Remember?" she said to Nick. "Jules used to love babysitting Luke for us, but whenever she wanted to use the car there was always some reason why she couldn't."

Nick nodded. "Yeah. He needed it for work, although he works in an office all day right next to their apartment building. Or it was being serviced, or one of his mates needed it. There was always something."

Classic controlling behaviour, thought Bonnie. "Nick, your father mentioned conversations you've had with Sam when the two of you were alone. Can you tell us about that?"

Nick traced a groove in the tabletop with his finger. "I try not to be alone with him, to be honest. The guy creeps me out. But yeah, there were a couple of times he was with his mates, and I was sort of involved in the conversation. Once at Jules's twenty-first, and another time – I forget where we were. But it was all that male bravado crap, you know?"

Bonnie did know, but she stayed silent. Soon enough Nick filled the void.

"They talk about women as if they're pieces of meat. Not Jules, not their own partners, but other women." He stared down at his hands, then looked up at Bonnie. "Look, I work on building sites. I know a lot of guys who talk like that, but for most of them it's just that – talk. They don't really think of women like that. But some guys... some of them believe their own bullshit, you know?"

"And you'd put Sam in this category?"

Nick nodded. "The first time I thought... hoped... it was just crap talk to impress his mates. But the second time... he's not the guy I wanted for my little sister, put it that way."

"So, what did you do about it?" asked Anik. To Bonnie's surprise he'd managed to settle the baby and walked over close to the table.

"Excuse me?" said Nick.

Bonnie shot Anik a warning glance, but it went ignored.

"If he wasn't the guy you wanted for your sister, what did you do about it? Did you confront him, tell him that sort of behaviour wasn't on? Did you discuss it with your sister?"

"Anik—" warned Bonnie.

Nick stood, his chair scraping along the timber floor. "Are you saying this is my fault?"

Anik switched the baby to his other hip, shrugged. "I'm just asking a question."

The two men faced off for a few seconds before Nick took his daughter from the detective's arms and handed her to Renee. Then he addressed Bonnie, hands on hips. "How is this helping find Jules?"

"We're trying to get a picture of Juliet's life in order to understand what may have happened to her," said Bonnie. "That involves us asking a lot of questions, some of them intrusive. Please, if you sit back down, the sooner we're done here the sooner we can get back out there."

Nick remained standing.

"Please, Nicky," said Dominic. "They have to ask." He tossed his head in Bonnie's direction. "She's on our side."

"There are no sides—" Anik started but shut up when he finally clocked that Bonnie was pissed at him. He picked up the photographs Ellen had left on the counter. "I'll go send these out, shall I?" He walked away without waiting for an answer.

"We're not responsible for this," said Renee.

"No-one's saying you are," said Bonnie.

"It's just... complicated." Renee sighed. "You can't always get involved in other people's business, you know? I asked Jules if she was all right a number of times. She always said yes. And it's not like we saw any evidence of physical violence, did we?" she asked her husband.

"I'd have done something if we did," said Nick, chest puffed out now.

"We've got our own family to deal with," Renee continued. "We've got three small kids, and we both work long hours. With Dom stepping back from the business..."

Bonnie nodded. "I get it. No-one's judging anyone here. We simply need to know as much as you can tell us about Juliet and Sam." She changed direction. "Does Juliet have any friends we can talk to? Anyone who might have seen her more recently than all of you?"

"You could try Gwen and Tess," said Ellen. "Those are her two closest girlfriends. I'll get their numbers for you."

"Thank you." Bonnie asked a few more questions but didn't get anything else useful from the family. They were becoming increasingly distraught, and once the baby started crying again Bonnie figured the interview was over. She left her card, and the usual instructions to call anytime.

Outside, Anik was standing by the car scrolling on his phone.

"What was that?" Bonnie asked as she yanked the driver's side door open and got in.

"What? I can't ask questions?" He slumped into the passenger seat.

"You can ask questions. You just can't ask questions that accuse a family of not looking after their daughter. Not when that daughter is missing. Come on, Anik. Time and place." Bonnie started the car. It took all her patience not to rev the crap out of it and speed away from the curb.

"When is the right time?" Anik fastened his seatbelt and stared at her. "Too many people do nothing. Say nothing. They know something's wrong, but they don't get involved. Then it's too late, and *we* have to get involved. If he knew his brother-in-law was a dodgy arsehole, why didn't he do anything about it?"

"It's not that simple, Anik."

"Isn't it? Why not? Nick's a decent-sized bloke. He's bigger than Sam Keller. Imposing enough. Why not have a little word?"

Bonnie didn't know what to say. The trouble was, she agreed. Why didn't people get involved if they felt something was wrong? But that wasn't going to help Juliet now.

"Look, I hear you," she said as she drove slowly through the suburban streets. "But we need these people on-side if we're going to build an accurate picture of Juliet's life."

Anik stared out the window, and they drove in silence for a few minutes. Bonnie thought back over the interviews. Ellen Wilson obviously believed her son-in-law was a stand-up guy, but she was in the minority. The rest of the family had formed the same opinion as Bonnie – that Sam Keller was not to be trusted.

"So where are we going now?" Anik asked, straightening in his seat.

Bonnie handed him the piece of paper Ellen had given her. "Gwen Sneijder and Tess Meadows. Juliet's closest girlfriends, apparently. Let's see what they think of the man she married."

25

The Homicide Squad room at Police Headquarters was much busier on Monday afternoon than it had been the previous day. Although she'd been there and witnessed it many times, Bonnie was still impressed by all the activity. This was clearly a place where things got done.

"How'd you get on?" Cooper asked when Bonnie and Anik joined him, Mars, and Kate in the incident room allocated to their case.

"My opinion of Sam Keller hasn't changed," Bonnie replied, taking the same seat she'd occupied yesterday. Anik sat beside her, and between them they described their interviews with the Wilson family.

"The mother seems to be on his side, from what you're saying," Mars commented. "Could it just be a male thing? The father and brother don't get on with Sam because he's a different type of guy than them?"

"You mean the lawyer versus tradie disconnect?" asked Bonnie.

"Yeah, something like that," said Mars. "Kate and I interviewed Sam and Juliet's friends, their social circle. They all mostly said the same thing – Sam and Juliet are a happy couple, no obvious issues. Juliet is quiet but seems lovely."

"I don't think so," said Bonnie. "Nick's wife, Renee, wasn't impressed with Sam at all. So, it's not just a guy thing."

Kate tilted her head at Mars. "To be fair, everyone we interviewed was Sam's friend first. Guys from school, rugby, etcetera, and their wives. None of them knew Juliet before she married Sam."

"So not an equal representation of their social circle, then?" asked Cooper.

"Well, that's just it," Kate continued. "All their friends – the ones they socialise with on a regular basis – are Sam's crowd. I couldn't find anything in her socials to indicate she'd seen her friends recently. The ones from her world before Sam."

"We managed to catch up with a couple of them," said Bonnie. "Gwen Sneijder and Tess Meadows, who she went to school with. But they hadn't seen her in almost a year."

"What was their opinion of her relationship with Sam?" asked Cooper.

"Tess called him Juliet's Prince Charming," said Bonnie, recalling the conversation she and Anik had had an hour ago with the young woman while she was on a break from work. "Apparently Tess and Gwen, along with another friend, Max, were there the night Sam and Juliet met. According to Tess, Sam swept Juliet off her feet."

"The women were both impressed at first," Anik explained. "The guy obviously had money, and he was older and more sophisticated than the rest of them. They thought Juliet had won the lottery."

Bonnie nodded, recalling how Tess had even admitted to being jealous of Juliet at first. But that wore off as they saw less and less of their friend. "Once Juliet and Sam were married, the friends started to drift apart. Weekly catch-ups became monthly, then blew out even more. The pandemic lockdowns didn't help, of course."

"What about Max?" asked Kate.

"Lives in Canberra," said Anik. "We called and spoke to him; like the others he hadn't seen Juliet for almost a year. He was pretty distressed to hear she was missing."

"Max and Juliet were quite close before Sam came along, according to Gwen," Bonnie explained. "But Max and Sam didn't get on at all, right from the start."

"The tradie thing again?" Cooper asked. "Different worlds?"

Bonnie shook her head. "Max is a suit. Politics, apparently. He works in the thick of it down in the capital. If any of Juliet's circle were going to have common ground with Sam, it should have been Max."

"All right," said Cooper. "We're building a picture of these two, this marriage, but we're light on evidence. The press are all over this story now. We need to get moving before Sam Keller is tried and convicted by the public. Even if he is guilty, that's the last thing we need. Where are Zach and Nora?"

"I'll find out," said Mars, reaching for his phone.

"I'll get coffee," said Anik.

Bonnie took advantage of the pause to gather her thoughts. Cooper was right; background information was starting to paint a picture, but they needed more if they were going to find Juliet and nail Sam Keller.

Ten minutes later the team was assembled again, this time with the additions of Zach, Nora, and caffeine. Bonnie was grateful for all three.

"What have you got," Cooper asked the tech duo.

"Security footage from the Keller's building," said Nora. She pointed a remote at the screen in the corner, bringing up an image of a parking area. A blond woman walked toward a dark-coloured SUV. "This is the carpark under the apartment block.

That's Juliet, on Friday afternoon. She makes multiple trips to the vehicle, each time adding stuff to either the boot or the front passenger seat area."

"Packing for their weekend trip," Bonnie surmised.

"Looks like it," said Nora. "Then this, shortly before six pm."

They watched as both Sam and Juliet entered the frame and walked to the car. Sam was carrying an esky cooler, which he placed in the boot before climbing into the driver's seat. Juliet had a handbag and a water bottle. She got into the passenger seat, placing the handbag at her feet and the water bottle in a pocket in the door of the car. She closed the door, and Sam drove out of the parking space toward the security door.

"I've watched it from all available angles, but there's nothing much else to see. Juliet packs the car, then they drive out together just before six."

"So, we know it was her in the car when they left the city," said Cooper.

"And unless they pulled some sort of weird switcheroo, she was still in the car when they went through the M5 tolls," Mars added.

"Doesn't mean she was there when they arrived in Bundanoon," said Bonnie.

"I might have something on that," said Zach. All eyes turned to him. "I haven't finished running my analysis on Juliet's phone yet, but I have tracked both it and Sam's phone over the course of the weekend. Both show something very interesting for that Friday night." He held out a hand to Nora. "May I?"

She gave him the remote and seconds later a map appeared on the screen. Zach used his cursor to point to a section of the map.

"This is a dirt road off the highway, approximately two kilometres south of the services at Pheasants Nest. Both Juliet's and Sam's phones show they were stationary some three hundred metres down this road between seven-fifteen and seven-thirty-seven on Friday night."

Bonnie sat up straighter in her chair. This was interesting. "Where does the dirt road go?"

"To a couple of farms, eventually, but there's nothing at the point where they stopped."

"Twenty-two minutes," said Anik. "What were they doing down that road for twenty-two minutes? In the dark?"

"And why didn't Sam tell us about it when we asked if they made any stops that night?" added Bonnie.

"Good questions," said Cooper. "What happened next?" he asked Zach.

"Both phones continued on to Bundanoon. They stopped at the pizzeria, then the holiday house, where they stayed until Juliet went to the grocery store the next afternoon."

"Until *her phone* went to the grocery store," Bonnie corrected.

"True," said Zach as his phone rang. He stepped away from the table to take the call.

"Sam lied," said Bonnie. "This changes things. No way he 'forgot' about stopping down a dirt road for more than twenty minutes. What were they doing down there? What was *he* doing down there?"

"It's not really long enough to dispose of a body though, is it?" asked Kate.

Bonnie shrugged. "Maybe he left her there, then came back to finish the job later?"

"Why?" asked Anik. "Why not get it over with while he was there?"

"Maybe he didn't have a shovel," said Bonnie, her mind racing now through possible scenarios. "We know Juliet was alive when they left the city. Maybe the dirt road is where he killed her. They have an argument, he kills her, then realises he can't take a dead body to Bundanoon. The car boot is full of their weekend stuff, so he can't easily stuff her body in there. So, he leaves her somewhere in the bush, goes to the house, calls in for the pizza to make it look like everything is normal, and sometime later he goes back with a shovel to finish the job."

"Or he killed her there, and somehow got her body into the car, then buried her later in the National Park," suggested Kate.

"Or maybe it's both," said Anik. "He killed her, hid her body, then went back later to retrieve it and took it to bury somewhere else."

"This is all speculation," said Cooper. "Good speculation, but again, we have no proof."

Zach ended his call and returned to the table. "We might have now," he said with a smile. "That was the techs working on the Keller's car. They found blood."

26

June 2019

Juliet was just finishing up the prep work for dinner when she heard Sam's key in the door. She grabbed a tea towel and wiped her hands, checked her reflection in the hall mirror, and stood ready to greet her husband.

"Hi, baby, how was your day?" She watched as he kicked off his shoes and dumped his bag inside the door.

"Busy," he replied, holding out a paper bag. "I got you something."

Juliet recognised the bag as coming from the local chemist and tried not to look too crestfallen. Sam had been randomly bringing home pregnancy test kits for months now, and every time she took them and only that single little line showed up, their evening had been ruined.

But saying no to taking the test would make things even worse.

"Thanks, honey," Juliet said as she took the paper bag and opened it to confirm her fears. It was, indeed, another test kit.

She kept her voice light and turned toward the kitchen. "I'm just working on dinner. I'll take it afterwards."

Sam pulled off his tie and flung it over the back of the couch. He grabbed Juliet by the hips and spun her around. "Can't you take it now? I've got a good feeling tonight." He leaned in and kissed her hard on the lips.

Juliet was pretty sure she wasn't pregnant. She'd had her period three weeks ago, and she just didn't feel pregnant. She'd spoken to Renee a couple of times, and Renee said when you're pregnant, you know. But then, weren't there all those stories about women giving birth and the whole thing taking them by surprise? Maybe some women just don't know.

She picked up the test kit, wriggled out of Sam's embrace with a smile, and headed off to the bathroom.

"That's my girl," Sam called after her. Juliet heard the familiar sounds of the fridge door opening and beer bottles clinking before she locked herself in the bathroom.

Ten minutes later she braced herself and went to deliver the news. Sam was lounging on the couch, scrolling through his phone, his first beer of the evening almost finished already. He looked up expectantly.

"I'm sorry, babe. Not today." She held up the offending test wand for him to see.

"Seriously? What the hell is going wrong here, Jules?" He straightened up as Juliet sat beside him.

"It's just not our time yet, that's all," she said, stroking his arm. "Good things are worth waiting for, aren't they?"

He drained the last of the beer and slumped back into the chair. "I guess." He picked up the remote and flicked the television on, searching through the channels until he found some type of sports talk show.

Juliet breathed a sigh of relief and stood. "Dinner will be ready in half an hour," she said. "I'll get you another beer."

"And some chips?" he asked, looking up at her with child-like eyes.

"Sure." She smiled down at him, planting a kiss on his forehead before turning for the kitchen.

Leaning into the fridge, Juliet pushed a packet of meat aside to reach for the beer. It was the last one in there; she'd better put some more in straight away. And one in the freezer, too, in case Sam wanted another tonight. Straightening up and turning away from the fridge, she came face to face with Sam.

"Oh!" she exclaimed, unable to help herself. "Sam, you scared me. I wasn't expecting—"

"Have you been taking the pill again?"

"What? No, of course not. Why would I do that? We're trying to have a baby."

"Are we? Are *you*?"

"You know I am." Juliet slowly reached out and slid the beer onto the counter. The fridge was still open behind her, but Sam was standing so close he was backing her into it.

"I'm not sure I know anything about you anymore, Juliet. 'It's just not our time'," he mimicked. "'Good things are worth waiting for.' That's bullshit stuff you say to losers who fail. Do you think I'm a failure, Juliet? Do you think I'm a loser?"

"No, of course not." She tried to look away but he grabbed her by the jaw and stepped closer, backing her further into the open fridge.

He yanked her head up. "Look at me, you lying bitch. Where are they?"

"Where's what?"

He tightened his grip on her jaw, and Juliet felt all the muscles in her neck and shoulders strain.

"Your pills. I know you're taking them. You must be, or you'd be pregnant by now. Where are they?"

Juliet's mind worked overtime as she tried to figure out what to say. She couldn't direct him to any contraceptive pills because there weren't any. It was just dumb luck she hadn't fallen pregnant yet. But if Sam was convinced she was lying, continuing to deny it could result in worse punishment simply because he didn't like to be proven wrong.

There was actually no way to win here, so she went with the truth.

"I'm not taking the pill, babe," she said slowly, his hand still squeezing her jaw. "I want to have a baby as much as you do." Okay, that part *was* a lie. She still wasn't ready to be a mother and wished he'd drop the whole thing. But she couldn't change how she felt; only how she acted.

He stared at her for a few more seconds before thrusting her head to the side and letting go. "Bullshit," he said, and started ransacking the apartment.

There was no stopping him now. Sam was a determined man, and when he got an idea into his head he wouldn't stop until he'd seen it through. Given there were no contraceptive pills in the apartment, Juliet could only imagine where this particular episode might end.

Silently rubbing her jaw, Juliet watched Sam methodically tear their home apart and tried to brace for whatever came next. She cursed herself for being so stupid. Why did she say those things? She should have known how her words would make Sam feel. She should have been more careful.

When he went into their bedroom, Juliet took the opportunity to put the extra beers in the fridge and freezer. Maybe, just maybe, he would calm down and they could salvage something of the evening.

She was preparing an icepack for her jaw when he came out of the bedroom waving a wad of cash held together with a stationary clip. "What's this?"

Oh no.

"It's…" She didn't have time to come up with a plausible story. "It's just some money I had left over from my allowance."

"Why was it hidden in the false bottom of a jewellery box?"

"I didn't want it to get stolen."

Sam laughed. "We live in a security building. Who the hell did you think was going to steal it? Jesus, Jules, you are stupid sometimes." He kept laughing as he counted the cash. "There's a couple of thousand here. I give you this to run the household and keep yourself nice." He looked her up and down. "I work hard for this money. Is this the thanks I get?"

"I… I was saving it for a rainy day."

He came closer, stopped laughing. He grabbed the front of her jeans and ripped them open, exposing her underwear. She was wearing the red silk, which he'd admired previously.

"Maybe this is why you're not pregnant," he said, fingering the silk and then flicking it away in disgust. "How am I supposed to be turned on if you don't put in any effort, Juliet?"

"I'm sorry, Sam."

"You will be." He threw the money to the floor. "Get in the bedroom."

27

B onnie had wanted to act as soon as they'd found the blood in the car, but Cooper said no. It was only a trace amount in the front passenger seat, not enough to indicate foul play, and with the media attention the case was now getting, Cooper wanted things done right.

The good news was the blood, along with the Friday night stop down a deserted dirt road, were enough to convince a judge to issue a search warrant for both the Keller's apartment and the family holiday house. So here they were, just before six on Tuesday morning, banging on Sam Keller's door.

"Police!" Bonnie called. "Sam, open up!" With any luck he'd still be in bed. Bonnie loved the element of surprise in a search like this. She raised her fist to bang on the door again, but it opened before she could do so.

"What the fuck?" said Sam. He was dressed in gym gear, some sort of smoothie concoction in hand. "This is a secure building. How did you—"

"We're the police," said Bonnie as she pushed past him. "Police trumps security building."

Anik, Kate, Nora, and Zach all traipsed in behind Bonnie, leaving Sam standing in the doorway looking from them out into the hall and back. Bonnie found herself hoping they'd made enough noise to wake all the neighbours. It was petty, she knew, but that's the kind of behaviour this man inspired.

"I'm guessing you're not here to tell me you've found my wife," he said, watching as the five of them stood in his living room and gloved up.

Bonnie handed him the papers. "We've got a warrant to search these premises, as well as the house in Bundanoon. A separate team are down there now."

"Search for what? Based on what evidence?"

"It's all in there. I expect you can read." She turned away from him to make a start on the search.

"You can't do this," Sam said, following her into his kitchen as he looked at the warrant. "Blood? What blood?"

"Ah, so you *can* read," said Bonnie. "Blood was found in the passenger seat of your car, Mr Keller. The same seat Juliet occupied when you left Sydney on Friday night. I'm expecting DNA tests will confirm it's Juliet's blood."

Keller narrowed his eyes at her while he took a long, slow drink from his smoothie. "She picked at a scab," he finally said. "Must have got some blood on the seat. Is that all you've got?"

"Nope. You lied to us, Sam."

"About what?"

"We'll get to that." Bonnie looked him up and down. "Going to the gym? You're not looking too concerned about your missing wife now."

"Working out helps me think," he replied. "I need to stay alert, stay strong. Juliet needs me." His gaze moved from Bonnie to Kate Riley, who was busy opening and searching every cupboard and drawer in the kitchen. Kate was twenty-five years old, blonde, and naturally beautiful, and Sam Keller was actually checking her out.

Bonnie shook her head. "Detective Jhaveri!" she called.

Anik appeared seconds later. "Yo."

"Take Mr Keller and wait with him in the hall, please. This apartment isn't big enough for all of us, and I don't want him getting in the way of the search."

"Are you serious?" Keller protested.

"Come on," said Anik, grabbing Sam by the arm.

"Get your fucking hands off me." He broke free of Anik's grasp.

"Do you want me to arrest you?" asked Bonnie.

"For what?" Sam spat.

"Assaulting a police officer. Foul language. Take your pick."

He laughed. "If you had enough to arrest me you wouldn't hesitate. I know you. Cops like you. You get off on the power, don't you?"

Pot? Kettle? Bonnie was desperate to wipe the smug smile off his face, but this had to be done right. She raised her eyebrows at Anik, who expertly guided Sam out into the hall without touching him this time.

Bonnie turned her attention back to the search. It was a beautiful apartment, immaculately presented and with views of the city streets which would soon be bustling with commuters. Right now, a few hardy joggers braved the cold wind that had made Bonnie glad to have skipped her own workout this morning.

But they weren't here to admire the view. While the others set about their professional search methods, Bonnie took the time to immerse herself in the space and try to get a feel for the missing woman.

Juliet was twenty-five years old. She'd come from a modest, suburban background, by all accounts been swept off her feet by a man used to the finer things in life and ended up in this fancy apartment surrounded by expensive furnishings and luxury appliances. Did she embrace this lifestyle? Feel lucky to have landed amongst all this money? Or did she find it ostentatious, or even embarrassing?

Bonnie ventured into the master bedroom, where Kate was now methodically working her way through the contents of the walk-in wardrobe. "You see much of this on her socials?" Bonnie asked the junior detective.

Kate shook her head. "Nothing inside the apartment, except a few close-up selfies of the couple which could have been taken here. Most of their posts were out and about – fancy restaurants, holidays, that sort of thing."

"Many followers?"

"No. Just friends and family, from what I can tell. She wasn't any kind of influencer, if that's what you're asking."

"Fair enough," said Bonnie. She started her own review of the wardrobe contents. A lot of designer labels on both sides, not much off the rack. Sam's suit jackets and shirts were lined up in order of colour, darkest to lightest. There must have been at least thirty shirts, all expertly pressed and hung on identical wooden hangers. Casual wear was folded and shelved so neatly it resembled a shop display.

Juliet's side of the robe was more colourful, but just as neat. Amongst the designer labels Bonnie noticed a few more down-to-earth pieces; gorgeous dresses and skirts that had no labels at all. She pulled out a stunning cobalt blue skirt and held the hanger at arm's length.

"She's altered that herself," said Kate.

"Really? How can you tell?"

"Look closely at the left seam." Kate turned the skirt inside out to show Bonnie what she meant. "It's an expert job, but you can tell it's been done. Either Juliet did it herself or got someone else to do it. There are a number of garments in here the same."

"Interesting," said Bonnie. It could mean nothing, or it could be an indication that Juliet wasn't always entirely comfortable in designer fashion. Either way, judging by this wardrobe she was very good at looking good.

Bonnie ventured into the en-suite bathroom. Here there were a few signs of Juliet's absence. The bathroom was clean; not enough time had passed for it to become the true victim of a single male, but the open bottle of aftershave and squished toothpaste tube spilling its contents onto the counter confirmed Juliet was not here to tidy up after her husband.

The kitchen was in a similar state. Sam had been home alone for two nights and one full day, and it showed. He'd ordered food deliveries both nights, the remnants of which were stuffed into the garbage with no thought given to separating recyclables. The sink held a couple of dirty plates and forks. Bonnie opened the dishwasher to find it full of clean dishes, presumably the final cycle before they left for the weekend. Sam obviously hadn't bothered to empty it.

Bonnie was starting to get a vibe. Juliet kept an immaculately clean and tidy household. There was order and structure to their lives, which had fallen down immediately once she was gone. That was understandable; a lot of couples had one partner who was neater than the other, and if Sam was the distraught husband desperate to find his missing wife that he claimed to be, tidying up would be the last thing on his mind.

But still. That wasn't the vibe Bonnie was feeling. She couldn't explain it, wouldn't be able to stand up in court and describe why, but Bonnie was completely creeped out by this apartment.

"Detective Hunter! We've found something."

Bonnie followed the voice to the corner of the living room,

where Nora was up on a stepladder with a ceiling vent open above her. Without looking down she held out a gloved hand to her partner, and Zach placed one of their cameras into it. Nora took a few photos, muttering under her breath, and then stared down at Bonnie.

"Pervert's got a camera up here," Nora said.

28

November 2019

"You know what to say," Sam whispered as he led her into the emergency department by her good arm. Juliet was thankful they lived so close to the hospital. She was sure she was about to pass out from the pain, so Sam needn't worry about what she may or may not say to any of the staff. "Help me, please," he called out once they were inside the sliding doors. "Help my wife."

Someone got a wheelchair under Juliet just in time, and she was wheeled farther into the waiting room. She closed her eyes and whisked her mind to another place.

"Where are you going?" she heard Sam say, and reflexively opened her mouth to answer before she realised he was talking to someone else.

"The triage nurse will be with you soon," said a male voice.

"We need help now," Sam protested. "My wife's arm... I think it's broken."

It was definitely broken, Juliet thought matter-of-factly. He'd made sure of that. It broke the first time he'd slammed it in the car door; she'd heard the crack of the bone. But he'd slammed it again three more times, just to be certain. Never one to do these things by halves, her husband.

The kind man who'd been so quick with the wheelchair had obviously left, as Sam didn't get an answer. "Bloody useless prick," Sam said, loud enough for the other patients in the waiting room to hear. Juliet kept her eyes closed. If she concentrated really hard, she could see the waterfall her family hiked to when she was a child.

"Be careful," her mother had said when they came upon the rope swing. "We will," Juliet and Nick replied in unison as they fought over which of them would have the first turn swinging into the pool at the base of the waterfall.

"Jules." Juliet felt Sam's hand lightly stroking her face. She opened her eyes; he was staring at her, full of concern. "Are you okay? Are you ready?"

Juliet looked up to see the door to the triage station open, a nurse waiting inside. She nodded, cradling her bad arm with her good one as Sam wheeled the chair into the little room.

"What's happened here then?" the nurse, whose name tag read Meera, said to Juliet once she'd taken her details from the Medicare card Sam provided.

"She got it caught in the car door," said Sam.

Meera looked from Juliet to Sam for a beat, then turned her attention back to Juliet with narrowed eyes. "Is that right?"

Juliet nodded.

"Let's take a look then." Juliet winced at Meera's touch, then cried out as the nurse manipulated the arm to assess the damage. "I'm afraid I'm going to have to cut this." Meera took the scissors to the sleeve of Juliet's top before she had time to protest. Not that Juliet would have; her clothes were the last thing she cared about right now.

"Is it broken?" Sam asked.

"I suspect so," Meera answered. "The doctor will take a look and order an X-ray to confirm. This is a significant injury," she said to Juliet. "How did you get it caught in the car door?"

"I... I wasn't watching what I was doing," said Juliet slowly, careful to get the story exactly as she and Sam had practiced. "I reached in to grab my purse just as Sam closed the door. He didn't see me..."

"I didn't see her," Sam jumped in, his voice cracking in just the perfect spot. God, he was a good actor. "I can't believe this happened. My poor Juliet, I can't believe I did this."

"It wasn't your fault," said Juliet, just as they'd rehearsed. "I wasn't paying attention. Ow, it really hurts."

"We'll be able to give you something for the pain as soon as the doctor has seen you," said Meera. She reached into one of the cubby holes in front of her desk containing bandages and dressings, and in less than a minute Juliet was sporting a sling on her broken right arm. "Keep it as still as possible," said Meera before opening the back door of the little room and calling an orderly over.

"How long before she sees the doctor?" Sam asked.

"They'll get to you as soon as they can," Meera replied before turning to the orderly. "Take Mrs Keller and her husband to bed six." She handed him a folder, and he took control of the wheelchair and pushed Juliet out into the main area of the emergency department.

Bed six was in the corner, and Sam watched as the orderly helped Juliet into the bed. When the man left, pushing the wheelchair away, Sam pulled the curtains around to give them some privacy.

"I'm sorry," said Juliet reflexively when he stared at her. She hadn't meant to be late home; she'd lost track of time. Stupid. She knew better.

"Hey, baby," said Sam, standing beside the bed and stroking

her hair gently. "Don't worry about all that now. The important thing is you're okay, and the doctors will get you all fixed up. If they ever get here." He turned and opened the curtain enough for him to see out, but Juliet's view was still blocked. She closed her eyes and returned to the waterfall.

"Three, two, one, go!" Nick called from the water, and Juliet dutifully ran and launched herself as high as she could before letting go of the rope and splashing down into the cool, clear pool.

"That's so fun!" she said, tossing wet hair out of her eyes.

"See, I told you. Nothing to be scared of." Nick climbed up the bank and readied himself for another turn.

Juliet watched as he expertly got hold of the rope, took it all the way back as far as he could, then ran and leapt so high into the air her breath caught. She held it until he safely emerged with the biggest grin on his face.

"Nicky! That was dangerous!" Juliet looked over at her parents on the picnic rug, expecting them to join her in admonishing such behaviour, but they were both engrossed in their favourite sections of the Sunday paper. Nick could get away with anything.

"Don't be such a baby," said Nick. "Go on, your turn again."

Juliet hesitated, but only briefly. Calling her a baby always had the desired effect, and soon enough they'd both been running as fast and jumping as high as they could. It had been a wonderful day, no-one had gotten hurt, and Juliet remembered feeling like her big brother could protect her from anything.

"Mrs Keller? I'm Dr Reed."

Juliet opened her eyes to find a short woman in surgical scrubs and a white coat standing next to the bed, her large glasses directly at Juliet's eye level.

"Hi," Juliet managed.

"About time," said Sam. "My wife is in pain."

Dr Reed looked across the bed at him. "Would you mind waiting outside, please?"

Sam stared back. "I'll stay."

"Please, can he stay?" Juliet asked.

"Of course," said Dr Reed after a beat. She pushed a button which lowered the bed, giving her easier access to examine Juliet. "Tell me how this happened."

Juliet went through the story again, wincing and trying not to cry as Dr Reed manipulated the arm and poked and prodded more than Nurse Meera had. When it was over, Dr Reed entered some notes into a tablet with a stylus pen, then cradled the tablet to her chest before addressing Juliet.

"I'm going to send you down for an X-ray to confirm, but it seems like a clean break to me. That's good news; hopefully, you won't need surgery. You'll be in a cast for six to eight weeks, though." Dr Reed looked up at Sam. "She's going to need some help at home. Are you going to be able to cover that?"

"We'll be fine," said Sam. "Thank you, Doctor. That is good news."

Dr Reed nodded. "Someone will be here to take you down to X-ray shortly, Juliet. I'm afraid you'll have to stay here," she added before Sam could ask. "The nurses will give you some forms to fill out."

Sam looked like he was going to protest.

"I'll be fine, babe," said Juliet quickly. She closed her eyes again.

"Can you at least give her something for the pain?" Sam asked.

"As soon as the X-ray is done and we're sure she doesn't need surgery," Dr Reed replied. "I'll be back as soon as I can after that." She opened the curtain and walked away.

Juliet kept her eyes closed, praying that Sam wouldn't make a fuss this time about not being allowed to go to the X-ray room.

He stilled for a moment, then finally dragged a chair closer to her bed, sat, and started playing on his phone. Juliet didn't need to open her eyes to know any of this, so in tune was she with the sounds and movements of her husband. Except, of course, when he didn't want her to be.

It could have been hours, or perhaps it was just minutes, before the same orderly as before came to wheel her down to X-ray.

"How long will she be?" Sam asked.

The orderly shrugged. "They're pretty busy. Could be a while. Cafeteria's open. You've got time to go and get a coffee, man."

"That's a good idea," said Juliet. "Don't worry, I'll be fine." She gave him a reassuring smile that to anyone watching would seem like a loving goodbye. Between Juliet and Sam, though, it was a private acknowledgement of the power balance in the relationship.

I won't say anything. I know what you're capable of.

29

B onnie made sure the interview was done by the book. Sam Keller may have agreed to come to the station for questioning, perhaps because the alternative of an even bigger police presence outside his apartment building hadn't been too appealing, but he was a savvy lawyer who would pounce on any little thing that could help get him off. The last thing they needed was a wife-killer to walk on a technicality.

"You're certain you don't want legal representation?" Bonnie asked for the third time.

"I've told you, I'll represent myself. I haven't done anything wrong, Detective. The sooner you work that out, the sooner we can both get back out there and find my wife."

It was just Bonnie and Sam in the interview room, along with a camera set up in the corner to record everything. Bonnie wasn't used to conducting interviews by herself, but for some suspects – particularly those who declined legal assistance – the more casual one-on-one chat was the most effective. She hadn't been sure what the best approach was for Sam Keller, so she'd deferred to Cooper's years of experience on this one.

"He'll want to get the better of you," Cooper had said. "He'll see you as inferior when it's just the two of you in there. Use that to your advantage."

Bonnie kept those words in the back of her mind now as she sat here with Sam. "Okay, let's get started. We have security footage from your building that proves you and Juliet left your apartment just before six pm on Friday."

Sam stared at her.

"Is that correct?" she asked.

He took a breath, then exhaled slowly. "Yeah. Jules packed the car, and when I got home, we left."

"We also have a picture of the two of you in the car taken as you went through the M5 toll."

Sam continued to stare, waiting for her point.

"So, we know Juliet was in the car with you at least until after the M5 toll point."

"What do you mean, 'at least until'? What do you think, I dropped her off somewhere and then faked her disappearance?"

Bonnie ignored the question. "We've traced both of your mobile phones for that period of time. At seven-fifteen pm, you turned down a dirt road and travelled approximately three hundred metres, where you stopped. What were you doing down an isolated dirt road in the dark?"

Sam shrugged. "Jules needed to pee."

"Why didn't you stop at the rest stop two kilometres earlier?"

"I'd already passed it before she said she needed to go."

"You're telling me Juliet had no need to urinate when you were approaching the rest stop, but within two kilometres – less than two minutes later – her need was urgent enough for you to find somewhere to stop?"

Another shrug. "It's what happened."

"Most people would just pull over, walk a little way into the bush. You drove three hundred metres down a deserted road."

"My wife likes her privacy, Detective. Look, I thought the

side street would be okay. It was a little dark, I'll admit, but Juliet is used to going in the bush. We go for bush walks all the time when we go down to the highlands."

Bonnie took a moment as she scratched an itch on the side of her face. "Your phones didn't move again until seven-thirty-seven pm," she said slowly. "That's twenty-two minutes later, Sam. Why did it take twenty-two minutes for Juliet to relieve herself?"

He paused before answering. "It didn't."

"So, what else were you doing?"

Sam leaned back, flung one arm over the back of his chair, and spread his legs wide. "Do I really need to answer that?"

"Yeah, you really do."

Sam looked down at his crotch, then back up to Bonnie. He grinned. "It was my birthday. My wife wanted to give me... a present."

It was all Bonnie could do not to vomit. She hated it, but she had to ask. "What did she give you?"

The grin widened. "She gave me a blow job, Detective. She's very good at it. I was happy to wait until we got to the house, but Jules was insistent. And that dirt road – it's private property, if I'm not mistaken. So, we weren't doing anything illegal, were we?"

Bonnie ignored his question. "Blood was the only bodily fluid found in your car, Sam. She can't be too good." She watched his face fall ever so slightly but didn't wait for him to respond. "Speaking of that blood, we've confirmed it matches Juliet's blood type. Can you tell me how her blood got on the front passenger seat of your car? And why it had been cleaned off?"

"I think I remember her saying something about scratching herself on a tree branch when she got out to go to the toilet," Sam replied.

"Really? Because this morning you said she picked at a scab. Which is it?"

He wasn't smiling anymore. "How should I know? What does it matter? It can't have been very much blood. I would remember if Jules hurt herself seriously. And she probably washed it off on Saturday because she likes to keep things clean. Look, I know you think I'm one of those monsters who hurts his wife. I'm not. I love Juliet. I would do anything to find her. I *will* do anything to find her. So, unless you have some actual evidence, can we wrap this up?"

"Soon," said Bonnie. "I just have one more thing. This morning my team found a series of hidden cameras in your apartment. Were you aware of their existence?"

He hesitated briefly before replying. "Yes. I put them there."

"Can you tell me why?"

"No."

"Why not?"

"It's not relevant, and it's none of your business."

"I think it's quite relevant, Mr Keller."

"My home, my cameras. I can do whatever I like in my own home."

"You've been filming your wife while she's home alone."

Sam didn't respond.

"Are we also going to find cameras at your holiday house? Sorry, your parents' holiday house?"

He stared at her.

"It's illegal to film someone without their knowledge. Did Juliet know you were filming her?"

Sam folded his arms; narrowed his eyes. "You'll have to ask her that when you find her. Are we done here?"

There was a knock on the door before Bonnie could answer. "Excuse me one moment." She paused the interview and quickly stepped into the corridor, closing the door behind her lest Sam decide to leave, which he knew full well was his right to do.

"What is it?" she asked Zach, who was standing before her, laptop open in his arms.

"I found a GPS tracker installed on Juliet's phone. He's been tracking her every move."

"For how long?"

"At least a year, from what I can tell. He's also had access to all her texts and emails, web searches. Essentially whatever she did on her phone, he knew about it. Or at least whoever installed this app did." He pointed to his laptop screen, which showed an outline of a mobile phone. "This is a clone of her phone. See this one here?" He pointed to a yellow app on the phone screen that seemed vaguely familiar to Bonnie. "It looks like one of the ones that comes pre-loaded on this type of phone, which most people just ignore."

"But it's not," said Bonnie.

Zach shook his head. "This is a very sophisticated app, not many people know of it. I've seen it before though, in other cases of domestic abuse. This app is a must-have for your modern-day coercive controller."

"And she wouldn't have known about it?" Bonnie asked again.

"I can't say for sure, but whoever put it here went to great lengths to disguise it."

Bonnie glanced at the closed door. The man behind it was a monster. She *had* to nail his arse. "How does it work? How does he see where she is?"

"The app sends all her data, as well as GPS info, in real time to a webpage. Whenever he logs onto that page, he can see where her phone is, and what she's doing with it. Unless it's turned off."

"Can he see if it's turned off?"

Zach closed his laptop. "Yeah."

Bonnie shuddered. Sam Keller filmed his wife while she was at home, and tracked her wherever she went. He read her emails, her text messages. Knew what websites she accessed. If she knew he was watching her and turned her phone off to escape his gaze, he knew that too. What must her life have been like?

She locked eyes with Zach; their mutual disgust of the man responsible for all this was palpable.

"We'll get him," said Bonnie.

Yeah, we will," the tech agreed. "Oh, Coop said there's someone here he wants you to talk to. She's from a women's refuge. Apparently, Juliet tried to leave Sam three years ago."

30

November 2019

The orderly wheeled Juliet through a series of doors, each of which he had to access with a swipe card. It was a full minute before Juliet realised they were no longer following the signs to the X-ray department.

"Where are you—"

"Shh," he interrupted, before stopping outside the door of a room marked 'Private'. He knocked, but didn't wait for an answer before wheeling her in.

It was a doctor's office, not unlike the one her and Sam's local GP occupied, with a desk, two chairs, and a patient examination table. Juliet hadn't known they had offices like this inside hospitals, but she supposed it made sense. Dr Reed got up from behind the desk and came over to Juliet. "Thanks, Andre." The orderly smiled at Juliet before leaving, closing the door behind him.

"I thought I was going for an X-ray," said Juliet. The pain was still clouding her ability to focus.

"We'll get to that, but I needed to speak to you alone." The doctor repositioned Juliet's wheelchair and then sat facing her. "Juliet, it's important you know I'm on your side here."

"I don't..."

Dr Reed held up a finger to stop her. "Your arm is broken in at least two places. There's no way that happened in the manner in which you described. Why don't you tell me what really happened?"

Juliet just wanted to go home. She was tired, in pain, and not capable of having this conversation right now. She stared at her feet resting on the little platforms at the base of the wheelchair. She was still wearing the red boots. What had possessed her to go grocery shopping in such footwear? Stupid. She'd been late home *and* wearing sexy shoes – what was Sam supposed to think? Could she really blame him for reacting the way he did?

"Juliet, I can get you out of this situation. Just tell me what happened."

Could she? The kind doctor meant well, Juliet knew that. But 'this situation' was her life. Her marriage to Sam was all she had. She loved him, and he loved her. He had a temper, and he got a little jealous at times. He was working on that. They both were. If she could just stop doing the stupid things that set him off...

"At least let me give you a full examination while you're here," said Dr Reed.

Juliet focused back on the doctor. "Okay," she said with a nod. "To the examination," she clarified. She wasn't ready to consider anything else Dr Reed was implying.

"Good. Now, can you stand for me?"

Juliet nodded and got to her feet. Dr Reed helped her over to the examination table, and lowered it so she could sit on the edge.

"I'm going to need you to take this off," said Dr Reed, indicating Juliet's high-necked jumper. The right sleeve was cut open all the way up to the shoulder, but the rest of the garment remained intact.

"Can't I just lift it up?"

Dr Reed shook her head. "You'll need to take it off for the x-ray, anyway. It'll be better if I help you; I've got a gown here we can get you into and blankets to keep you warm." Dr Reed started lifting the jumper before Juliet could protest further.

The bruising around Juliet's neck from when she'd bought Sam the wrong brand of aftershave had almost faded, but not quite. She hadn't had time to apply concealer this morning, which was why she'd opted for the high-neck turquoise jumper. It wasn't helping her now, though. Dr Reed snapped on a pair of gloves and examined the area.

"Is your husband responsible for this?" she asked as she gently touched Juliet's neck.

"I... he..." Juliet stuttered. "I really don't want to talk about it."

Dr Reed continued her examination without missing a beat. She didn't ask more questions about Sam, just the occasional 'does this hurt?' or instructions to turn this way or take deep breaths. Once she was finished, she helped Juliet into a gown, then got her back in the wheelchair and draped a blanket around her shoulders.

She returned to the chair and sat facing Juliet. She spoke slowly and clearly. "I know you don't want to hear this. But Juliet, I am very concerned for your safety. As well as the badly broken arm you've presented here with today, there are marks on your body consistent with an ongoing campaign of physical abuse."

Juliet didn't respond. What was she supposed to say?

"It's hard, I know," said Dr Reed. "But you have to understand, men like this are dangerous. Choking in particular is a red flag for future homicide."

Juliet stayed silent. Dr Reed didn't know what she was talking about. Sam wasn't 'men like this'. He was her husband.

"Those marks on your neck... how many times has Sam choked you?"

Too many. The words formed on Juliet's lips but refused to come out. *But I deserved it. I just need to do better, remember what to do. And what not to do.*

"Tell me this," Dr Reed continued. "Are *you* concerned for your safety?"

Was she? So many times she'd done the wrong thing, set Sam off. Staying 'in line', as Sam called it, was exhausting. Could she really ask more of herself?

Dr Reed was waiting for an answer. Juliet looked into the woman's kind eyes, and for the first time saw her as an ally, a friend, rather than a doctor. With all the strength she could muster, Juliet nodded.

That was all the encouragement Dr Reed needed. "Okay. I have a contact, she works at the local women's shelter. If I call her, will you come back here to my office after your X-ray and just listen to what she has to say?"

"Sam will be waiting for me," said Juliet. She knew how he got if she kept him waiting, and she didn't think she had the strength to cope with that right now. She just wanted to go home, take some pain killers, and let Sam look after her the way he always did when she... got hurt.

"Don't worry about Sam. I'll have Andre tell him you're held up in X-ray. He can't get back here."

"I guess..." It couldn't hurt to hear what the shelter woman had to say. If it would get Dr Reed to let her go home.

"Good." Dr Reed pressed a button on the phone on her desk,

and almost immediately Andre was there. "I'll see you soon," said the doctor, already holding the handset to her ear and dialling a number by the time Andre had the wheelchair turned around and headed for X-ray.

31

Ruth Mason stood by the window, looking out over the streets of Parramatta. She turned when Bonnie entered the room. "Detective Hunter? Thank you for seeing me."

She was mid-fifties, shoulder-length brown hair, and an average-looking woman in all respects – except for the large scar which ran from her right cheekbone all the way down to her jaw.

"I'm told you have some information about Juliet Keller," said Bonnie, gesturing to a couple of chairs and doing her best not to stare at the scar.

Ruth nodded as they both sat. "When I saw her picture on the news... and then that smug bastard appealing for help..." She shook her head. "I think we failed that woman."

"Tell me what you know," said Bonnie.

Bonnie listened as Ruth described getting a call from a doctor at Sydney Hospital about Juliet. Sam had broken Juliet's arm in two places by slamming it in the car door, and Ruth had taken her out the back way of the hospital while Sam still waited in Emergency. The police had been called, but Ruth heard later that no charges had been laid.

"What happened to Juliet?" Bonnie asked.

"We had no space available at the shelter that night. I got her a room at the Carrington – that's a motel we use short-term for overflow. I was hoping it would only be for a night or two, that we could get her into the shelter soon. But a lot of women need our services. Anyway, I went back the next afternoon to see how she was doing, and she was gone."

"Did you follow up at all? Go to her home?"

Ruth shook her head. "We do our best, Detective Hunter. We don't have enough rooms for all the women who do want help, without forcing those who don't. These men... I shouldn't say that, they're not all men, although the overwhelming majority are... these *coercive controllers*, they get their partners so far under their control, the partner feels that they have no other options."

Bonnie had seen enough domestic abuse in her time to know exactly what Ruth was describing. The patterns of the perpetrators, the techniques they used to control their victims, it was horrifying to think of the lengths some people would go to dominate and hurt the person they supposedly loved. Manipulation, isolation, gaslighting, surveillance, not to mention physical harm. If Sam Keller had been controlling Juliet enough to make her go back to him after he put her in the hospital three years ago, what had it escalated to now?

"Did you ever hear from Juliet again?" Bonnie asked Ruth.

"No. I'm sorry, but like I said..."

"I know," Bonnie finished for her. "There are too many. You can't help everyone."

"We failed her, didn't we? I failed Juliet, and now she's probably..." Ruth raised a hand to her face, fingers tracing the scar on her cheek.

Bonnie softened. "It's not your fault." She reached for Ruth's hand, held it away from her face. "I'm sure there are many women out there today who wouldn't be if it weren't for you and your organisation, Ruth. Keep doing what you do. Keep doing your job – it helps make mine a little less unbearable."

Ruth nodded, standing. "Thank you, Detective Hunter."

"Please, call me Bonnie."

"Bonnie. If there's anything I can do to help you lock him up for good, please let me know. Men like Sam Keller don't deserve to walk this good Earth."

Bonnie couldn't agree more. She saw Ruth out of the building, then phoned Kate as soon as she was on her way back to the interview room.

"Cooper had me check into it," said Kate when Bonnie asked her about Juliet's visit to the emergency room three years ago.

"Was a DVSAT done?" Bonnie asked, her pace quickening as she walked. The Domestic Violence Safety Assessment Threat had been rolled out across NSW jurisdictions since 2015 as part of a series of reforms to address domestic and family violence. Bonnie was a strong proponent of the reforms – anything to help stop men like Sam Keller and Ian Bessell ruining the lives of their families – but three years ago it was still in its infancy. Not all officers attending domestic violence callouts were as enthusiastic as Bonnie, with many seeing the DVSAT as just extra paperwork.

"No," Kate replied. "Sam Keller was interviewed, denied having anything to do with Juliet's injuries. Juliet had left the hospital before she could be interviewed. The responding officers went to the motel room the next day, but she was already gone. By the time they caught up with her at the Keller's apartment, she refused to answer the DVSAT questions."

Damn. "Thanks, Kate," Bonnie said, hanging up before diverting into a nearby ladies room. "Fuck!" She slapped her palm against the door to one of the stalls. It bounced off the wall and crashed closed again, almost hitting Bonnie in the face. She caught hold of it and steadied herself. She couldn't let this slime bag get to her like this.

After using the facilities, Bonnie composed herself in the mirror. The tracking app on Juliet's phone should be enough to convince a judge to give them a warrant for Sam's phone and computer. If they could find evidence of him logging onto the website used to monitor Juliet's movements, they could arrest him for using a tracking device to determine the geographical location of a person without that person's permission. That offence alone carried a maximum penalty of five years, which was a start.

Bonnie reached the door to the interview room where she'd left Anik with Sam Keller.

"Detective Hunter, about time," said Sam. "I have things to do you know. What is this urgent new evidence you just had to question me about? Although I fail to see how urgent it could be if you were happy to run off and leave me with your babysitter here."

Anik threw Bonnie an exasperated look as he rose to leave.

"Please stay, Detective Jhaveri," said Bonnie as she took her seat next to Anik. Play time was over; Sam needed to see they meant business.

Anik resumed his seat.

Bonnie once again went through the formalities of starting the recording and introducing all present. When she was done, she paused, clasping her hands together and resting them on the table between her and Keller.

Keller leaned back, opened his hands in a 'what?' gesture.

"Sam, technical analysis of Juliet's mobile phone has uncovered an application we believe has been used to trace her movements and monitor her activity. Do you know anything about this app?"

She had to hand it to him, he was a bloody good actor. He didn't react at all.

"I do not."

"You didn't install this application on Juliet's phone? Use it to track where she went? What she did?"

"I did not."

"Yet you admit to installing surveillance cameras in your home?"

"Security cameras. As we have already discussed, it is perfectly legal for me to install cameras in my own place of residence. But what you're suggesting, an application that tracks a person's location and monitors their data without their consent, that would be a breach of the Surveillance Devices Act, as I'm sure you're aware. I would do no such thing."

"So how do you explain the presence of such an app on your wife's phone?"

Keller folded his arms. "I can't. As you say, it is *my wife's* phone. You'll have to ask her when you find her. *If* you find her."

"*If* I find her? Why do you say it like that, Sam? Did you do that good a job at hiding her body?"

"Be very careful, Detective Hunter."

Bonnie stared him down.

"I am merely referring to your incessant questioning of me," he continued. "How are you expecting to find my wife if you're spending all of your time on me?"

"I'm following the evidence. I'm not satisfied you're telling me the truth, Sam."

Keller rolled his eyes, leaned back in his chair again, and rested his hands on his head. "What else can I tell you?"

"How about you tell me how Juliet's arm got broken in November 2019?"

Sam sniffed. "That was a misunderstanding."

"How is a broken arm a misunderstanding?" asked Anik. "What happens when you two really get going?"

For a second Bonnie thought Sam was going to launch at Anik across the table, but Anik raised his hands palm out in apology, and Sam backed off.

"I mean it was a misunderstanding on the part of the doctor treating Jules," he clarified. "It was an accident. They tried to make it look like I was this monster who hurt his wife. It was ridiculous."

"According to our records, Juliet was referred by the hospital to a shelter, who arranged emergency accommodation," said Bonnie. "Doesn't sound like a misunderstanding to me."

"That bitch doctor..." Sam checked himself. "That doctor and the social worker woman, they ganged up on Jules. She told me later they withheld treatment until she agreed to go to that crappy motel."

"Then what happened?" Bonnie knew the official story, but she wanted to hear Sam's version.

"Jules came home. She told me how they treated her. I was so mad, I wanted to sue the hospital. But Jules didn't want to make a fuss. She said it was over, she wanted to leave it behind us. So, I let it go. I shouldn't have. I should have sued their arses. I knew this crap would come back to bite me one day."

He was right about one thing, it was crap. His story was completely different to the version Ruth Mason had just told, and Bonnie knew which of them she was inclined to believe. But without Juliet herself there was no way to prove Sam broke Juliet's arm. Bonnie could only work with hard evidence.

She checked her watch. "The app on Juliet's phone is enough for me to get a warrant for your phone and computer. If I find anything that proves you accessed any of the data gathered by that app, I'll arrest you immediately. You might want to reconsider that decision to represent yourself."

Sam smirked. "Knock yourself out, Detective."

32

November 2019

By the time Juliet had finished in X-ray and been wheeled back to Dr Reed's office, she had been ready to tell the doctor and her women's shelter friend that it had all been a big misunderstanding. But Ruth – that was the woman's name – and Dr Reed had already set things in motion, acting like they knew what was best for Juliet.

"We don't have any beds at the shelter right at the minute," Ruth had said. "But there should be one opening up in a day or two. In the meantime, we've found you a room at the Carrington Motel. It's a little way out of the city; we find it a safer option to move clients a decent distance from their abusers in the first instance."

It was hard for Juliet to concentrate on what Ruth was saying, on account of the massive scar running down the side of the woman's face. She tried to focus on the words coming out of Ruth's mouth, but her eyes kept coming back to the scar. What had happened to this woman?

They had set Juliet's arm in a cast, and Dr Reed had finally given her some painkillers, which provided some relief, but talk of clients and abusers and procedures and safe houses was all too much to process. She just wanted to go home.

Ruth had driven her here, to this motel room in a suburb of Sydney Juliet was unfamiliar with. She'd given her some money and vouchers for food and personal items then told her she'd be in touch as soon as a room at the hostel was available. She was kind, Ruth, and Juliet was sure she'd been a big help to a lot of women. Women who had really abusive husbands. Other women. Not women like Juliet.

They hadn't told her what had happened to Sam. As far as she knew he was still at the hospital, waiting for her to come back from X-ray. That was silly, though. It was over eight hours ago. He'd know she wasn't coming back by now.

She couldn't imagine what Sam had said when he realised what was happening. Had he got angry? Or had he been calm, nice even, the way he usually was with other people? Was he saving it all for her for when she finally came home?

Home. She wasn't going home, that's what Ruth had said. And Dr Reed. Could she really survive on her own? Did she really want to? She should call her parents. Or Nick. But that would mean telling them what had happened. She wasn't ready for that. Her mother loved Sam, but her father and brother weren't that fond of him. They were just different, that's all. They didn't understand Sam.

When was the last time she'd spoken to her family?

Sam had broken her arm in two places. She wasn't an idiot; she knew what he did was wrong. He'd really frightened her this time. But she hadn't helped the situation. She glared at the red boots, discarded in the corner of the shitty motel room. She'd picked them up at East West Vintage the day before and cleaned them up so well they looked brand new. She knew Sam would love them, but she wanted to test them out first to see how comfortable they were. She should have been home well before Sam, in time to change out of them and into her sensible shoes, but the grocery shopping took longer than she'd thought, and Sam was home early.

He didn't mean to hurt her. Sam worked hard, and he saw a lot of bad things and bad people in his job. Sometimes that spilled over, and he took it out on Juliet. Their marriage was a partnership, and if she didn't go out to work every day like he did, the least she could do was be there to help him when he got home.

Juliet was tired. She'd been in this motel room since just after midnight, and it was now close to three am. Dr Reed had given her something to help her sleep, but she didn't want to take it as well as the painkillers. Sam didn't like her taking drugs unnecessarily.

She lay back on the bed and stared at the ceiling, trying to ignore the throbbing pain in her arm. This was crazy. Sam wasn't the type of man Dr Reed had described. He wasn't going to kill her. He loved her. She should be at home right now, letting him take care of her. Juliet allowed herself a smile, knowing how well he would have looked after her once he'd driven her home from the hospital. He'd have made her a cup of tea, set her up in bed with pillows to support her arm, and stayed awake all night just so he didn't bump her in his sleep.

She missed him. She missed his smile; the way he smelled when he came out of the shower every morning. The kisses he planted on top of her head. The way he yelled at the television when his rugby team wasn't doing well, which was often.

Juliet must have drifted off to sleep at some point. Despite the cold, she hadn't bothered to get under the covers, and was still lying on top of the bed when the thumping woke her from a hazy dream. She opened the door before she was fully awake.

Sam stepped inside the room, closed the door, and pushed her back onto the bed all in one swift movement.

"Sam!"

"Shut up." He looked around, as if he were fascinated by the tiny motel room with its grey carpet and beige walls, its mini-fridge, its kettle and toaster.

"Sam, I..."

"I said shut up. Seriously, Jules. Is this what we've come to? You'd leave me for a dump like this? I thought you loved me."

Juliet wasn't sure whether to speak. She waited a beat, until she was sure he was waiting for an answer.

"I *do* love you. Those people... they don't understand us." The tears came involuntarily.

His voice softened. He came closer. "What did they make you do?"

He was giving her an opening, and she took it. "They wouldn't let me go back to you," she said, wiping her eyes. "After the X-ray, they put this cast on and then brought me here. They said it was for the best. They didn't give me any choice. I'm so tired, Sam. I don't even know where I am."

He sat on the bed beside her and reached for her hand. She folded her good arm into his.

"Some crappy motel in hicksville," he said, shaking his head. "These people... they think they can interfere in our lives. Take my wife away from me." He turned to her and gently touched the cast. "You told them it was an accident, right?"

"Of course," she lied. "I don't know how they got the wrong idea."

Sam shook his head. "Morons. You know they sent the police after me?"

"Oh no. What happened?"

"Nothing. Don't worry about it, it's sorted." He stood, pulling her up off the bed with him. "Come on, let's get you home."

Juliet glanced at the boots in the corner of the room, then turned and followed Sam in her stockinged feet. No need to keep a reminder of this episode.

As Sam guided her out into the morning sunlight, a thought occurred to her. "Sam, how did you find me?"

He pulled her close and whispered into her ear. "You're my wife, Jules. I'll always be able to find you."

33

January 2020

There were two lines on the test stick. Not that she needed to see them; Juliet had been pretty sure she was pregnant for almost a week now. Turned out her sister-in-law had been right; you just know.

Juliet wiped away the tears and shoved the test stick deep into the bathroom rubbish bin. Then she pulled it out again because Sam had gotten into the habit of searching the bins lately. Goodness knows what he was looking for, but she certainly didn't want him finding this.

She wrapped the offending stick in toilet paper and took it to the bin in the kitchen. It was almost full, so it was perfectly plausible that she'd take it out to the rubbish chute during the course of her day.

Juliet stopped; stood in the middle of the kitchen. Was she really trying to hide the pregnancy from Sam? He'd be over the moon when he found out. They'd been trying for ages; he was so desperate to be a father. He'd make a good father, wouldn't he? And maybe, during the pregnancy at least, Juliet would see more of the protective, caring man she'd married. So why was she burying the positive test in the garbage?

As she closed the lid of the bin, Juliet's right arm began to throb. The cast had come off weeks ago and Dr Baird – they'd gone to a different hospital this time – had said it was healing well, but every now and then it still hurt. She assumed it would be better by the time the baby was born. A new mother needed two fully-functioning arms.

Was she ready for this? She was only twenty-three. She'd be twenty-four by the time it was born, but still. She didn't feel ready.

What were her friends going to say? Tess and Gwen were both still single, still partying every weekend. Gwen wasn't even finished medical school yet. No way either of them would be getting pregnant at this age. And Max, almost finished his first year at his fancy job down in Canberra. He had a girlfriend now. What was her name? They'd been together almost a year, and Juliet hadn't even met her yet. She felt so different to her friends, so far away.

Juliet shook the negative thoughts from her head. This was crazy. She was a married woman, and now she was going to be a mother. Her own mother had had Nick by the time she was Juliet's age. Everything was going to be fine.

She had a couple of hours before Sam was due home. Juliet checked her meal plan for the week, and quickly decided to change things up. Sam liked order in their household, and now that she understood his routines and planning systems, she had to admit she liked it too, but he also wasn't opposed to mixing things up when the occasion called for it. A baby on the way should definitely call for a little spontaneity.

She'd make beef stroganoff, with full fat cream, one of his favourite treat meals. A nice bottle of red to go with it – except, no, she couldn't drink now. Sam still could, though. The red would be for him. But he'd pour her a glass as soon as he got home; expect her to drink with him. She'd have to tell him why she couldn't, and he'd know she'd done the test without him.

He wouldn't like that.

She could put the bottle in the cupboard, maybe. Pull it out after she'd done another pregnancy test, revealed the big news.

Juliet steadied herself, both palms flat on the kitchen bench. She needed to think this through. She knew she was pregnant. Had done a test to confirm it. Should she just tell Sam as soon as he walked through the door? Or did she need to put on a show for her husband, let him be a part of the moment?

There was a chemist a few blocks away, in the opposite direction to Sam's office. She could go and get another test kit now. Yes, that was the best plan. No stroganoff, no bottle of red. Just a regular Thursday night at home. A regular Thursday where she realises her period is late, maybe she should do a test?

She was going to have a child. Juliet Keller, wife, mother. It was time to be decisive. Time to grow up.

Grabbing her keys and purse, Juliet was almost out the door before she remembered the garbage bag. She went back for it and, after shoving it in the chute she let the lid close behind it with a satisfying thud.

34

Bonnie pulled off her boxing gloves and threw them into the tub, each one making a satisfying thwack sound as it landed on top of the rest of her workout gear. She took a long swig of water, then grabbed her towel and used it to wipe down the punching bag before heading outside into her little courtyard. Taking a seat, she wiped her face and neck and enjoyed the cold night air on her bare skin mixing with the feeling of complete exhaustion.

Sam Keller had gotten to her. She'd spent the better part of an hour of her evening punching his face in – well, metaphorically at least. It wasn't helping.

They hadn't needed a warrant for his phone and computer – Sam had surprised Bonnie by handing them over voluntarily, including his work computer. Nora and Zach had stayed back to work on them, but Bonnie wasn't hopeful. Sam wasn't stupid; he'd never hand over anything that could incriminate him that easily. He must have used another source to access the website tracking his wife's every move.

The forensic team searching the Bundanoon holiday house hadn't found anything. No hidden cameras, nothing to suggest

Juliet had been held captive or harmed there over the weekend. Again, not a surprise to Bonnie. The house belonged to Richard and Yvonne Keller, not Sam. She couldn't see him getting away with installing cameras at his parents' retreat. There'd be no reason to – he could keep an eye on her in person when they were on holiday.

The real disappointment of the day was the search of the location where Sam and Juliet had pulled over for twenty-two minutes on Friday night. Forensics had searched thoroughly within a one-hundred-metre radius of the site, and uniforms had completed a line search all the way to the farmhouses and as wide as they could reasonably get into the bush. They'd found nothing, and a few hours ago Sam Keller had walked out of the station freely with that smug look on his face.

Bonnie was starting to shiver. She packed her remaining workout gear away and hit the shower. The hot water stung her cold skin at first, but quickly became soothing as she washed away the sweat and grime of the day. She would have stayed under the spray for hours, if not for Edna's voice somewhere deep in her head reminding her to be water-wise.

They'd made an unlikely pair of housemates, Edna and Bonnie. The secretive old woman and the sixteen-year-old runaway. But it worked, and Bonnie missed her friend every day.

She didn't allow herself to think of those days often. Too much pain. But every now and then, it helped. Out of the shower, dried, and dressed in jeans and a t-shirt, Bonnie grabbed a beer and some leftover pasta and settled herself at the kitchen table.

For a long time after Edna died, Bonnie hadn't been able to settle in this house. Even though they'd lived there together for almost five years before that night, the house felt alien once Edna was gone. Bonnie went through stages – not being able to eat at the kitchen table because it reminded her of Edna, not being able to relax in the lounge room at the front of the house. She stayed in the smaller of the two bedrooms, leaving Edna's bedroom untouched for almost a decade. But a couple of years ago that all changed, thanks largely to Charlie Cooper.

"Life's too short," Cooper had said when the dust had settled over Homicide and he came to visit with his wife and kids one summer's day. "And this place is too small to only be using a quarter of it. Grow up, Hunter. Edna left you the house because she wanted you to have it. All of it." His four kids had chased each other up and down the hall, broken a vase, and managed to convince Bonnie that their father was absolutely right.

Cooper was the only person she'd really spoken to about Edna. She'd been twelve years old when she was removed from her mother's care and put into her first foster home. They were a pretty good family, in most regards, and she'd done her best to fit in. But the eldest son didn't like her, and their conflict eventually wore the parents down.

By the time Edna found her she'd been through six – no, seven – more foster homes. The last foster father had been particularly bad – a controlling arsehole who ruled his family with an ongoing campaign of violence, threats and intimidation. Bonnie had stayed with that family for five months, only lasting that long because she felt sorry for the biological kids and thought she could protect them. But when he started coming into her room at night, Bonnie figured it was time to leave.

Problem was, there was nowhere to go. She was sixteen, she'd been through eight different families in four years, and the system didn't want her anymore. She had no choice but to take her chances on the street.

Bonnie finished off the pasta and beer and washed up her dishes. She thought of Sam Keller, and how much he reminded her of that last foster father. She only put up with the abuse for five months; she couldn't imagine Juliet dealing with it for five years.

What if they'd been looking at this all wrong? What if Sam was telling the truth? He was an abusive husband, of that Bonnie had no doubt. But he wasn't acting like a typical guilty abuser. Bonnie had interviewed plenty of men who'd hurt their intimate partners. Too many. They all said the same things. 'It was her fault. She made me do it.' Sam wasn't saying those things.

True, Juliet wasn't in a hospital bed, all banged up. Or worse, at least as far as they knew. She was missing. It was easier for Sam to deny all involvement. But Bonnie had interviewed men whose wives were missing before. The ones who were responsible always had theories. 'Someone's taken her', 'she's run off with Joe from down the street', or 'she's gone back to England to stay with her mother'.

Sam wasn't trying to explain his wife's disappearance. No, he kept insisting they stop wasting their time focusing on him and get out there and find her.

Juliet had been in a bad marriage for five years. She'd already tried to leave once, that they knew of. She must have felt trapped. In Bonnie's years in the system, in bad places, when she felt trapped, what did she do? She ran.

What if Sam didn't kill Juliet? What if she got the better of him?

What if she ran?

35

February 2020

"What about this one?" Juliet pushed the black and red stroller around the stacks of baby clothes and nappy bags.

"Sure, babe, looks good," Sam replied.

He wasn't looking, though, he was way too engrossed in the vast array of baby monitors. He'd been trying to find the right one for almost an hour, and Juliet was getting tired. It had been Sam who'd insisted they come to this place. He'd read online it was the best store for baby stuff in the city, and his son would only have the best. Not that they'd found out the sex yet. They'd only known she was pregnant for three weeks. It was far too early for any of this. But Sam was so excited, and he kept calling the baby his son as if just wishing for it to be a boy would make it so.

"What's the difference between these two?" Sam asked the patient assistant one more time. Juliet had had no idea how many different types of baby monitors there were. They didn't just let you know if the baby was awake. They had video screens so you could see the baby sleep, they monitored its breathing, they even had an alert for if the baby rolled over. It all seemed very high-tech. Sam was in his element.

Juliet tuned out. She parked the stroller back in its place in the line and went to look at onesies. They were so cute, and so *tiny*. She felt her hand go to her belly, even though she was nowhere near showing yet. How was she going to cope with such a tiny little thing?

Sam had been amazing these last three weeks. He'd been so excited the night they did the pregnancy test together, and he'd been the most caring and attentive husband ever since. They'd gone to see the doctor, and Sam had asked questions Juliet hadn't even thought of yet. He was going to make an excellent father.

"Jules! Where are you?"

Juliet put the onesie she'd been holding back on the rack and followed the sound of her husband's voice.

"There you are." He held a box up for her to see. "We'll go with this one."

Juliet suppressed a smile. It was the first one he'd looked at, the most expensive. The one she knew an hour ago that he'd eventually choose. But Sam had to go through his process when making a purchase decision like this. Who was she to argue? In the three years she'd known him, Sam had never had any trouble with an appliance.

"Good choice, babe. Can we go now? My feet are getting tired."

"Of course." He led her to the most expensive in a line-up of rocking chairs. "Here, you sit in this while I go pay. See how it feels. We're going to need one of those, too. Is there anything else you wanted?"

Juliet shook her head. "Not today. We have plenty of time."

. . .

Back at the apartment Sam got busy with the baby monitor while Juliet fixed lunch. There was a rugby game on later that afternoon, and she wanted to make sure they had plenty of time to eat and she could clean up the kitchen before it started so Sam could watch the game in peace.

"Would you like a beer?" she asked as she placed the two bowls of chicken salad on the dining table.

"Ah, fuck! Fucking thing!" Sam threw the monitor and the screwdriver across the room. The monitor hit the wall and landed with a thud on the hardwood floor, its screen smashed. The screwdriver ended up under the television cabinet, as if it knew what was coming and had found its hiding place.

Juliet had no such luck.

"What's the matter?" she asked, wondering whether she should retrieve the broken monitor and throw it in the bin before it caused any more offence.

"Stupid fucking thing!" Sam repeated. "How is that supposed to be the best on the market when you have to put it together yourself? It's a monitor, for fuck's sake. Bloody ridiculous."

Juliet had to agree. What kind of baby monitor required such difficult assembly? She'd picked up the box and pulled out the folded instruction leaflet before she'd realised what she was doing.

"What? You think you can do better?"

"No, I just—" She didn't get a chance to finish the sentence. Sam tore the instructions from her hand and slammed her up against the kitchen bench. She felt the sharp edge of the marble dig into her back before he wrenched her forward and threw her to the floor.

"You. Think. You. Can. Do. Better?" Each word punctuated by a kick to the stomach.

"No! Sam!" Juliet tried to turn away from him, all her

instincts screaming at her to protect her child. "The baby! Sam, stop!"

He stopped. Juliet cradled her stomach, and Sam turned away and started kicking the couch instead. He managed to split the leather before he finally calmed down and stood over her, breathing heavily.

"You'd better not have harmed my son," he said, before grabbing his keys and walking out of the apartment.

When he finally came home hours later, reeking of alcohol and pissed off because his team had lost, he found Juliet sitting in a pool of blood on the bathroom floor.

"It's gone," she said. There were no tears. She couldn't cry for this baby. She couldn't even cry for herself.

Sam sighed, as if he'd just found out the dishwasher was broken, or a friend had cancelled a pub afternoon. As if this was just another of life's mundane disappointments. "It wasn't good enough," he said matter-of-factly. "Wasn't strong enough. Come on." He held out a hand and she took it, let him pull her to her feet. "Let's get you cleaned up. The next one will be better."

36

Bonnie had time for a quick morning swim before Anik
was due to pick her up for their second drive to Castle
Hill in three days. She hit the water at dawn, and was
out to Shelly Beach and back before some of the stragglers had
even pulled on their goggles.

"You're in a hurry this morning."

Bonnie turned to find the guy in the Speedos from two days
ago grinning behind her.

"Yeah, got a big day." She nodded in the direction of the surf.
"Bit calmer today. Sorry, I've forgotten your name."

"Steve," he said with a wave. "So, what's got you rushing off,
Bonnie? Big corporate job in the city?"

Bonnie laughed. "Do I look like a desk-job kind of girl?"

"Fair point. Not really." Speedo Steve looked suitably chas-
tened. "I guess today's not the day I buy you that coffee, then."

"Afraid not, Steve." She noticed he was still dry. "Besides,
you've got to get out there and earn it."

"Another fair point." He pulled his goggles onto his head.
"I'll catch you next time, non-corporate Bonnie."

Bonnie smiled and waved him off into the surf, then turned and jogged home.

Fifteen minutes later she and Anik were in the car on the way to Castle Hill to reinterview Juliet's parents, and Bonnie had offered up her new theory of Juliet on the run.

"She's already tried to leave Sam once," Bonnie explained as Anik drove.

"But didn't that shelter woman say she went back to him?"

"Did she go back voluntarily, or did he make her?"

"He would have had to find her first." The red light they'd been crawling up to for the last five minutes turned green, and Anik made the turn onto the freeway. Bonnie finally felt like they were getting somewhere.

"We know he's been tracking her for at least a year," she said, thinking out loud. "Maybe he was tracking her back then, too?"

"Maybe."

Bonnie picked up on the scepticism in his voice. "You don't think so?"

Anik shrugged. "I just find it hard to believe one person could have that level of control over another for so long. If that was the case, why didn't she just leave?"

It was the age-old question from someone who'd never had any first-hand experience with domestic abuse and coercive control. Bonnie got it, with the number of DV callouts she attended every week – every day, sometimes – even she still caught herself asking the same question from time to time. But it was never that easy.

"How much do you know about coercive control, Anik?"

"It's when the abuse isn't just physical, right? When they control what their wives or partners do, what they wear, who they see. Access to money. That sort of thing."

Bonnie was impressed. He knew more than most.

"Yes, that's all part of it. But at its worst it's about total control, total domination."

"Again, why don't they just leave?"

"Because it doesn't start out that way, Anik. When a man like this – like Sam Keller – meets their future partner, they go all in. Love-bombing, it's sometimes called. Remember what Dominic said about Sam and Juliet's relationship in the beginning?"

Anik nodded. "He said Sam doted on her. Bought her expensive presents, brought flowers and wine to dinner all the time."

"Exactly," said Bonnie. "The whole family loved him. Shit, Ellen is *still* sticking up for him, even when it looks for all the world like he's killed her only daughter. Juliet's friends all called him Prince Charming. It didn't take long for Juliet to fall for him."

"The love-bombing," said Anik.

"Right. There would have been no abuse then. We can't know exactly when it would have started, but back before they were married, and no doubt in the honeymoon stage, he would have been the perfect man."

"So, then what happened?"

"Isolation," said Bonnie, recalling what she'd learnt from her extra-curricular research on the subject. "Once these men have their victims where they want them – completely in love with them – they then start to make them dependant on them, as well. They start isolating them from their family, their friends. It's subtle at first – making excuses for not attending family gatherings, telling her he needs her to do something for him rather than go out with her friends. Then he might start bad-mouthing her friends and family, making her choose between him and them."

"Some prince," said Anik.

Bonnie recalled the last foster-family she lived with. Mother and father, two biological kids. She wasn't the only foster-kid they'd taken in, apparently, but she was the only one there at the time. In the five months she was with them, she never once came across any extended family or friends. They were never visited by anyone but her social worker, never went out, no family barbecues. She and the other kids were instructed to come straight home from school every day. Weekends they sometimes went to the beach, or a local park, but it was only ever the five of them. Bonnie hadn't noticed it at the time – it was only years later that she made the connection.

"She can't see what he's doing?" Anik asked.

Bonnie shook her head. "Like I said, it's subtle. All of it is. Once she's isolated from everyone else in her life, he can monopolise her perception. Start making her think any outburst from him is her fault. If she wasn't so forgetful, or messy, or clumsy, whatever, then he wouldn't get so mad. That sort of thing. Remember, she loves him now. He's swept her off her feet. She believes what he says, and she's got no-one else around her to tell her any different. He's made himself her world."

"Yeah, but once he starts hitting her…"

"By the time she realises what's going on, who he really is, it's too late. Then there are any number of reasons she won't leave. *Can't* leave."

"For example?"

"She may feel like she has nowhere to go. If he's successfully isolated her from her family and friends, her life with him is all she has. It may be harder to leave than to stay. Particularly if he's controlled her access to money as well.

"She may think she can fix him. He might promise to get help, get counselling or whatever, and she sees it as her duty to stick by him, help him fix the broken part of him that is abusive. It's not violence every day with these men, you know. They can be the loving, caring husband she thought she married."

"Or maybe she thinks if she leaves, he'll come after her," said Anik.

"Exactly," Bonnie agreed. "Which I think is where Juliet found herself after five years with Sam. I think that time he broke her arm and she left him, he found her. Whether it was through a tracker or maybe he used his contacts in the police, I don't know. But I think he found her and brought her home and threatened to do worse if she ever left him again."

Anik put his indicator on to change lanes. They were getting close to the Wilson's house. "But you think she's left him now?"

"I think it's possible," Bonnie replied. "Sam Keller is not your garden variety domestic abuser. He's been tracking Juliet's movements and monitoring her online activity for at least a year. He's got cameras in his home so he can watch her while he's not there. He's put her in the hospital once that we know of. And he got away with it. Juliet tried to leave him, and he brought her back. That was three years ago. Imagine what her life was like after that. Imagine what things were like for her through COVID, when he would have been working from home. The two of them stuck in that apartment together all day every day, isolated from the rest of the world. We know domestic abuse skyrocketed the last two years."

Anik pulled up outside the Wilson's house. He cut the engine and turned to face her. "So, in order to leave him for good, you think she staged her disappearance? Made it look like he killed her?"

Bonnie slowly nodded as she came to the realisation. "That's what I would do."

37

Bonnie didn't have time to elaborate on her theory. Ellen Wilson was working in the front garden and came over to the car as soon as Anik and Bonnie pulled up.

"Have you found her?" Ellen asked, pruning clippers poised in mid-air.

Bonnie shook her head as she exited the vehicle. "Not yet, Ellen. Do you mind if we come inside? We have some more questions for you both." Dominic's work ute was parked in the driveway, so she assumed he was home.

Ellen put the clippers in the front pocket of her apron. "Of course. Anything we can do to help." She gestured to the half-pruned hedge. "I've been trying to keep myself busy."

"That's not a bad idea," Bonnie agreed.

Inside the house, Dominic was in the kitchen making coffee. Bonnie and Anik both accepted the offer of a cup, and the four of them settled once again around the large dining table.

"What can you tell us?" Dominic asked, his large hands wrapped around a steaming mug.

Bonnie filled them in as much as she could on the investigation so far. She made them aware of Sam's controlling behaviour but didn't reveal the specifics of the cameras in the apartment or the tracking app on Juliet's phone. Dominic was a protective father who'd already tried to intimidate Sam once, and Bonnie didn't want to give him any reason to interfere in the investigation again.

"I don't understand," said Ellen. "You're telling us Sam has been abusing our daughter... controlling her, keeping her from us. But you haven't arrested him?"

Bonnie chose her words carefully. "He's very smart, Mrs Wilson. He's a criminal lawyer; he knows how to stay on the right side of the law."

"Or you have it all wrong," she countered.

"He broke her arm!" said Dominic, shaking his head at his wife. "I knew Juliet wasn't telling us the whole truth back then. Are you so taken in by that slimy bastard you can't see what he's doing to our daughter? What he's *done* to her?" Dominic stood but didn't move away from the table. "I can't..."

"Calm down, love," said Ellen. She subtly moved the coffee mug out of his reach.

"Mr Wilson, it would help us a lot if you could sit back down," said Bonnie.

"Why? He's killed her, hasn't he? That bastard has killed my little girl." Despite his protests, Dominic resumed his seat.

He was a broken man, and Bonnie wasn't sure what to do. Should she share her theory? Get their hopes up that Juliet might still be alive when there was nothing to base that on but a hunch? But what was the alternative? They had no evidence he'd killed her, either. As it currently stood, Juliet Keller was missing and they had no proof of anything other than that her husband was a controlling monster.

In the end it was Anik who spoke. "We have no evidence that Juliet is dead, Mr Wilson. It's important we hold onto that. And if we're going to find her, one way or the other, we need your help."

Bonnie thanked him with her eyes as she took a sip of coffee. It was black and instant, far from her usual preference of a soy latte, but it was surprisingly good.

"We need to ask you both some more questions about Juliet in general terms," she said. "In cases like these, when we're struggling to find answers, it helps for us to get as clear a picture of the missing person as possible. Remember, we've never met your daughter. Tell us about her, and her life, both before and after she met Sam."

Ellen started. "She's a strong girl, our Juliet. Always has been. Full of laughter, too."

"But she works hard," said Dominic. "Well, she did. Got a part-time job when she was still at school, as soon as she was old enough. We told her we'd help her out with a car, match whatever she put into it. She saved up for two years, and that Corolla was her pride and joy."

"What Corolla?" As far as Bonnie knew, the Kellers only had one car – the black BMW.

"She sold it once she moved to the city," said Ellen.

"He made her sell it, you mean," said Dominic.

"He didn't *make* her sell it," Ellen countered. "They only have one parking spot in the building," she explained to Bonnie and Anik. "Juliet's car had to stay here when she moved in with Sam after they were married. No-one was driving it; it didn't make any sense to keep it."

The Wilsons spent another fifteen minutes describing their daughter, her work ethic, her love for clothes and desire to design her own range of workout wear. They talked about how she loved her nephews and niece, and how little they saw of her lately.

Dominic reached for his coffee, took a sip. "We saw her less and less once she moved to the city. Then when all this lock-down stuff started, we didn't see her at all."

"We spoke on the phone during lockdown," said Ellen. "We all found that time quite difficult. Well, I guess the whole world did, didn't they? Anyway, Juliet had Sam working from home, and in an apartment – even one as nice as theirs – you can imagine that got a little tricky."

"There was tension in their household?" Anik asked.

"Of course, there—" said Dominic.

"No more than—" said Ellen at the same time.

Bonnie figured they wouldn't get anything useful about Sam and Juliet's lockdown experience out of conflicting stories from two people who weren't there, so she changed the direction of the conversation. She recalled Ellen had last seen Juliet in November, six months ago. She asked about Juliet's demeanour that day, and whether Ellen had noticed anything out of the ordinary.

"She was her usual, happy self," Ellen replied. "It was good to see her, of course. We had lunch at a nice cafe in the city."

"Did Juliet arrange the meeting or did you?" asked Anik.

"Oh, she did. She called a few days before, asked me to come into the city."

"Was that usual for your meetings?" asked Bonnie.

"Well, it was the first time I'd seen her in so long, we didn't really have a *usual* thing. But back when Juliet was first married, no, I'd have to say she came here most often. I went in there a few times, sometimes to the apartment and sometimes to a cafe. But mostly she came out here so she could see her father and brother, too. And the kids, of course."

Bonnie was starting to get a picture. "So once lockdown ended, Juliet called and asked you to come and meet her in the city for lunch."

"That's right. Oh, she also asked me to bring some papers of hers."

"What papers?" asked Bonnie.

"Her birth certificate and passport. We keep all the family documents like that together in a safe place, and we still had Juliet's because she hadn't needed them."

Bonnie felt her heart rate increase ever-so-slightly. "Why did she need them now?"

"She said she and Sam might head overseas once that was allowed again, and she still hadn't changed her name on her passport. She thought she'd better get it done, because she said with COVID and no-one having travelled for two years, every-one's passport will have expired. She said there'd be so many people trying to renew their passports now that there'd be a long wait. She was right, wasn't she? Val next-door told me her daughter waited four months."

Bonnie exchanged a look with Anik; she could tell he was thinking the same thing. Had they found a birth certificate and passport among Juliet's things?

Or were they part of her escape plan?

38

May 2020

Juliet was careful to remain outside the field of vision of Sam's computer screen as she placed his ten am coffee on the coaster beside him. He was wearing headphones, so she could only hear his side of the conversation he was having with Ollie and another guy over Zoom, but it was pretty heated. Not that that was anything unusual.

Sam had been working from home for six weeks now, and Juliet wasn't sure how much more of it she could take. He'd set up his office on one end of the dining table. She'd tried to encourage him to use the second bedroom, for privacy, but he wasn't having it. The whole country was locked down, no-one was going anywhere, he reasoned, so it wasn't like they were going to have visitors. He didn't want to be locked away in a back room with no view.

So that back room with no view – the room they were in the middle of setting up as a nursery – had become Juliet's lock-down retreat. Well, it was less of a retreat and more of a constant reminder of her failure to produce a son for Sam, but at least it was quiet.

Juliet closed the door and settled into the rocking chair they'd had delivered last week. She placed her herbal tea on the side table next to her Kindle and thought about diving back into the book she'd been reading. It was the latest crime novel from one of her favourite authors, one she'd been looking forward to for months, but now she was struggling to get into it. She'd been struggling to get into anything, to be honest. But she wasn't alone there.

They were saying the pandemic could last months, or years, even. The best scientific minds in the world were working on a vaccine, but by all reports it would be a long time before things went back to normal. Before Juliet got her living room – and her life – back.

She loved Sam. She had to keep reminding herself of that. It wasn't his fault he was stuck at home all day, having meetings with his staff and clients over Zoom. The client meetings were especially tricky, with him having to maintain client confidentiality. She wasn't allowed in the room when Sam was meeting with a client, and as their living room, dining room, and kitchen were all one big open-plan space, it meant she was confined to either their bedroom or the nursery.

At first, she'd chosen their bedroom because it had the ensuite, so she could use the bathroom without tiptoeing down the hall, but there was nowhere to sit in there other than on the bed. It felt lazy and wrong to be lying on the bed for long periods of the day, so she'd started coming into the nursery instead.

The iPad Sam had bought three months ago – after she'd lost the first baby – rang to indicate an incoming call. Juliet lunged for it and silenced the ringer. Sam hated when his meetings were interrupted.

It was her mother, trying to FaceTime. Juliet thought about

answering but caught a glimpse of herself in the wardrobe mirror. She rejected the call, then sent her mother a quick text to say Sam was on a work call and she'd catch her later. It wasn't a complete lie.

Juliet turned back to her reflection in the mirror and raised a hand to her face. She was getting good at hiding the bruising, but this round was accompanied by a cut just below her cheekbone; impossible to cover with makeup. It probably should have been stitched, but Sam had said they couldn't go to the hospital because of COVID. He didn't want either of them getting sick, not when they were trying to get pregnant. So, he'd gone out to the chemist and returned with some of those butterfly strips, and they'd made do.

The iPad was originally purchased so Juliet could shop online for all the baby stuff to fill the nursery now that most of the big stores were closed. But she was starting to get the impression it was really supposed to be a research tool. Sam had his heart set on becoming a dad. Every night, once he closed his laptop and opened his first beer, he asked how her day had been, and every night the conversation came back around to what she was doing or could do – or not do – to get pregnant.

The tips and tricks from countless websites were like an endless playlist in her head. Know your ovulation cycle. Have sex regularly. Stay in bed for fifteen minutes after sex. Exercise, but not too much. Don't drink alcohol. Reduce stress. Avoid caffeine. Avoid lubricants. Eat food high in antioxidants. Take multivitamins. Juliet didn't believe most of it, but her continued research helped convince Sam they were on the same page.

Were they on the same page? Juliet had loved being pregnant, she knew that much. It may have only lasted a couple of weeks, but she'd felt like she had a purpose. That she wasn't just there to look after Sam, to keep the house clean and the cupboards stocked and be his glamorous wife whenever that was called for.

She'd felt like she wasn't alone.

But was that the right reason to bring a child into the world? Into this world, now, in the middle of a pandemic? Maybe she should try talking to Sam again. It wouldn't be the worst thing to put off having a baby for another year or two. She was still only twenty-three. They had plenty of time.

Juliet finished her herbal tea and examined her face in the mirror again. Last night, when Sam had asked about her day, she'd mentioned an article claiming that couples who were trying to get pregnant had more chance when both parties cut down on alcohol. It was her own fault, really. He'd had a tough day and was already on his second beer. You have to pick your moments for that sort of conversation. When was she going to learn?

The yoga mat spread out on the floor mocked Juliet. She poked her tongue out at it and picked up the Kindle. She made it through half a page before Sam bellowed a request for food from the living room.

39

Back at Headquarters, Bonnie grabbed a sandwich and a juice from the cafe in the foyer before heading up to Homicide where the team had assembled in the incident room. Mars and Kate were discussing something over their lunch at one end of the table; Nora and Zach were busy on their laptops. Bonnie took a seat and was halfway through her sandwich when Anik joined them with the kebab he'd bought from up the street.

"Ah, that's the business," he said as he unwrapped the meat-laden feast. "Best kebabs in the country."

"That's a big call," said Mars.

"I speak only the truth. You want a bite?" Anik offered.

Mars screwed up his nose. "No, thank you. That looks disgusting."

Anik glanced at the salad Mars was working his way through and raised one eyebrow. He opened his mouth to say something but wrapped it around his lunch instead when Cooper walked into the room.

"What have we got?" Cooper asked, taking a seat at the head of the table.

"Bonnie thinks Juliet's alive," Anik said through a mouthful of kebab.

"I think it's a possibility we need to look into," Bonnie clarified. She was excited about the theory, but at this stage that's all it was. She didn't want the investigation to completely change focus away from Sam and his abusive behaviour.

"Explain," said Cooper.

"Everything we've found so far on the Keller's marriage points toward an ongoing campaign of domestic violence and coercive control." Bonnie counted off on her fingers. "Love-bombing at the start of their relationship; isolation from her family and friends by moving to the city and getting rid of her car. Suspicion by Juliet's father that Sam was physically violent. Then the broken arm, the involvement of police and a women's shelter, culminating in Juliet's attempt to leave at that point. And now we've found cameras in the apartment, and the tracking app on her phone. I don't think any of us have much doubt about the kind of relationship Juliet and Sam Keller have."

She waited for argument; none came. "So, I got to thinking – what if Juliet decided she wanted out, and the only way she felt she could safely do that was to disappear?"

"You think she staged the whole thing down in Bundanoon?" asked Mars. "Made it look like someone took her?"

"Or like Sam killed her," said Anik.

Although she'd admitted to Anik it was what she'd likely have done herself, Bonnie wasn't ready to accuse Juliet of setting her husband up for murder just yet. "Let's just look at the staged disappearance as a possibility for now," she said.

"Do you have any tangible evidence to base this theory on?" asked Cooper.

"Maybe," Bonnie replied. "We spoke to the Wilsons this morning." She filled them in on Ellen's story of Juliet wanting her passport and birth certificate so she could change the name on her passport to her married name.

"I'm on it," said Nora, fingers already tapping away on the keyboard.

"Okay," said Cooper. "Zach – can you get the crime scene photos up on the screen? Bonnie, talk us through how it could have happened."

Bonnie waited a moment until Zach was ready, then asked him to scroll to the photo with the best overall view of the Kellers' car parked across the road from the Bundanoon IGA.

"We have no witnesses who saw this car arrive, no-one able to identify who drove it here and who got out of it. That made us suspicious that it could have been Sam who left the car here, threw the keys and Juliet's phone into the grass and walked away, wanting to make it look like Juliet had been taken. But what if it wasn't Sam who did that, but Juliet herself?"

"Where would she have gone?" asked Kate.

Bonnie had given that aspect some thought but hadn't come up with a good theory yet. "She's young, fit. She could have walked a fair distance."

"Not along the roads, not without being seen, at least," said Mars. "Bundanoon is a small town. To get out of it and to somewhere bigger, like Moss Vale or Bowral, she'd have had to walk along the country roads. A woman walking alone at night out there would have been seen by multiple cars, and with all the attention this case has had, someone would have come forward."

He was right. *Damn.*

"What if she had help?" Kate suggested. "A friend who was in on the plan, waiting somewhere close by to pick her up?"

"That's a possibility," Bonnie agreed.

"We've talked to her friends," said Anik. "They've barely seen her recently."

"We've talked to the friends we know about," said Bonnie.

"The friends Sam and her family have told us about. What if there was someone new in her life?"

"Like a lover, you mean?" asked Anik.

"Or just a friend." Bonnie thought back to her days in foster care, to the connections she made that she never told her foster families about. And earlier, when she'd latched onto anyone who could make the reality of her homelife disappear even for an hour or two. "Haven't you ever made a friend you wanted to keep to yourself?"

Anik made a face like he'd just eaten a sour lolly. "Not really."

"*I* know what you mean," said Nora without looking up from her screen.

Bonnie continued, encouraged by the idea. "Someone she met at a cafe, or gym. Or just out shopping. Someone she didn't have to share with Sam, so she didn't have to worry about him driving them away. Or maybe she had every intention of introducing them to Sam at first but once she decided to run she guarded the friendship so she could use their help to escape."

Cooper didn't seem convinced. "So this person was in on the plan, picked her up in Bundanoon, whisked her away, and is hiding her now?"

"It's just one possibility," said Bonnie. "The point is, we may have been wrong. She *could* have got away." She wasn't sure whether she was trying to convince the team, or herself.

Cooper's phone pinged, and he picked it up and started swiping and scrolling.

"I don't know," said Mars. "My money's still on murder. How do you explain the blood in the car? Sam stopping for twenty-two minutes out in the middle of nowhere?"

"The blood in the car was minimal," Bonnie replied. "It could easily be explained by a cut or scratch. And twenty-two minutes isn't long enough to hide a body. Not out there, in the dark, and well enough so that a forensics team found no trace."

"No, but it's enough time to kill someone," said Mars. "He had a full twenty-four hours to hide the body before his friends arrived."

"Nothing was found at the holiday house, either," said Zach.

"He could have left the body in the car," Mars countered.

"In the front seat?" asked Anik. "That's risky."

"Boot?"

They all looked to Zach.

"No blood found in the boot. A few of Juliet's hairs, but it's their car. You'd expect that."

"So, nothing conclusive either way," said Mars. "Look, I know none of us want it to be the case, but to me this is pretty clear. There doesn't need to be much blood for someone to die. And I don't need to quote the stats on domestic homicide. The simple facts are that Juliet Keller is missing, and Sam Keller is a slimy toad of a man who has demonstrated a propensity for violence."

"Exactly the kind of man someone would go to great lengths to escape," said Kate.

"So, you agree with me?" Bonnie asked.

"I agree it's a possibility," Kate replied. "Mars and I have been looking into the Kellers' financials. Shortly after they got married Juliet closed her personal bank account. They have one joint account, but there's not much in it and very few trans-actions."

Bonnie sighed. She'd been afraid of this. "So, Juliet had no money of her own? No credit card?"

Kate shook her head. "Sam has a credit card that was used extensively for household items during each of the lockdowns, but outside of those times the activity suggests it was only him using it. He withdraws large amounts of cash on a regular basis, although the amounts have reduced over the last six months. He must have given her cash to buy groceries, other household stuff. It looks like she was completely reliant on him financially."

"Another aspect of coercive control," said Mars. "He snapped and killed her. Must have."

"Not so fast," said Nora, raising her eyes over the top of her screen. "There's been no application made to change the name on Juliet's passport."

"You sure?" Bonnie asked. Passport control was federal, it usually took weeks to get any response from those guys.

"Called in a favour," Nora explained. "Juliet's passport is still valid for three more years, and still under the name Juliet Wilson. No application anywhere in the system for any changes."

"Maybe she didn't get around to it yet," said Mars.

Cooper looked up from his phone, suddenly interested. "Did we find the passport and birth certificate during the apartment search?"

"No," said Zach.

"Should we talk to Sam again, see if he knows where they are?" Anik asked.

"No," Bonnie and Cooper chorused. "Juliet got them from her mother six months ago," Bonnie went on. "If she was planning to run back then, she would have kept them hidden from Sam."

"And if she has run," Cooper added, "we don't need to alert him to the fact."

"Exactly." Bonnie sat straighter in her seat, and she wasn't the only one. There was a buzz in the room that hadn't been there a minute ago. Even Mars looked open to the possibility Juliet was still alive.

"So, what now?" asked Kate.

Bonnie had an idea. "Zach, the tracking app on Juliet's phone. Can we access the data?"

"Sure. I'll send it to you." He got straight to work.

"What are you thinking?" Cooper asked.

Bonnie smiled. "That app has been tracking all Juliet's movements, her communications, and all the websites she accessed. If she's been planning her escape for six months, maybe there's a clue somewhere in there."

40

October 2021

Juliet took a deep breath of the fresh, morning air before fixing her mask back onto her face. Mask mandates were no longer in force in Sydney, and she'd been vaccinated, but she wasn't taking any chances. She couldn't imagine trying to look after Sam and run the household while sick; it was hard enough as it was. Besides, she'd become used to hiding behind the mask.

It was all bullshit, according to Sam. It wasn't that he didn't *believe* in COVID-19, Juliet told herself. He wasn't stupid, not one of those crazy anti-vaxxers that were protesting against lockdowns and masks. Sam just didn't like being told what to do. Juliet, on the other hand, was perfectly fine with being told what to do. She was just glad they could both finally get out of the house.

Sam had gone to work at the city office today for the first time in months. He'd hated working from home, almost as much as Juliet had hated having him there all the time. *No*; she checked herself as she walked down Pitt Street. Hate was a strong word. She didn't *hate* having Sam at home all the time. She didn't *hate* her husband. She just needed some space. That was understandable, wasn't it? That was normal, after four years of marriage?

Juliet turned into King Street and passed a few of the boutiques where Sam liked her to shop. They were open, but she couldn't bring herself to go in yet.

Four years of marriage. At times if felt like only a minute, at others, a lifetime. She still hadn't got used to the crazy amounts of money Sam liked her to spend on clothes. She pulled her handbag in tighter, hyper-aware of the large amount of cash he'd handed over this morning.

"It's Freedom Day, baby!" he'd declared, standing in the middle of the bedroom in his underwear and waving the cash around like he was the Wolf of Wall Street. "Time for you to get out there and spend my money!"

Juliet had been in her underwear, too, staring into the wardrobe trying to decide what to wear. She wasn't sure that she'd done it consciously, but she'd realised a couple of months ago that her clothes were all arranged in groups according to how much of her body they covered. Today, even though the forecast said it was going to be hot, she needed something with at least three-quarter length sleeves.

"This one," Sam had said, reaching over her shoulder and pulling a blue dress from the rack. He took her face in his hand and kissed her gently on the lips before his hand moved down and lightly traced the fresh bruising on her arm. He stared into her eyes. It was the morning-after moment, his way of saying sorry.

It was over in seconds.

Sam threw the cash onto the bed. "Get yourself some new summer dresses today," he said as he got busy picking out his own outfit. "And some sexy underwear too. It's time you started looking nice for me again. I'll have you pregnant before the end of the year!"

Juliet had hoped he'd moved on from giving her cash. One of the few benefits of lockdown had been using his credit card to shop online. She'd dropped some subtle hints, mostly about how much safer it felt to use cards instead of cash, but they'd obviously fallen on deaf ears. So here she was again, walking through the city with thousands of dollars in cash secreted in her purse.

Her stomach grumbling in protest at having skipped breakfast, Juliet paused outside a café she didn't recognise. It looked cosy. There were shelves of books lining the walls, and tables and chairs that didn't match each other at all. Sam would hate this place, the complete lack of symmetry and order. Juliet smiled and pushed the door open to enter.

"Good morning," said the woman busy steaming milk at the coffee machine behind the counter. "Takeaway, or do you want a table?"

Juliet looked around at the inviting tables and shelves full of books. She was sick of takeaway coffee in paper cups. "I'll take a table, thanks."

"Perfect." The woman's smile helped Juliet to relax. "Sit anywhere you like, I'll bring a menu as soon as I'm done here."

Juliet chose a table in the back of the store near the biography section. She loved reading fiction; relished the escape it provided from real life, especially during the last year and a half. But lately she'd been seeing ads on her iPad for biographies – what was the one that had caught her eye yesterday? It was about a Holocaust survivor, and the reviews had been excellent. She checked the shelves to see if she could spot it.

"There you go."

Juliet turned to see the smiling waitress had placed a menu on her table. "Looking for anything in particular?"

"Actually, yes." Juliet described the book, and the waitress nodded knowingly.

"The Happiest Man on Earth," she said, pulling the book from the shelf and placing it on the table next to the menu. "It's brilliant."

"You've read it?"

"Oh yes. This is my favourite section, the biographies. Some of the stories... I love reading about what regular people are capable of. It's a good thing I get a staff discount – I spend half my pay in this section sometimes!" She pointed to the menu. "Give me a wave when you've decided."

Juliet thanked her and picked up the menu. The toasted sandwiches sounded delicious, but Juliet was conscious of the extra kilo she'd acquired during the latest lockdown. She should probably go for a salad.

Still undecided, she picked up the book the waitress had found for her. The author, Eddie Jaku, was pictured smiling on the front cover. She recalled one of the reviewers describing how Eddie's optimism and hope had completely changed the way she looked at life. Juliet stared at the old man's smile and thought, fuck it. *He'd* order a toastie.

She ordered coffee and the most decadent-sounding toasted sandwich on the menu, and told the waitress she'd be buying the book as well. Then she settled in to read how Eddie Jaku became the self-professed happiest man on Earth.

A few hours, two coffees, and three designer-dress stores later, Juliet found herself in East West Vintage. She'd managed to pick up enough new clothing to keep Sam happy, including the sexy underwear he'd demanded this morning, but it had been so long since she'd been to her favourite second-hand store and she didn't want to go home without checking it out. She wasn't even sure they'd still be around, so many retail outlets having fallen victim to the pandemic, but both Samira and East West Vintage were apparently going strong.

"Juliet! How the bloody hell are you?" Samira hadn't changed a bit.

"I'm well," Juliet replied, focusing all her energy on not touching the bruises on her arm. They were covered by the sleeve of her dress, but still, Samira was perceptive; her noticing would mean never being able to return to East West Vintage again and Juliet couldn't stomach that thought. Not today, not now she finally had her freedom back. Such as it was.

"Wow, is that the dress I sold you back... when was it?"

"January last year, and yes, it is," Juliet replied, pleased that Samira had noticed. She considered this dress one of her finest accomplishments – a few alterations and the sly addition of a designer price tag before he got home and Sam had never suspected it was a second-hand piece.

"You're amazing," said Samira as she circled Juliet, admiring her handiwork. "You know, you could do this professionally. Make some extra cash. I've got an online store—"

Juliet held up a hand to stop Samira before she got carried away. "Not going to happen, my friend."

Samira laughed. "I don't blame you. If I had a husband like yours, I'd spend all my time keeping myself looking fabulous, too!"

Juliet laughed with her, but she was thankful when another customer entered the store and demanded Samira's attention. *If only you knew.*

There was nothing in East West Vintage that caught her eye today, and time was getting on. Juliet waved goodbye to Samira and exited the store. As she headed for home, Eddie Jaku's words played over and over in her mind. 'Life can be beautiful if you make it beautiful,' and 'happiness is something we can choose.'

Eddie's life seemed so far removed from her own. He'd lived through hell and come out brave and smiling. She lived a life of luxury and privilege but was becoming more and more fearful and sad every day.

Sunlight streamed onto the shop windows as she walked by, and Juliet caught sight of her reflection in one of them. She stopped and stared, the harshness of the black mask covering her face contrasting with the bright blue dress. Eddie's words in her head were replaced with Samira's. 'You could do this professionally. Make some extra cash.'

Samira was right. If she could alter clothes to make something new and unique for herself, there was no reason she couldn't do it for others. Not that she needed extra cash right now. She had enough trouble spending what Sam thrust upon her every month.

But maybe one day. Maybe one day she could be brave and happy, too.

Life can be beautiful if you make it beautiful.

41

"Right about here," said Anik, checking his phone as he and Bonnie stood on King Street, the bitter wind tearing a path across the city. "The tracking app has Juliet spending at least an hour here every Friday morning."

Bonnie pulled her coat tighter and looked around. Allowing for the accuracy level of the app, the only place within range that was appropriate for someone to spend at least an hour every week was a bookstore with a cafe inside.

"That's got to be the place," she said, and headed for the door.

It was blissfully warm inside the cafe, and Bonnie made sure Anik closed the door behind him so it would stay that way. It was Thursday morning, just before ten am, and there were a few tables taken but it looked like the morning rush was over.

"Hi," said the woman behind the counter. "Table for two?"

Bonnie shook her head, held up her badge. "We're making enquiries about a woman who possibly frequented your cafe." She held out Juliet's photo.

The woman's smile disappeared. "Juliet. Yes, she came here every Friday."

"You knew her by name?" Bonnie asked.

The woman shook her head. "No, not at the time, but I've seen the news. Do you have any idea what's happened to her? Oh, sorry, I guess I can't ask that. I recognised her as soon as I saw it. Her photo on the news, I mean. She was always so lovely. I can't believe she's missing. And what they're saying about her husband. It's just awful. He seemed so nice. Do you really think – sorry, I'm babbling."

"It's okay. What's your name?"

"Rebecca. Bec, but you probably want my full name. Rebecca Amos."

Bonnie conjured up her most reassuring smile. "Thanks, Bec. Why don't we take that table after all. Have you got a minute to join us?"

Bec looked around, caught the eye of another staff member. "Thanh can handle things without me for a little while." She led them to a table in the back near the biography section.

"What can you tell us about Juliet?" Bonnie asked when they were settled.

"This is her table," Bec replied. "Well, most of the time. She came in every Friday, like I said. If this table was free, she'd sit here. She'd have a coffee, sometimes two, occasionally something sweet but not often."

"Was she always alone?" Bonnie asked.

"Every time I saw her, she was. But I have one Friday a month off, so I can't be certain of those days."

"What about other customers," said Anik. "Did anyone else talk to her while she was here? Any other regulars she might have struck up a friendship with?"

"I don't think so," said Bec. "She usually just got to work on her laptop as soon as she'd ordered. That was why she liked this table." Bec pointed to a power point on a nearby wall.

Bonnie straightened a fraction. "Laptop?" There was no

laptop found at the apartment, nor at the holiday house. Sam said Juliet didn't have a computer, only an iPad and her phone. Maybe that's what Bec meant. "Are you sure it was a laptop, not an iPad?"

"No, it was definitely a laptop. I noticed because it was pretty chunky, not like some of the fancy looking ones we see. We get a lot of people working over a coffee in here. We have free Wi-Fi, although most people hotspot to their phones these days. Sorry, babbling again. I remember Juliet because she was here every Friday like clockwork, and she always left a generous tip."

"Okay," said Bonnie. "One more thing. You said Juliet's husband seemed nice. Did you meet him? Did he come in here with her?"

Bec shook her head. "I don't think he was ever here with her. But he came in yesterday, asking the same questions. Do you really think he—"

"What did you tell him?" Bonnie interrupted.

"Same as I've told you. He seemed pretty distraught, was saying you guys weren't doing everything you could to find her. I didn't believe that, of course—"

"Did you tell him about the laptop?"

"Yeah. Should I not have?"

Bonnie and Anik exchanged glances. Bonnie's first instinct was to race out the door and find Sam, but that wasn't going to help Juliet. She needed to think.

"It's okay," she told Bec. "You know, maybe we will have a couple of coffees and sit for a while."

They took Bec's details and then gave her their coffee orders. When they were alone at the table Bonnie let some of her tension out.

"Damn it, we should have realised Sam had access to the same information we did from Juliet's phone."

"At least this proves he's accessed it, right?" asked Anik.

"It doesn't prove it, no. He could easily argue he knew Juliet used to come here. Where she has coffee every Friday morning would not necessarily be a secret she'd keep from her husband. We'd have no chance of proving otherwise."

"But her using a laptop here could be."

"Exactly," Bonnie agreed. "Given that we haven't found one among her possessions, and Sam said she didn't have one, either she kept it from him or he's lying and hiding it himself."

"But then would he have been in here asking questions if that were the case?"

"Probably not." Bonnie smiled. "We're on the right track, Anik."

Bec brought their coffees, and a donut for Anik. Red jam squirted out the side when he bit into it.

"Shit," he said, using a napkin to unsuccessfully wipe the red mess from the cuff of his shirt sleeve.

Bonnie left him to it and sipped her coffee. She was now more convinced than ever that Juliet had staged her disappearance to get away from her abusive husband. Good for her. But where did that leave them?

Anik threw the red-soaked napkin onto the plate and finished the rest of the donut more carefully.

"Worth it?" Bonnie asked.

"You bet," he replied, grinning. "I love donuts. So, Juliet was coming here for six months, right?"

"Yes."

"What I don't get is if Sam's been tracking her all this time, he knew she was coming here. Why didn't he follow her and see for himself she had a laptop behind his back?"

It was a good question. "Maybe he didn't need to," Bonnie replied. "The tracking was about possessiveness and control. He had the tracker so he didn't *have* to follow her. He could sit back in his office or watch his phone, or however he accessed the app, safely knowing where his little woman was at all times." Bonnie felt her anxiety levels rise as she went on. "As far as he was concerned, she was out and about doing household-maintaining things, and keeping herself nice for him while he was being the big protector and breadwinner at work. It's that whole male superiority thing."

"I don't think I'll ever understand men like that."

"The only people who understand men like that are other men like that," said Bonnie. "Unfortunately, there are still way too many of them out there. Education programs for young men are doing something, and the stigma of family violence and abuse is changing, but not fast enough. This is a problem that'll take generations to stamp out."

Anik pulled the sleeve of his jumper down over his shirt to cover the stain. "Sounds like you've had your share of experience with men like Sam."

"Too many times," Bonnie replied, with a look that signalled it wasn't a conversation she was prepared to get into now.

Anik took the hint, thankfully, and they drank the rest of their coffees in silence.

Bonnie tried to take heart in the positives. It was looking increasingly likely that Juliet Keller was still alive, and for every Sam Keller in the world, there were men like Anik and Charlie Cooper. Good, decent men.

It wasn't nearly enough, but it was something.

42

"So where to now?" Anik asked as they prepared to leave the cafe.

"Show me the map again," said Bonnie.

As well as sending them the raw data from the tracking app on Juliet's phone, Zach had prepared a digital map of the locations Juliet had frequented. They worked out that in addition to grocery shopping multiple times a week at the Coles supermarket in World Square, she'd attended a yoga class three times a week, visited her hairdresser monthly, and a nail salon fortnightly. Mars and Kate were currently out visiting those last three establishments but hadn't reported anything of interest so far.

Bonnie and Anik were tasked with the supermarket, as well as following Juliet's Friday routine, the most interesting part of which they'd thought was the bookstore cafe. But now that they knew she arrived here with a laptop, Bonnie was curious as to where the laptop came from. Bec said it had been 'chunky', so if she was hiding it from Sam, as they suspected, it was unlikely Juliet would have risked keeping it at the apartment.

Anik unfolded the paper version of the map he'd printed

before leaving Headquarters last night. They each had Zach's digital one on their phones, but it was easier to get an overall view this way and Bonnie found herself thankful once again that Anik wasn't a typical Millennial when it came to technology.

"What are you thinking?" he asked, rocking back and forth in his chair like an excited child.

"I want to know where she kept that laptop," said Bonnie, studying the map. "Where did she go as soon as she left the apartment on Friday mornings?"

"Their apartment is here, on Park Street," Anik explained as he pointed. "She departed there on Fridays at around nine am, presumably after Sam left for work. She would walk two blocks south to World Square, where she was mostly on the move for around thirty minutes or so, shopping, we assumed. Then she'd head four blocks north to the cafe here on King Street."

"Did she go back to World Square before returning home?"

Anik nodded. "Sometimes she'd go straight there down Pitt Street, other times she'd go via George Street and the Queen Victoria Building."

"*That's* her shopping," Bonnie surmised. "Judging by her wardrobe she visited a lot of boutique-type places like the ones in the QVB."

"Yeah, that seems likely. But she always started and ended up in World Square. The Coles there is the closest grocery store to her apartment. Sam told us Juliet shopped there multiple times a week, as she liked to buy fresh ingredients to cook, but she did a bigger grocery shop for bulk items on Fridays. It would make sense to do that last, before heading home."

"She wouldn't have carried bulk groceries home on foot, though."

"No, I guess not. She could have had it delivered?"

"But then why go there at all? Why not do it all online?" Bonnie could think of a number of answers to her own question.

To get out of the apartment, for one thing. Juliet probably enjoyed her time out and about, and wanted it to last as long as possible. Plus, Bonnie was building a picture of Juliet as a very thorough and organised person. She'd have to be, to live with Sam. So, she wouldn't want to leave her grocery shopping to the whims of online ordering, where other people chose her products and items could be substituted without her approval. No, she'd want to do that herself.

"He gave her cash," said Anik. "No card. Hard to spend cash online."

"Good point," said Bonnie. "But I think there's another reason. We need to go to World Square."

Thanking Bec on their way out, the two detectives braced themselves for the cold, four-block walk. At least it wasn't raining.

"You think she got a cab sometimes?" Anik asked as they made their way through the Pitt Street Mall.

"Probably, on days like this."

"Should we try and find out? Maybe talk to the cab drivers?"

Bonnie gave it a moment's thought. "I don't think so. I doubt Juliet would have said anything on a short cab ride that could help us. And we already know her movements."

"Fair enough."

As they walked, Bonnie considered Juliet's habits. She shopped at World Square multiple times a week, bringing home fresh groceries every few days to make their meals. Then on Fridays, she had her mornings in the cafe but not before walking two blocks in the wrong direction to World Square. For what? It couldn't have been for groceries, as she went back there again after the cafe for that. It could have been for the other shops, but again, why go both before *and* after the cafe?

Bonnie could only think of one explanation, and it filled her with hope. "There must be a storage facility at World Square," she said to Anik when they got to a cross walk with a red light.

"Yeah." Anik was already looking it up on his phone. "That must be where she kept the laptop. Yep, here it is. Mottley Storage, World Square."

"Show me," said Bonnie, holding out a hand for his phone as the cross walk light turned green. Anik handed it over, and Bonnie scrolled as she walked. Mottley Storage had all sizes of storage options, down to cubic metre lockers that could be rented by the day, week, or month. She gave the phone back to Anik. "That's where we start."

Mottley Storage was located in the basement of the World Square shopping complex in the heart of the CBD. After waiting ten minutes for him to return from a break, Bonnie and Anik were able to interview the owner and manager, Pete Mottley.

"There are some pretty strict privacy laws I'm obliged to follow, Detective," said Pete when Bonnie showed him Juliet's picture. He was a big guy in food-stained overalls who was well-suited to his name, at least in looks. Bonnie sensed he wanted to help. "You'd need a warrant to get any information or search any storage unit that young lass may or may not have rented from me."

"We're working on getting one," Bonnie confirmed, intending to do just that as soon as they left. "But is there anything you can tell us that might help in the meantime?"

"I can tell you her husband was here yesterday asking the same questions," Pete replied. "He didn't like it much when I gave him the same response. Got quite upset, I'd go so far as to say. Nothing at all like the distraught husband I saw being interviewed on the television. Hard to believe it was the same guy."

"But you didn't tell him anything?" asked Anik.

Pete shook his head. "Like I said, privacy laws. Same reason I can't tell you anything. But...seeing as you're the police and all, I should probably mention the special we have going at the moment for emergency workers."

Bonnie was about to politely decline, but something about Pete's half-smile and tilt of the head told her to play along.

"Go on."

Pete guided them to a wall of lockers as he spoke, quoting prices Bonnie had no interest in. "Most people rent by the month," he went on, fishing a master key out of his pocket. "That's what these lockers here are good for. They have a combination lock, so no need to carry a key." Pete opened one of the smallest lockers. "This one here, for example, came available last Friday." His single raised eyebrow spoke volumes.

"Is that so," said Bonnie, playing along.

"Yep. And all we need is a name, phone number, and one month in advance."

"You take cash?" asked Anik.

"Of course."

Bonnie pushed her luck. "This particular locker, you say it came available on Friday. I assume that's because someone else was finished with it?"

"I believe that's correct, yes."

"And this person, they were satisfied with their rental experience, would you say? I mean, if I'm considering using your facility, and in particular this locker here, it'd be helpful to know that others before me had had a positive experience."

"Well, we don't really have a feedback form as such, Detective, but perhaps the fact that this person rented the locker for nearly six months might help?"

Bonnie smiled. "It does indeed." She had a good look inside the locker. It was certainly big enough to hold a laptop and more, but it was completely empty now. "Thank you, Pete, you've been most helpful. Can I ask a favour?"

"You can always ask, Detective."

"Maybe hold this locker for me? Just for a day or so."

"I'll do my best." Pete closed the locker and secured it with his key before leading them back to the exit.

"Thanks again," said Bonnie as she and Anik walked out. "We'll be in touch as soon as we have that warrant."

"Fair enough. You know, sometimes people don't want to be found."

Bonnie turned back to face him. "Sometimes they don't have a choice."

Pete nodded. "Then you'd better find her before he does."

43

February 2022

Juliet enjoyed the cool breeze as she rode the escalator down to Mottley Storage. She'd taken her time to stroll through the shops this morning until she'd been certain Sam wasn't following her. Not that he followed her too often – just enough so she knew she could never let her guard down.

He had a tracking app on her phone. She didn't know how long it had been there, but she was glad she'd figured it out before she rented the storage locker. She'd been going to get one at a place out on Kent Street because it was cheaper than Mottley's, but it was too exposed. Sam would have realised what she was up to instantly.

She hadn't been completely sure he wouldn't find out about this one, but with it being in the basement of a building full of shops, she figured as long as he wasn't following her it would look on the tracking app like she was just in the shopping centre. So far that theory seemed to hold.

The cool breeze disappeared as soon as Juliet reached the

bottom of the escalator, replaced by the warm air that reminded her of Town Hall train station. She smiled as she remembered catching the train home to Castle Hill after a night out in the city with the girls. Sam wouldn't even think about letting her get on a train now. 'Too many lowlifes on trains,' he'd say.

With one last glance over her shoulder to see that she was alone, Juliet headed for her locker. She punched in the code and opened it before reaching into her handbag for the cash she'd managed to save, which she then added to one of the ziplock bags already in the locker. If anyone was watching this, or found her locker and opened it, they'd think she was dealing drugs. She was up to four ziplock bags full of cash now, as well as the one that held her passport and birth certificate. It wasn't enough yet, but it was a good start.

Juliet had first had the idea to start building an escape plan late last year. Samira had planted the seed. *You could do this professionally. Make some extra cash.* She'd been talking about the blue dress Juliet had altered. It was the first time in a long time Juliet had thought of herself as talented, with something to offer that other people might actually pay money for. By the time she'd gotten home that day, she'd created a thriving business in her mind – a little corner shop where people could bring their clothes for alterations, where she could sell clothes she'd upcycled, and where perhaps she could work on some of her own designs, too.

She'd made the mistake of mentioning the idea to Sam. After the big splash of cash on his so-called Freedom Day, the amount he'd been giving her to spend had become less and less. He seemed more stressed than usual, too. Juliet worried they might be having money problems, and thought an alterations business might be a way she could help.

"I could start by working from here," she'd suggested when explaining the idea one evening in late December.

"What? You want strangers coming to our home? Oh, I can just see that, Juliet. Women standing on boxes in my living room while you stick pins in the bottom of their dresses." He'd laughed, the nasty laugh that made her feel so small and insignificant.

"I just thought…"

"You thought what?" he yelled.

"I thought I could help. I thought we might need the money."

That one had cost her a black eye, so she'd dropped the matter. The idea that she could start a business had stuck, though, and it gave her hope that if she did ever leave Sam, she could find a way to support herself.

She was going to need a lot more start-up cash than this, though.

Juliet's fingers danced over the laptop and phone she also had stashed in the locker. As well tracking the movements of her phone, Sam had some way of knowing everything she did on both her phone and the iPad he bought her. So, as soon as she had enough money saved, she'd bought the second-hand laptop and cheap phone.

She longed to take them with her, go and sit at her table in the biography section of the bookstore cafe, and continue her research on how to disappear. But today was Wednesday. Friday was the only day of the week it was safe to visit the cafe; the day Sam's office had their regular weekly staff meeting he complained about but could never miss. The only day she could be sure – well, as sure as possible – that she wouldn't be followed.

With a last check that all the contents were still there, Juliet closed the locker and turned to leave. She pulled up quickly with a gasp when she saw Pete, the owner of the place, standing behind her. Not right behind her; Pete had always been good about giving his customers their privacy. But he was an imposing figure, and she hadn't been expecting him to be standing there staring at her.

"Pete, hi. Is everything okay? I didn't think my rent was due yet."

"No, you're all good. Sorry, didn't mean to give you a start."

Juliet waved him away, her composure returned. "It's okay. I thought I was the only one down here."

"Usually that's my trick. Hey, can I ask you... I don't want to pry, but..." Pete pointed to her locker. "Is everything okay?"

"With the locker? Yes, fine. It's exactly what I need. Just the right size." Juliet held her breath, praying that was all he was talking about. She knew she was out of place down here, the twenty-something woman in designer clothes paying cash to rent a basement storage locker by the month. Pete was the kind of guy who had that fatherly protective look about him, which was lovely, but really the last thing Juliet needed right now.

"That's not... ahh, sorry, pet. Like I said, I don't mean to pry. I just... are you safe?"

Juliet dug deep and gave him her brightest smile. "I will be, Pete. I will be." She walked past him and stepped onto the escalator before he could ask any more questions.

Upstairs in the shopping centre, Juliet went through the motions as she did every week. She picked up a basket and pulled out her shopping list, which had all the ingredients to make tonight and tomorrow night's dinners. She'd shop again on Friday for the weekend.

Starting in the fresh produce section, she selected the best-looking tomatoes and mushrooms for tonight's pasta dish. Wednesday night was experiment night, where she liked to try something new from one of the many recipe books she'd collected the last couple of years. Juliet enjoyed experimenting but learned pretty quickly that Sam was only good for one new meal per week. Wednesdays seemed to be his least stressful day at work, which meant he came home in a relatively happy mood. Of course, it always paid to have something in reserve just in case. She could usually tell as soon as he walked through the door whether to go with a new meal or a tried and tested favourite.

Soon, she was going to have to start experimenting with meals for Christmas in July. Sam's family had a holiday house in Bundanoon, in the Southern Highlands. Juliet loved visiting the house, especially in winter. The cold seemed to suit the area, with its country atmosphere and charm. And there were no cameras in the holiday house.

The Keller family hosted a big Christmas in July weekend every year. Sam was an only child, but there were family friends in attendance and it was always a big occasion. The main meal, a lunch on Sunday, was always catered, but Saturday night was a more informal gathering which Yvonne usually cooked for herself. This year, for the first time, Yvonne had entrusted Saturday night's dinner to Juliet.

Juliet thought the Christmas in July weekend might be an excellent time to disappear.

44

The afternoon was getting on by the time Bonnie and Anik arrived back at Police Headquarters in Parramatta. They picked up a quick coffee and bite to eat and met the rest of the team in the incident room.

"Where are we at?' asked Cooper.

Bonnie explained their findings from the cafe and the storage facility.

"He was definitely trying to tell us something without telling us anything," she said of Pete's cryptic offer to rent them a locker. "I've lodged the application for a warrant but based on what he said plus the data from the tracking app, I think it's safe to assume she rented a locker there."

"For six months," Anik added.

"So, she's been planning this for at least that long," said Kate. "Good for her."

"It still doesn't mean she got away with it," said Mars. "What?" he added when the three women in the room shot death stares at him. "I *want* her to have got away from him, of course I do. But we have no physical evidence that says she did."

"We have no physical evidence that says she didn't," Bonnie countered.

"Okay, settle down," said Cooper. "Let's talk through what we *do* have."

"I've been through her web history on both her phone and iPad," said Nora. "It's mostly social media, recipe sites, clothes, magazine sites, news. Nothing helpful. But that's to be expected, now that we know she had a secret laptop. Anything to do with planning an escape would be on that."

"Do you think she knew Sam was tracking her?" asked Kate.

Bonnie had been wondering the same thing during the drive from the city. "I think there's a good chance," she said. "Why else have a secret laptop stashed in a storage locker?"

Anik nodded. "That would explain using the place in World Square, too. It would have looked to Sam like she was just in the centre, not specifically down in the basement."

"What we *do* have," Cooper reminded them. "*Physical* evidence, not supposition."

Bonnie sighed. She knew they didn't have much.

"The fact that she's missing," said Nora.

"Blood in the car," added Zach, barely looking up from the laptop he was perpetually glued to.

"Footage of her in the car when they left Sydney Friday night," said Mars. "Twenty-two minutes parked down an isolated road. And no-one saw Juliet in Bundanoon."

"No crime scene," Bonnie countered. "The blood in the car was minimal, nowhere near a fatal amount. Nothing found at the house."

The table went silent.

"I don't think we can stick to the physical evidence here, Coop," said Kate. "There isn't enough to paint a picture either way."

Cooper nodded his agreement. "All right, talk through your

theories, then. Let's see what makes the most sense. Mars, you start."

Mars pushed his empty coffee cup away and clasped his hands together on the table in front of him. "I think he killed her down that dirt road. I don't think he planned it. Something made him snap. Maybe he hit her initially, that's where the blood came from. Then he saw the dirt road, thought he'd give himself some privacy. But once he was down there, he went too far. Strangled her or killed her some other way without leaving evidence at the scene. Or he cleaned up the evidence at the scene. Got her back in the car and continued on to the house. Or maybe he even did it in the car. The X5 is a decent size vehicle; there's enough space. However he did it, I think he got back on the road and continued to Bundanoon, calling and stopping for pizza to make it seem like everything was normal."

"With a body beside him?" asked Anik.

"It would have been dark by then," Mars reasoned. "His car has tinted windows. She could have looked like she was sleeping."

"So, he gets her body to the house," said Cooper, "then what?"

"Then, like I said, he has twenty-four hours to get rid of the body. And he knows the area; apparently that house has been in his family for generations. He knows the National Park. He could have waited until the early hours and then taken her down one of the fire trails. Plenty of places to hide a body out there."

Bonnie had to admit, this was the theory she'd been stuck on for days. But that was before she knew Juliet had been actively planning her escape.

"If all this is true, why is he now looking in the same places we are?" she asked.

"That's a good point," said Anik. "He's been to both the bookstore cafe and the storage unit."

"Plus, he didn't take the cameras in his apartment down," said Nora. All eyes turned to her for further explanation. "He went home from Bundanoon to the city on Sunday night, right? We didn't turn up with the warrant until Tuesday morning. He had thirty-six hours to remove those cameras, but he didn't."

"Yeah, that doesn't make sense," said Anik. "If I'd been stalking my own wife and then I killed her, I'd be pretty quick to remove any evidence of the stalking."

"Fair point," said Mars. "But he's cocky. Maybe he didn't think we'd get a warrant for the apartment? Or maybe he was convinced his 'security cameras' explanation was good enough?"

"Maybe," said Bonnie, but she didn't believe it. The more she thought about it, the more she was convinced Sam Keller wanted to find his missing wife as much as they did.

"Okay," said Cooper. "Let's talk it through based on the theory that Juliet planned and successfully executed her disappearance. What's the first thing she does?"

"The birth certificate and passport," said Bonnie. "We know she asked her mother for those in November last year."

"Why?" asked Anik. "She has a driver's licence. If she wanted to disappear, why did she need her true identity documents? Wouldn't she be looking for a fake ID instead?"

"Good point," said Bonnie. "Let's come back to that. If we assume Pete Mottley was trying to tell us something without actually telling us, then Juliet rented the storage unit for six months. That makes it November last year, which coincides with getting the ID documents from her mother. Pete said all he needs is a name, phone number, and one month in advance."

Kate clicked her fingers and pointed at Bonnie. "But she couldn't risk giving him the number of the phone Sam was tracking."

"Exactly," Bonnie replied. "She needed a new phone. And you need ID to buy a phone. Ellen said Juliet wanted the passport and birth certificate because she wanted to change the passport over to her married name. But what if she wanted to use them to get a second phone under her maiden name?"

"It's not exactly cloak and dagger stuff," said Mars.

"Doesn't have to be," said Bonnie. She was thinking on the fly now, considering Anik's earlier question. "Juliet didn't need a fake ID because she wasn't trying to break any laws. All she wanted was a phone she could use without her husband's knowledge."

"So, where's that phone now?" asked Kate.

"Same place as the laptop, probably," said Nora. "With Juliet. God, I hope she pulled this off."

"Go back a step," said Cooper. "Do we know when exactly in November Juliet met with her mother?"

"I've got that," said Anik, flicking back through his notebook. "November fifth. A Friday. They had lunch at a Japanese restaurant in the city, but Ellen couldn't remember the name of it."

Bonnie followed Cooper's thinking. "She needed the phone to get the locker, and she needed the ID documents to get the phone. She probably didn't waste any time once she got the documents from her mother. She wouldn't have wanted to risk bringing them back to the apartment where Sam could find them."

"On it," said Zach, fingers flying across his keyboard, two steps ahead of them. "World Square again. According to the tracking app Juliet was there from around midday on Friday November fifth until just after four pm. That's a long lunch."

"They could have gone shopping afterwards," Mars suggested.

Bonnie shook her head. She could picture the day in her mind now; what she would have done herself in the young woman's shoes. "No. Juliet had a plan. She got the documents from her mother, then the new phone, then the locker. Is there a Telstra shop in World Square?"

Zach nodded. "Both Telstra and Optus."

"I'll make the calls," said Kate, picking up her phone and stepping away from the table.

Mars folded his arms, his expression still sceptical. "So, she got a second phone and rented a storage locker back in November. Does that mean she was trying to escape, or just that she knew Sam was following her and she wanted some breathing space?"

Bonnie answered. "At some point, she also bought herself a laptop, which I think she stored in the locker as well. She visited World Square as both her first and last stop of the day every Friday."

"And she was going to this bookstore cafe on Fridays to work on the laptop?"

"Every Friday like clockwork, according to the waitress we interviewed. Juliet was definitely working on something, and now she's disappeared without a trace. And her husband is looking for her."

Cooper stood. "I think Bonnie's right. Sorry Mars, but it makes more sense. Sam Keller is obviously using the data from the app and coming to the same conclusions as us, which he wouldn't be doing if he'd killed her given that he claims to have no knowledge of the app's existence. And in the absence of any evidence of foul play, I'm afraid we have to assume Juliet is out there somewhere."

"You're afraid?" Kate questioned. "You make it sound like a bad thing."

Bonnie realised where he was going. "Coop, you can't..."

"I don't have a choice, Bon. No foul play. No body. No crime."

"What?" Kate's eyes widened as she realised what Cooper was saying. "Does this mean…"

Cooper blew out a breath. "We're Homicide. I can't justify all this manpower if no crime has been committed."

"So, you're pulling us all off the case?" asked Anik.

Cooper nodded gravely. "There is no case."

45

Friday, May 13th, 2022

"I wish I could blow it off," said Sam as he fixed his tie in the bedroom mirror. "We could get away early, have more time to ourselves." He finished straightening the tie as he spoke, the businessman in the suit feigning boredom with the every-day grind.

Juliet knew it was complete bullshit. Sam loved the corporate world, the handshakes and deals, the boys' club testosterone. He hadn't taken a single day off in the five and a half years she'd known him. She called his bluff.

"I'd love that! I still need to go grocery shopping, though. You could come with me?"

Sam laughed and pulled her in for a kiss. "Nah, I'd better go in. Those fools have no idea."

"Fair enough," said Juliet, taking his hands in hers and squeezing. She had showered but was dressed only in her underwear. Sam liked it when she farewelled him in as little attire as possible, and today was all about keeping him happy.

"I'll have everything ready so we can just jump in the car and go as soon as you get home."

"That's my girl." He pulled away and donned his suit jacket before heading into the living room. "Don't forget my new blue shirt. I want to wear it for dinner tomorrow night."

"It's ironed and ready to go." She followed him down the hall like the dutiful wife. If he had a briefcase, this would be the moment she would hand it to him, along with a packed lunch, fifties-housewife style. At least a semi-naked version of the fifties housewife.

Thirty-three hours, Juliet told herself. *Just get through the next thirty-three hours.*

"You going to your book cafe this morning?" Sam asked as he stopped by the door.

For the last six months, ever since she realised Sam knew her every move, Juliet had cultivated a lifestyle befitting the stay-at-home wife of a big-shot lawyer. She'd also made sure to tell him all about it. Her shopping expeditions – designer stores only, no more East West Vintage – the yoga classes, and especially Fridays at the bookstore. She came home with at least one new book every week, and described how much she enjoyed sitting at her favourite table, reading and sipping coffee and watching the world go by. She also never failed to mention how lucky she was to have a husband who worked hard so she could live this perfect life.

So far, it had worked. In six months, Sam had not felt the need to leave his all-important Friday morning meeting and come check on her at the cafe.

"There's a debut novel I want to get my hands on," she said to answer his question. "There's been a lot of press around it, and I'm keen to find out what all the fuss is about. And maybe I can pick up a little something for someone's special birthday, too." She gave him a sultry smile and leaned forward for a kiss.

Sam smirked and grabbed her arse as he kissed her hard. He pulled back and his eyes roamed possessively over her body.

Thirty-three hours.

He looked at his watch. "Gotta go. See you this afternoon, wife."

Juliet plastered on a smile. "Can't wait, husband."

When he was gone, all she wanted to do was wash the remnants of him from her body. But she'd already showered, and another would look odd when he watched his private little peep show later. And he *would* watch, she knew, checking all his camera angles and obsessing over everything she did this day. Her last day in this apartment. Her second last day in this marriage.

It had to be business as usual.

Juliet dressed and made herself a cup of peppermint tea. She checked all the usual magazine and news sites on her iPad as she drank, making sure to click on stories of celebrity gossip and anything to do with the three-fs – fashion, food, and family. She had zero interest in any of those things, but it was all part of the perfect-wife persona for Sam.

When she'd finished her tea and racked up enough vacuous media consumption, Juliet readied herself for the day ahead. She checked the time; just after nine-thirty. Sam should be in his meeting by now. She grabbed her bag and keys and headed for the door.

The World Square shopping centre was two blocks from the apartment in the opposite direction to Sam's office. It was a two-block walk Juliet had become very familiar with. Every day that she left the apartment on foot for the last six months, no matter what she was doing, she first walked these two blocks to this shopping centre. She also made sure to mention a number of times to Sam how much she enjoyed the smoothies from a particular stall inside this shopping centre, so it would seem perfectly natural that this would be her first stop on any outing.

Juliet felt a tingle of excitement mixed with the ever-present fear as she walked today. She managed to restrict herself to just three glances over her shoulder, quite an achievement for any Friday, let alone this one.

Her first stop was a sports store, where she picked up two water bottles identical to the ones she used for her yoga classes. Lately, she'd been making sure to leave these bottles out in the open or in the car where Sam saw them frequently. By now, hopefully he just associated the solid pink and white bottles as hers and thought nothing of their presence.

Once she had the bottles, she made her way down to the storage lockers. Although it would be easier if he wasn't, Juliet found herself hoping Pete would be there. Not that they'd ever exchanged more than a few sentences, but she'd come to feel just a tiny bit protected by this big bear of a man in his dirty overalls.

"There she is, regular as clockwork," came the deep voice as the escalator brought Juliet to the basement storage business.

"Hi, Pete. How's things?"

"Can't complain. You?"

"No-one'll listen."

It was the same conversation they had most Fridays, and Juliet felt some of the tension release from her shoulders.

"Another month?" he asked as she approached.

"Actually, no," she replied, stopping just short of his desk. "I think I'm done. Do you mind?"

Pete shrugged. "Of course not. I'll miss you, though. Moving on?"

Juliet nodded. "Something like that."

He stood, came out from behind the desk. The look on his face so sincere, but also grave. "You stay safe, you hear me?" He looked like he wanted to take hold of her, give her a hug, but that wouldn't have been appropriate even in the pre-pandemic world.

Juliet gave him the brightest smile she could muster. "That's the plan, Pete."

They stood there for a moment, awkward, but understanding. Juliet found herself hoping Pete had a nice family at home, maybe a daughter he could protect and treat like a princess. Then the moment was gone, and Juliet was cleaning out her locker.

The sky had come over quite dark outside, and Juliet pulled her coat tighter as she walked to the cafe. The wind made it feel a lot cooler than the actual temperature, but at least it wasn't raining.

"Morning," said Bec as Juliet entered the cafe. "Usual?"

"Yes please," Juliet replied as she headed for her table. It was vacant, but the remnants of someone else's morning tea were still scattered about.

"Here, let me get that for you." Bec busied herself cleaning the table, and Juliet smiled her thanks. Many a time over the last six months Juliet had stopped herself from engaging in more than small talk with this woman. Bec was thoughtful and kind, the sort of person Juliet could see herself becoming friends with, but it was too risky. As far as she could tell, Bec didn't even know her name. Juliet only knew Bec's because she'd heard her interacting with the other staff.

She was going to miss this place.

Juliet pushed the thought aside and got to work on the next step of her plan. On a previous visit she'd googled how to wipe the hard drive of her computer, and now the time had come. It had served its purpose, this clunky machine she'd picked up from a second-hand shop nearby, but it was too bulky to take with her.

After copying the last of her files to her Dropbox account, Juliet did what she needed to do to wipe everything from the computer and restore the factory settings. As the laptop did its thing, she sipped her coffee and scanned the nearby bookshelves for something appropriate for Sam's birthday. A book on sports and business – two of Sam's favourite things – seemed like the obvious choice.

When the laptop had finished Juliet packed her things and took the sports business book to the counter.

"We've got that mystery you were asking about last week," Bec said as she rang up Juliet's tally.

"Oh, thank you!" Juliet followed Bec's pointed finger to the stack of books by the door. She'd almost forgot. Going home without what she'd told Sam she was coming specifically to get could have been disastrous today.

I've got to be better than that, she thought as she grabbed a copy of *Before You Knew My Name*, by Jacqueline Bublitz.

"Such a beautiful cover," said Bec as she scanned the barcode on the back of the book.

"Have you read it?" Juliet asked.

"It's next on my list. Maybe we can swap notes next time you're in?"

Juliet smiled. "I'd like that."

46

B onnie followed Cooper into his office. "If he finds her first, he'll kill her." Anik had trailed behind, and now stood nervously in the doorway.

"My hands are tied, Detective Hunter." Cooper sat behind his desk; wiggled his mouse to wake the sleeping computer. Once they'd reached the conclusion that Juliet Keller was most likely still alive, he'd reassigned the team elsewhere.

How could he just dismiss the whole case like that?

"Jesus, Coop, you practically begged me to come onto this case. Now I'm all in, a woman is in danger, and you won't let me do anything."

Cooper sighed but said nothing.

Bonnie took a seat in front of his desk. "How many domestic homicides have you attended in your career?"

He looked up. "Too many."

"Exactly. We're always there too late. How many times have you wished things could have been different? That you could have got there in time? That you could have prevented the bloodbath?"

Cooper's eyes narrowed. "I can't have this conversation, Bon."

Bonnie knew she was cutting close to the bone, but she pressed on. "This is nothing like the vigilante, Coop. We have a chance to do something here, legitimately, to save a woman's life. Surely you can find some way, some loophole, to let us keep looking for Juliet."

Anik slid into the chair beside Bonnie. "Please, boss. I mean, Coop. Bonnie's right. We're close. We need to save her."

Cooper stared at Anik, then switched his gaze back to Bonnie. Bonnie held firm, already thinking of her next steps. If Cooper stuck to his guns, then she was done with her second-ment to Homicide and she could do whatever the hell she liked anyway. It would just be a lot easier with Homicide's resources.

"Two days," Cooper finally said. "And it's just the two of you. I need Mars and Kate on the Rafiki murder."

Bonnie smiled. "Can we still use Deadpool?"

If Cooper was shocked by her use of the nickname for Zach and Nora, he didn't let on. "Sparingly." He lifted his head to the door. "Close that on your way out. I've got a year's worth of paperwork to do before I leave here tonight."

They were back in the incident room, alone, before Anik spoke. "I've never seen anyone change his mind like that."

Bonnie shrugged. She didn't like taking advantage of Cooper's weakness but needs must. She certainly wasn't going to explain that to Anik, though.

"Let's get to work," she said as she started pacing the length of the room. "We know Juliet planned her escape for six months. She probably used that time to save a stash of cash, too. What we need to do is figure out where she went once she left the car outside the grocery store in Bundanoon."

"And what she took with her," said Anik.

"Yes, good point. Whatever she took, it would have to have been either on her person when she left the house, or in the car."

"She packed the car back in Sydney on the Friday afternoon, didn't she?" Anik asked.

"She did."

"Do you think she stashed a bag then?"

Bonnie considered the idea. Juliet had tried to escape Sam in the past, when he'd broken her arm and she'd been put in a motel room by the women's shelter. She'd been unprepared back then, and whatever had happened – whether Sam found her or she went back to him by herself – she would have remembered that experience when planning this time.

"She would have been prepared, but I don't think she would have had a bag ready to go. If Sam found it... well, I doubt she would have risked that. This was her big chance to get away. Perhaps her only chance. She would have prepared only what she absolutely needed – money, the phone, maybe the laptop."

Anik found the security camera footage Nora had shown them of Juliet packing the X5 on Friday afternoon. Bonnie pulled up a seat beside him and they watched it again together, closely this time. Juliet carried a couple of matching tote bags down first and put them in the boot. She appeared to open one of the bags and fish around in it for a couple of seconds, before zipping it closed again. On her second trip to the car, she added four full grocery bags to the boot. Third trip: hanging clothes and coats in the back seat. Finally, she made a fourth trip to the car, this time with a green shopping bag, the contents of which she emptied into the front passenger seat.

"She does all that before five o'clock," said Anik. "Then shortly before six they both come down together and leave." He played that section of the recording, and Bonnie watched as Juliet placed a water bottle in the pocket of the front passenger door. She remembered thinking nothing of this when first viewing the footage three days ago. But now...

"Go back," she instructed Anik. "Back to when she was

packing the car alone. That last trip she made when she put stuff in the front seat."

Anik did so, and they watched again. It was hard to see because of the angle and the way she was leaning into the car, but it was definitely there.

"She takes two water bottles from that bag and places them inside the car," said Bonnie. "The one she puts in the door later when Sam is with her, makes three. Who needs three bottles of water for a two-hour drive?"

Anik replayed the scene and squinted at the screen. "You're right. Sports drink, maybe? I've seen athletes with different bottles for different drinks."

"When they're training or racing, sure. But not when you're just driving to your holiday house on a Friday after work." Bonnie thought of her own vehicle. There were at least two discarded water bottles in her back seat that she'd been meaning to retrieve. An idea started to form. "No-one notices an empty water bottle rolling around in the car. Or maybe underneath the seat. The ones with solid walls would make perfect hiding spots for smaller things."

"Like a mobile phone, or a roll of cash," said Anik.

"Exactly."

"So, what does that tell us?" Anik asked. "She left of her own accord. She possibly had a couple of water bottles full of cash and a mobile phone. Then what?"

Bonnie recalled the location. The car by the side of the road, the keys and Juliet's phone – the one Sam was tracking – discarded in the grass nearby. The shops, the fence, the train line.

The train.

Could it be that simple?

"Were there any trains running around the time of her disappearance?"

Anik opened a new browser window and started typing. A moment later he had the timetable for the NSW train network on screen. "Looks like there was one to Goulburn at eighteen twenty-nine, and another to Central at nineteen-thirteen. Bit risky to hang around that long – the station isn't far from where she disappeared."

"Maybe," said Bonnie. "But it was getting dark. She could have found a hiding spot. There was nothing earlier?"

Anik shook his head. "Train to Central at two pm. She was still at the house then. There are buses. Could she have got on one of those?"

"I doubt it," said Bonnie. "A bus driver out that way would know his or her locals. Juliet would have stood out, and they'd have come forward as soon as her picture was on the news. We can canvas, but it's not likely."

"What do we do now then?"

Bonnie pushed back her chair and stood. "We need to go back to Bundanoon."

47

Friday, May 13th, 2022

Juliet's next stop was the reseller. She'd only bought the laptop from them six months ago, and was hoping it still held some sort of value. Even a few extra dollars to add to her stash would be helpful. Having to bring her plan forward by two months meant she needed every dollar she could get.

"I can probably give you fifty bucks for it," said the bored guy with the tufty beard behind the counter.

"Really? I paid five times that for it here just months ago."

"Things move fast in the tech world, lady. I can't resell this. It's barely even good for parts. Fifty is a gift, take it or leave it."

The store sold all manner of electronic devices, not just computers, and Juliet was about to agree to the price when something caught the corner of her eye.

"Is that charged?" she asked, indicating a cordless electric shaver languishing in the corner of a bottom shelf.

The guy leaned forward to see what she was pointing at. "Dunno. There's a cord with it."

An idea started to form. It hadn't been part of her plan, but the shaver was the exact same one as Sam's at home. She only needed to get it into the car and hide it there for what... thirty hours. If by some chance he found it, maybe he would just think it was his.

"Can you plug it in and charge it for me?" Juliet asked. "I'll leave the computer, come back in a couple hours, pick up the shaver and we'll call it even. Deal?"

The guy thought for a minute, shrugged. "Sure, why not."

She still had the grocery shopping to do, but this store was on her way back home so it shouldn't look too odd on Sam's tracker. There was a dress boutique right next door – the reason she'd chosen this place back when she'd first bought the computer – and she didn't think the tracker was *that* accurate.

How had her life come to this? Her every move followed, her privacy invaded in her own home. By the man who was supposed to love her. When had she become his possession?

Thirty hours.

Juliet shook the thoughts away and concentrated on the tasks at hand. Do the grocery shopping in time to have it delivered before four o'clock. Pick up the shaver and the cash. Find a public toilet and use the privacy to stash her money, phone – make sure it's turned off – and identity documents in ziplock bags inside the two new water bottles, scuffing the bottles a little so they didn't look new. Return home and pack their bags for a normal weekend at the country house.

Check and recheck every part of her plan. And avoid doing anything that could set Sam off.

It was after four-thirty by the time she was ready to pack the car. First their tote bags, matching, gifts from Sam's parents last Christmas. Juliet had managed to slip the new shaver into hers while her back was to the bedroom camera. After placing the bag in the boot of the car, she leaned in, unzipped the bag, and removed the shaver, careful not to bring it outside the confines of the car boot. There were security cameras in the parking garage, but none close enough to make out what she was up to as long as she was careful. She tucked the shaver into a corner of the boot, praying it would be dark by the time they reached Bundanoon and Sam wouldn't see it. She also hoped it would retain its charge for a few days, because she'd already thrown the charging cable away.

Next, she brought the grocery bags down to the car and stacked them in front of their totes, making sure to leave space for the esky full of cold items. Sam would bring that down when they were ready to leave. Then the hanging clothes, including Sam's perfectly ironed blue shirt and her dress for dinner tomorrow night. The dress Sam said she'd wear to his birthday dinner party because it showed off her 'fine arse'. One of the many outfits she hated because it made her feel like a trophy.

Hopefully, it was a dress she'd never have to wear again.

Back up in the apartment it was time for the final stage of Juliet's preparation. She'd discovered the cameras around the same time she'd realised Sam was tracking her phone and iPad. He just knew too much; was too easily able to find things she'd hidden or put away. She'd been lying in bed one night, unable to sleep, events of the evening playing over and over in her mind. He'd come home from work early and gone almost straight to the cupboard in the kitchen; pulled out the dress he'd told her to get rid of because it reminded him of some bitch at work. It was such a nice dress, all she'd wanted to do was take it down to Samira at East West Vintage the next time she went out, but Sam... anyway. At least that incident had resulted in the useful intel of the cameras.

There were three in the open plan living area – two covering the lounge and dining rooms, and one in the kitchen. There was no avoiding them, but she could work with their angles. She pulled the two new water bottles out of her handbag and did her best to make it appear as though they were empty. She positioned herself in front of the sink before screwing the cap off the top of the first one. Angling it so the mouth of the bottle was pointed away from the kitchen camera, Juliet turned on the tap to a trickle and slowly filled the space around the ziplock bags with water. She repeated the process with the second bottle, then placed the full bottles and some other snacks into a green grocery bag.

Down at the car, Juliet emptied the bottles and snacks out of the grocery bag and into the passenger side. The snacks she placed within easy reach, but the water bottles she secured underneath the seat. She'd bring a third one down with just water in it for the drive, not wanting to risk Sam picking up either of these two.

It was as much as she could do. Bringing the plan forward two months had cost her valuable savings and planning time, but there was no choice. Juliet had to act now.

For both their sakes.

48

Friday, May 13th, 2022

The punch came hard and fast and right on the edge of her chin. Juliet shouldn't have been surprised by the level of force Sam was able to put behind his fist in the confines of the car. He'd had enough practice by now. But he still had the knack of springing an attack when she wasn't expecting it.

The second blow split her lip.

"You have to do it, don't you?" Sam spit, his face full of rage. "Why do you always provoke me, Juliet? It's Friday night, I've had the week from hell, and we're still an hour away from the house. Can't you just once..." He finished the sentence by shaking his head and examining his fist. The grazes on his knuckles would be Juliet's fault, too. They always were.

Twenty-three hours.

Juliet wiped the blood from her lip with her left hand, looked around for a tissue. There were none. Some of the blood dripped onto the leather; she watched as it ran down the side of the car seat. Sam couldn't see, so she let it run its course.

It had been a simple question that set him off. Or rather, the repetition of a simple question. She'd asked about Amanda, Ollie's latest girlfriend, wondered how they met. Sam said he didn't know, then she asked whether they met at work. That would qualify as asking the same question twice, a trait Sam abhors.

Stupid.

Juliet had needed the toilet for about twenty minutes now, but she forced herself to push it to the back of her mind. She couldn't ask Sam to stop, not in this mood. She had to make it to the house in Bundanoon. She had to make it through the next twenty-three hours.

"Did you pack my razor?"

Juliet looked over to find her husband scratching at his chin as if nothing had happened, as if he hadn't just punched her twice in the face without taking his eyes off the road.

"I did. And the spare blades, too."

"That's my girl." Sam accelerated around a slower car, and some of the tension released from his shoulders. He reached across and gently stroked Juliet's leg. "What did my lovely wife get up to today?"

This was the way it went – the sudden burst of violence, release of the day's aggression, and then he was back to the agreeable version of himself. Juliet relaxed ever-so-slightly. Plastered on a smile.

"Just my usual Friday. A morning smoothie from Bunches, then I walked down to the cafe before grocery shopping and then home to pack the car. With some window-shopping along the way, of course." Better account for the time hanging around the second-hand store where she sold the computer.

"Did you buy any books?"

"I got the new novel I was after, yes. Plus, I might have

bought a little something for someone's birthday tomorrow, but you'll have to wait and see."

Sam nodded, satisfied. He liked presents.

"Should we just get a takeaway pizza tonight? You look tired."

"I do have a bit of a headache," Juliet replied, switching to little-girl-who-needs-looking-after mode. It was amazing how effortlessly her actions and reactions adjusted to suit Sam's mood. Some couples were so in tune with each other they subconsciously dressed the same or randomly found themselves sitting in the same pose. Juliet's version of this was to seamlessly slip into the role her husband's behaviour required.

"Do you mind making the call?" she asked, knowing he needed to be the protector, the hunter.

Sam stroked the side of her face. "No problem."

As Juliet listened to Sam order their usual from Benny's, somewhere in the back of her mind the thought registered that it could work in her favour if no-one actually saw or heard from her this weekend.

The idea had been to just disappear. To escape the prison her marriage had become, the control Sam exerted, the violence and fear he inflicted. But she knew he'd never let her simply leave.

The last time she left, when that doctor and the woman from the shelter put her in the motel and Sam had found her, he'd made it very clear she wasn't the only one he'd hurt if she ever left him again. Juliet pictured her nephews and niece, wondered how much they'd grown since she last saw them. She turned to the window and stared out into the darkness as a single tear escaped and trickled down her cheek.

Wiping the tear away, Juliet refocused on the job ahead. The only way to make sure Sam didn't come after her, and guarantee her family's safety, was if he thought something had happened to her. The plan was to make it look like she was taken. All of her research, her preparation, the money she'd saved, the phone. He could never know about any of it. To Sam, she must be the dutiful wife who suddenly disappears. 'Met with foul play', isn't that what the police say?

But... was there another way? An even better way?

What if the police thought Sam was responsible?

Juliet glanced down at where the blood had seeped into the car seat. Her blood. Whenever a woman went missing, the husband was always a suspect. She knew that much from the crime dramas she watched and read. Was there a way to set Sam up for this?

No. It was too risky. Fabricating evidence might fool the rest of the world, but Sam would know the truth. Which meant he'd know she was still out there, and unless she could do a good enough job to have him locked up immediately, he'd stop at nothing to find her and make her pay. She couldn't let that happen. She had to stick to the plan, disappear, and hope he believed she'd been abducted by a stranger.

And she couldn't break any laws in the process. Because then the police would search for her, too.

The urgency in Juliet's bladder was becoming desperate, and she didn't think she'd be able to hold on until Bundanoon. She glanced over at Sam, singing his heart out along with his favourite rock gods, and decided it was worth the risk.

"Honey, do you mind if we..."

She stopped talking as his face turned, but it was too late.

"Are you seriously going to make me stop right now? Fuck, Juliet. I just want to get to the house. What is it with women? You can't go two hours without pissing? You're like dogs, pissing on every fucking tree in the street."

They'd been approaching a rest stop, and Juliet had thought if she timed the request just right, he'd say something like 'no problem, babe', and swing into the carpark. But they sped on by, and her heart sank.

Twenty-two hours.

Sam put the indicator on, but there was nowhere to pull over. His face was set in the hard, don't-fuck-with-me stare Juliet was truly afraid of. He wrenched the wheel and suddenly they were bouncing down a dirt road, narrowly missing a tree as he made the turn.

It only took a few hundred metres for the darkness of the bush to swallow the car. Sam braked hard, jerking them to a stop, and stared at Juliet.

"Well go on then. You want to piss, don't you? I'll leave the lights on for you." He turned the music up and resumed his off-key sing-along.

Juliet didn't know what to do. Squat near the car, or walk away? In front of the headlights, where he could see her, or off to the side, in the darkness?

She settled on a place on the outskirts of the beam of the headlights, in the shadows but with enough light to see what she was doing. She turned her back to the car and squatted, music blaring so loud she didn't hear Sam's door open. He was on her before she'd finished, underwear still around her knees as he laid into her.

The Eagles sang their song about drugs and excess as Sam punched Juliet again and again. She asked him to stop, begged him to think of his friends coming tomorrow, but it was no use.

Twenty-two hours.

Maybe.

Juliet focused on the words of the song as she wrapped her arms around herself, trying to absorb the blows. She listened as the lead singer told her she could check out any time she liked, but she could never leave.

God, he'd better be wrong.

49

I t was just past five o'clock when Bonnie and Anik reached the outskirts of Bundanoon. A little later in the day than when Juliet had disappeared, but not much.

"Right there." Bonnie pointed to the spot the X5 had been parked, and Anik pulled over. A car drove out of the IGA across the road, and Bonnie recognised the owner of the store at the wheel. She gave a wave, then the car was gone and they were alone in this section of the street.

"It's cold," Anik said as they got out of the car. He was only wearing a suit jacket, no coat in sight.

"Cold, almost dark, and deserted," Bonnie elaborated as she pulled a pair of woollen gloves from her coat pocket. "Perfect for disappearing."

Anik took a few steps toward the fence. "The keys and phone were over here somewhere?"

Bonnie nodded, followed him. The stick Senior Constable Curran had inserted into the ground to mark the spot was still there. She pointed it out to her partner.

While Anik looked around, Bonnie stood by the car and thought about what she would have done in Juliet's shoes. Juliet had the two water bottles in the car, presumably – hopefully – filled with the money and identification she needed to start a new life somewhere. She'd been wearing a jacket – according to Sam she'd taken his big winter coat, complete with beanie and gloves, when she left the house to run to the grocery store. Sam had told them the coat lived at the Bundanoon house, a permanent fixture on the rack by the door. The Southern Highlands got very cold in winter.

Juliet had been smart, then. She had the warmest winter coat available to her, a beanie, gloves, and two water bottles. Bonnie glanced into the unmarked car she and Anik had driven down in, spotted the empty chip packet and muesli bar wrapper from the snacks they'd grabbed before setting off. She thought back to the recording from the Keller's building carpark, the one where Juliet emptied the contents of a green shopping bag into the front seat. There'd been snacks along with the water bottles. Driving snacks, or snacks for a longer journey?

"The train station is just over there," said Anik, pointing.

Bonnie locked the car. "Let's go."

They walked past Benny's, saw the staff inside setting up for the evening trade.

"No-one remembers seeing her walk by," said Anik.

"No, but remember what she was wearing. She could have tucked her hair up inside the beanie. Hunched over, hands in the pockets of Sam's big black coat. In the dark she'd look like just another local making their way home in the cold. Add a mask, she'd be anybody and nobody."

"True," Anik agreed.

As they approached the train station, Bonnie looked for somewhere a person could stay out of sight for a couple of hours. There were a couple of spots that might work.

"There are cameras on the platform," said Anik as they made it to the station. "I'll call Deadpool."

It would take time for Nora or Zach to contact the rail authority and get hold of the footage from the station. But the position of the camera angles meant that no-one could get on or off a train without being seen, so they should be able to confirm definitively whether Juliet left Bundanoon by rail on the night she disappeared. Importantly, Sam Keller would not be able to access that information.

While Anik made the phone call, Bonnie continued walking around the corner from the station, following signs pointing to the Morton National Park. There were a few more shops, outside of which was a water cooler designed for both drinking and filling up your own bottles. According to the signage, the township of Bundanoon prided itself on being the world's first bottled water-free town, having banned the sale of bottled water back in 2009.

An idea started to form in Bonnie's mind. Juliet had been a regular visitor to this town, so she must have known about these water coolers. What if she didn't get on a train straight away? She was dressed warmly enough. What if she filled her pockets with snacks from the car, removed the cash and whatnot from her water bottles, and filled them up here at this cooler? She'd have all she needed to survive at least a couple of nights.

"Hey, where are you going?" Anik called to Bonnie as she continued walking.

"National Park," she replied without turning.

"Shall I go back for the car?"

Bonnie shook her head. "Juliet was on foot. I want to see whether this was doable."

"Whether what was doable? Walking to the National Park in the dark? It's freezing out here, Bon."

Bonnie turned, took in his slender, suited frame complete with fancy shoes. "Why didn't you bring a coat?"

"I wasn't expecting to be traipsing around the bush at night in the coldest place on Earth."

"Policing one-o-one, dude. Be prepared."

"I thought that was the Scouts motto."

Bonnie nodded, turned back and kept walking. "Knew what they were doing, the Scouts. And this is far from the coldest place on Earth. It's not even the coldest place in New South Wales. Come on. Walk faster and you might warm up a bit."

Houses on either side of the street thinned out as the blocks got larger and bush dominated the landscape. After about a kilometre there were no more streetlights, and Bonnie activated the torch on her mobile phone.

"You really think she came down here?" Anik asked, rubbing his shoulders as they walked in an effort to generate some warmth.

"I don't know. Maybe. She'd have to know Sam would come looking for her when she didn't return. When did you say the next train was?"

"Six twenty-nine, over an hour and a half after she left the house."

"I think that's too long. She would have assumed Sam would come looking before then, and the train station is too close. She couldn't afford for him to find her. Plus, she knew his friends would have arrived by then, and even if Sam didn't, *they* would have insisted on calling the police. I don't think she would have risked waiting at the station and getting on a train with everyone looking for her."

"Zach's checking, but he says it'll most likely be tomorrow before we get anything from the rail authority."

"That's frustrating."

They finally reached the outskirts of the National Park. There was a parking area which allowed overnight stays, with a few vans in residence tucked up in the corners. Bonnie and Anik knocked on doors, asked questions, but only one of the vans had been there since the weekend and the couple inside didn't remember seeing anyone walking alone around the time in question. But it was cold, they said, and they stayed inside their van with the curtains drawn after dusk.

Bonnie and Anik kept walking down a seemingly endless dirt road, spotting the occasional signposted track leading off into the bush. The scrub was thick and uninviting, but the further they got the more convinced Bonnie became of her theory.

"Juliet could have easily made it down here unnoticed," she said, stopping in the middle of the road. "We've been walking for over half an hour and no-one's passed us. No vehicles, no-one on foot."

"Even if we did see someone coming, we could have hidden pretty easily," said Anik. "Turn off your torch for a second."

Bonnie did so, and they stood in the darkness for a moment until their eyes adjusted. The moon was almost full, and once they were used to it there was plenty of light to walk by.

"How full was the moon on Saturday night?" Bonnie asked.

Anik checked his phone. "Full moon was Monday and Tuesday. Saturday it looked like that." He pointed to his screen, displaying a handy calendar which showed the phase of the moon for every day of the month. Saturday night was apparently 'waxing gibbous', or in Bonnie's language, about three-quarters full.

"Enough to see by," she concluded. "I reckon we're onto something, Anik. If I were Juliet, and I had my chance to get away from that abusive prick of a husband, I would have come down here."

"Then what?" Anik asked.

"I'd have laid low for a couple of days, then made my way back to the train station and jumped on a train out of town." She started the long walk back out of the park. "Call Zach again, will you? We need footage from the station for every train that left since five pm Saturday."

Anik did so, and Bonnie took out her own phone and sent a text message while they walked. She needed eyes on Sam Keller, had to make sure he wasn't still one step ahead of them. Mars was technically off the case, but he was the only person she could ask to do this.

His reply came back immediately. *Been parked outside his building since five.*

Bonnie was starting to like this homicide squad.

50

The warrant for the storage locker came through first thing Friday morning. Bonnie called Pete, who had one of the last remaining fax machines in the city and asked for the warrant to be faxed through. Fortunately, Headquarters also had one of the archaic machines, and she was able to enlist the help of a couple of administrative assistants to comply with his request with minimal swearing and cursing.

"Did it come through yet?" she asked him for the fourth time.

"No, nothing... hang on, it's starting up. Yes, here it comes. Ah, excellent. Thank you, Detective Hunter."

"My absolute pleasure," Bonnie lied. She mouthed a thank you to the support staff before heading back to the Homicide Squad room. "Now, what can you tell me about Juliet Keller?" she asked Pete as she walked.

"Julie Wilson," Pete replied.

"That the name she used?"

"That's the name she put on the application form I have in front of me. Julie Wilson, and an address out in Castle Hill." He read off the address, and Bonnie mentally matched it to that of Juliet's parents.

"Thanks, Pete. Is there a phone number?" Bonnie reached the incident room and clicked the lid off a whiteboard marker. Nora and Anik watched in silence as she wrote the number on the board. Bonnie locked eyes with Nora who nodded and got to work on her laptop.

"What else can you tell me?" Bonnie asked Pete.

"Julie— sorry, Juliet, rented the locker since November last year, paid cash monthly, and was always a pleasure to deal with. I got the feeling she was in trouble, but I never wanted to pry. We get all walks of life down here, Detective."

"I can imagine," Bonnie agreed. "When did she terminate the rental?"

"Last Friday morning. She spent a few minutes emptying everything out, then said goodbye to me. I told her to stay safe, she said that was the plan. And then she was gone."

"She didn't say anything about where she was going?" Bonnie asked.

"No. But I wasn't surprised to see her picture on the news. Her husband was abusive, wasn't he?"

"I can't—"

"No, I suspect you can't give me details of an ongoing investigation. It doesn't matter, I know what I saw."

Bonnie's grip on her phone tightened. "What did you see, Pete?"

"I deal with people every day," he replied, speaking slowly. "I know what it looks like when someone isn't having a good time at home. That young lass... let's just say there were bruises that did not look like accidents. Long sleeves and scarves in the middle of summer. Sunglasses down here in my little underground world. And she was constantly looking over her shoulder. Always on edge. So, I wasn't surprised when she turned up on the news. I was a little surprised when the husband fronted up down here. Pleasantly surprised, of course."

"Of course," Bonnie agreed. Pete had obviously reached the same conclusion as them – if Sam was following the tracking data and visiting places Juliet had frequented, it could only mean he was looking for her, too. Which meant he hadn't killed her.

"You *are* going to find her before he does, aren't you, Detective Hunter?" It sounded like less of a question and more a demand.

"I'm going to do everything I can," Bonnie assured Pete. She thanked him again for his information and ended the call, before quickly bringing Nora and Anik up to date.

"Julie Wilson," said Anik. "So, she just reverted to her maiden name, dropped one letter from her first name, and used her old address. Not much of a criminal mastermind."

"I don't think she was trying to be," Bonnie replied. "She wasn't trying to break any laws, set up a fake identity. She just wanted to get away from her husband." She turned her attention to her phone, punched in the number Pete had given her for Julie Wilson.

"Anything?" Anik asked.

The phone didn't ring. "Straight to voicemail," Bonnie replied as she listened to an automated voice message telling her the person she was calling was not available. She left a message and her number but wasn't hopeful of Juliet returning the call.

"It's a Telstra phone," said Nora. "Kate got onto them yesterday, but they couldn't give her much without a warrant. But now you've got the name and number I should be able to get the call log today."

"Good," said Bonnie. "Hopefully she's called somebody for help, might give us a location."

"I can probably help with that," said Zach, bustling into the room with his laptop open in his hands. He sat and connected to the monitor in the corner. "I leant on the rail authority, got this through early this morning." He rubbed his eyes with one hand without missing a keystroke with the other.

"You found her?"

"I think so. It's a pretty quiet station, so it didn't take me long to go through each train that picked up there. I started with the day she went missing and searched forward from there. You were right, she definitely didn't get on any train on Saturday night."

He finished typing, and on the screen, Bonnie recognised the Bundanoon train station platform she'd stood on yesterday. "When's this from?" she asked.

"Monday night," said Zach.

"Two days after she went missing." Bonnie watched as a train approached the platform. She couldn't see anyone waiting, but Zach wouldn't be showing them nothing. As the train drew to a stop someone stepped out of the shadows. Even with the long black coat and beanie, Bonnie could tell it was the figure of a woman. She turned in the direction of the camera and Zach paused. It was hard to see in the limited lighting of the platform, but it definitely looked like Juliet's face. The white running shoes also matched the description Sam had given them. All that was missing was Juliet's long, blonde hair.

"She must have tucked her hair up inside the beanie," said Anik.

Bonnie looked closer. There was no tell-tale bulge at the back of the beanie. She smiled. *Clever girl.* "I don't think so."

"You don't think it's her?" Anik asked. "It certainly looks like her."

"Oh, it's her," said Bonnie. "But her hair isn't tucked up in the beanie. It's part of her disguise. I think she's shaved it off."

They watched as Juliet got on the train.

"It's the seven fifty-two to Canberra," said Zach. "Monday evening."

Bonnie stood. "Send her picture to every station that train stopped at along the way. I don't think she got off, but if she did, I want to know where."

"Doesn't she have a friend in Canberra?" asked Nora.

"Yes, Max Reeves," said Anik. "We spoke to him on the phone, he said he hadn't seen or heard from Juliet in months."

"Maybe it's time we asked him in person then," she said, gathering her things and taking in her partner's slightly more practical attire. "You prepared today?"

"I have a coat, if that's what you mean."

"Good. If you thought the highlands were cold, you're not going to love Canberra."

51

Monday, May 16th, 2022

J uliet watched the darkness of the night slide by as the train made its way to Canberra. The carriage was close to empty; a few workers in suits making their way home to the capital from a busy day in Sydney, a mother and young son with suitcases piled on the seats, and a slouching teenager in a black hoodie whose music Juliet could hear three seats away despite the best efforts of his headphones. She could only imagine how loud it must be in his head.

She received some attention from the mother and son when she removed her beanie and scratched her bare scalp. The boy, who couldn't be more than five or six years old, stared openly, while the mother chastised him and gave Juliet an apologetic smile. Juliet smiled back. She couldn't blame the young fellow, she must look quite a sight.

There was a sign near the door to the carriage claiming the toilet was at this end. Juliet had never been on a train with a toilet before, the city trains not having any facilities. But it made sense for longer journeys such as this, and she went off in the direction of the sign. The station at Bundanoon had been unmanned, which was why she'd waited until this late train, but it meant the toilets there had been locked.

The toilet on the train was basic but clean, and even included a mirror. Well, a shiny metal surface in place of a mirror, presumably for safety reasons, but it was enough for Juliet to assess her appearance after two days and nights in the bush.

She'd done okay with shaving her scalp, under the circumstances. The shaver had fortunately retained enough charge, and, working by feel, she'd made a pretty even job of it judging by the reflection staring back at her now. The shaver hadn't come with any of the attachments, so there was no chance of giving herself a 'number two' all over or any such thing. She'd been hopeful she'd end up looking like a cancer patient. Judging by the reactions of the mother and son in the carriage just now, it looked like she'd pulled it off.

Juliet felt bad masquerading as something she wasn't. She'd read a story about a woman who'd pretended to have cancer and duped a lot of people out of a lot of money. She'd wondered at the time how anyone could do such a thing. Imagine making the people you loved think you were going to die?

The train slowed, and Juliet realised they must be coming into a station. She braced herself against the wall until it came to a complete stop, then took the opportunity to wash her face in the hand basin. The water was cold but refreshing, and made her feel slightly better. She put the beanie back on her head as the train started off again. She'd pick up a couple of bandannas in Canberra. It didn't matter what she looked like, she reasoned with her reflection. As long as she didn't actually *say* she had cancer, surely, she wasn't doing anything wrong.

Back in the carriage, Juliet noticed one of the workers and the young music aficionado had departed at the last stop. She retook her seat with a smile at the mother and son, and thought about her own family. They'd been foremost in her mind these last two days. Her mum and dad, Nick and Renee and the kids. She wished she could have told them her plan, but it was too risky. Her mother wouldn't have understood, still so taken in as she was by Sam's charm. She'd have told Juliet she was being silly, that husbands and wives need to work out their problems together.

Her father and Nick would have been a different story, but probably even less helpful. They'd have wanted to intervene. She could just see the two of them setting off to find Sam and *give him a taste of his own medicine*. That would not go well for anyone.

Perhaps she could have spoken to Renee, but her sister-in-law was so busy with the kids these days. It wouldn't have been fair to involve her, ask her to keep a secret from her own husband.

No, this was Juliet's mess and she had to sort it out for herself. She'd find a way to get a message to them at some point, let them know she was safe. And then maybe, once Sam had moved on... no, she couldn't allow herself to think that far into the future. There was still such a long way to go.

"Why don't you have any hair?"

Juliet hadn't noticed the small boy sidle up to her seat.

"Oh, hello," she croaked, then cleared her throat, realising these were the first words she'd said out loud since calling goodbye to Sam two nights ago. "What's your name?"

"Joshua!" his mother called before he could answer. "Sorry, love, he's too bloody quick. I can't close my eyes for a second."

"It's okay," Juliet replied, glad of the distraction. She pulled off her beanie and winked at the boy. "I'm trying out a new look, what do you think?"

"I think it's cool," he said. "Mum, can I have no hair too?"

The woman rolled her eyes. "Maybe. Come back here, please. Leave the nice lady alone."

Joshua gave an exaggerated sigh but did as he was told. "It's boring," he said as he slumped back into his seat.

His mother handed over her mobile phone, and Joshua sat up straighter and started playing some sort of game.

"You got any?" the woman asked.

Juliet shook her head. As much as she wanted human contact, it was better to avoid too much conversation with strangers right now. She knew Sam would have reported her missing, but spending the whole time isolated in the national park she had no idea the extent to which anyone was actually looking for her. Was there a wide-scale search happening as they spoke, or had she barely rated a mention deep into the six-o'clock news last night?

"You want one?" the woman asked, this time with a smile. Joshua, who was clearly still listening despite being engrossed in his game, glanced up and frowned at his mother.

"One day," Juliet replied, and turned to stare into the darkness out the window. Her hand went instinctively to her belly, and she was glad the mother and son couldn't see the gesture behind the seats separating them.

52

Bonnie called Mars as Anik drove. "Any movement?"

"Not before six am," Mars replied.

"What do you mean? Aren't you still there?" Bonnie was afraid she knew the answer already, but she'd hoped...

"I had to get to work, Bon. I can tell you he entered the building carpark around seven last night, and he hadn't left either by car or on foot before I called time at six this morning. Sorry, but I'm not on the case anymore. You know that. Cooper would have my balls if he knew where I'd been all night."

"What you do on your own time—"

"Is all well and good unless it affects my ability to do my work," Mars finished. "I can't back up after a night without sleep too often, Bonnie."

"I know. Sorry, Mars. I appreciate it, really I do. Hopefully, we'll find Juliet today and then we can all get some sleep."

"I heard you're on your way to Canberra. You think she's there?"

"I hope so."

Bonnie ended the call and brought Anik up to speed. "It's

almost ten now. So, he could have left for Canberra anytime in the last three or four hours. Dammit."

"Yeah. But we have no reason to suspect he knows where she is, do we?"

Bonnie had spent her own sleepless night trying to answer this very question. On the one hand, Sam Keller was a civilian who didn't have access to phone records and Rail Authority CCTV footage. On the other hand, he was a criminal lawyer with friends in high places and contacts in low ones. The more she thought about it, the more concerned she became for Juliet.

"I'm going to call his office, see if he came in to work today."

She stared out the window as the phone rang. They were on the same highway Sam and Juliet had travelled last Friday night, and Bonnie spotted the police tape still marking the entrance to the dirt road where the couple had spent twenty-two minutes in the dark of the bush. *What had really happened down that road?*

The receptionist at Sam's firm informed Bonnie that Sam had – understandably, of course – taken leave for most of this week. He was dealing only with matters of urgency, and then working from home for most of those matters. She'd only seen him in the office once, looking completely distraught. The woman expressed her deepest hopes that Juliet would be brought home safely into his loving arms very soon. Bonnie thanked the woman and ended the call, shaking her head. How many people did this guy have fooled?

"He's not there," she told Anik. "Working from home on only the most urgent cases, apparently."

"So, he could very well be on his way to Canberra, if he's found out what we have?"

"Let's hope he hasn't," Bonnie replied. "I'm going to try phoning again."

She'd been calling Juliet's new phone number since they'd got it from Pete this morning but so far, no luck. Either the phone had been switched off, or Juliet had discarded it already. Bonnie suspected the former – hopefully Juliet wouldn't have gone to all the trouble to get a new phone if she wasn't going to keep it.

Bonnie had also been calling Max Reeves with the same result, although his number at least rang before switching to voicemail. She left the same urgent message she'd left multiple times for Juliet.

"Why aren't they answering? Or at least calling me back?"

"Do we know where Max works?" asked Anik. "Perhaps you could call the office directly."

"Good idea." Before Bonnie could check through her notes to find Max's place of work, her phone rang.

"I've got her call log," said Nora. Bonnie put her on speaker so Anik could listen in. "Besides a few businesses, the only calls Juliet made were to Max Reeves. You're on the right track, guys. How close are you?"

"Still two hours out," Anik replied.

"Max isn't answering his mobile," said Bonnie. "Do you know who he works for?"

"Hang on a sec." Bonnie heard Nora typing. "Okay, got it. I'll text you the number."

"Thanks, Nora."

"No problem. Here if you need anything else."

Bonnie ended the call. As soon as Nora's text came through, Bonnie called the rather generic-sounding PMC Consulting, only to be told that Max was out on client visits this morning and was only contactable on his mobile. Bonnie expressed how urgent the situation was, and after more convincing than should have been necessary the woman on the other end of the phone promised to do her best to contact Max and have him call Bonnie. Bonnie had her doubts.

"How long?" she asked Anik.

"Five minutes less than the last time you asked. I'm going as fast as I can, Bon. It's not a lights and sirens situation, you know that."

"Yeah, I know."

Bonnie tried to relax. Tried to convince herself that Sam Keller still had no idea where his wife was. That Juliet was safe, Bonnie would get to her first, and they could work together within the system to have Sam held accountable for all of the horrible things he'd done to Juliet.

There were laws against coercive control now. Laws that could protect women like Juliet. Too many women had had to die or have their lives completely ruined by men like Sam Keller in order for these laws to come about. The system was far from perfect, but it was getting better, and Bonnie knew it would be on her side as she did everything she could to prevent Sam ever hurting Juliet again.

As long as Bonnie got to her in time.

53

J uliet ran her hand over the five days' worth of stubbly growth on her head.

"Do you want me to shave it for you?" asked Cai.

"Maybe later," Juliet replied, fixing on one of her new bandannas. She quite liked the orange and yellow tones in this one, although she had to admit she wouldn't have chosen it for herself. Or at least she wouldn't have chosen it for her *old* self. But Cai was all about colour, vibrant purple streaks highlighting her own glossy black hair, so it was no surprise she'd gone out and purchased three of the brightest bandannas Juliet had ever seen.

Cai had been so good to Juliet these last four days, looked after her as if she were a stray dog or fallen bird in need of nursing back to health. It had been a long time since Juliet had been pampered and cared for, and she'd unashamedly allowed it to happen. But she couldn't stay here forever, would need to start her new life soon if she had any hope of surviving – and keeping this friendship intact.

Cai pushed her laptop off her crossed legs and onto the

couch beside her. "It's got to be morning-tea time, don't you think?"

Juliet smiled. "We've only just had breakfast!"

"It's Friday," Cai replied with a wink. "That's close enough to the weekend, right? And weekends are for treats. Like cookies!" She unfolded her legs and headed off to the kitchen, returning minutes later carrying a tray loaded with an assortment of cookies and two steaming mugs of coffee.

"You know how much I appreciate all this, don't you?" said Juliet as she took her coffee and cradled it in her hands.

Cai put the tray down on the couch between them. "Stop it. We've been through this. Any friend of Max's is a friend of mine. And besides, you're famous."

Cai had a wicked sense of humour, which Juliet hadn't known how to take at first but had warmed to now. And it was true, Juliet was famous. Sort of. She'd been all over the news for a few days, not that she'd seen much of it herself. Hiding out in the bush and changing her appearance had been the right thing to do, as it turned out. With all the publicity surrounding her disappearance, it would have been unlikely for her to have made it to Canberra without being recognised.

Now, almost a week after her disappearance, the news stories were less frequent. Sam had been on a few times, appealing for information and saying how he just wanted to know that his 'baby' was safe. *Why, so you can fix that once and for all?* Juliet chastised herself for even thinking of him. This was her shot, her clean break. Sam had been inside her head for too long. He didn't belong there anymore.

She sipped her coffee, picked up one of the choc chip cookies and examined it.

"Speaking of Max," she asked Cai, "is he still coming over today?"

Cai nodded. "Should be here soon. He's got a meeting he

couldn't get out of this morning, but then he said he was taking the rest of the day off. He's very keen to see you."

Juliet couldn't wait to see her friend either. He'd been so great these last few weeks. She hadn't wanted to involve him in her plan, hadn't want to put him at risk. She knew Max's would be the first place Sam would look for her. But when she had to bring things forward, she had no choice but to call him.

He'd thought of everything. "I know just where you can stay," he'd said. "My friend Cai. She's a gorgeous person, loves helping people out. She'll fawn over you, mark my words. And if you go straight to her there's no way Sam can get to you. He doesn't even know she exists."

Juliet hadn't known Cai existed, either. She wasn't sure whether Max and Cai were involved, or just friends, but whatever the relationship status, they were very close. Juliet had hated that her best friend had such a bond with someone and she hadn't known. Hadn't cared enough to know. No, that wasn't true. She cared about Max, of course she did. She cared about all her friends, and her family. That's *why* she'd kept her distance. Sam was her husband. Her mess. Until now.

"He'll come to you," Juliet had said. She couldn't put Max in harm's way.

"Don't you worry about me, I can handle your husband."

Juliet took a bite of her cookie and immediately regretted it. The coffee had been sitting okay, but food was clearly a step too far. She raced off to the bathroom.

When she finally returned to the living room, Cai handed her a cold face washer and a glass of water.

"Thanks." Juliet eased herself back onto the couch.

"How far along are you?"

"That obvious?"

Cai nodded. "It's okay, I won't tell anyone. But one woman to another, you're not going to be able to hide it much longer."

"Yeah. I think I'm about thirteen or fourteen weeks." Juliet took a sip of water and held the washer to her forehead. "It's why I had to leave sooner than I'd planned. I couldn't risk Sam finding out about the baby."

"I hear that. Right piece of work, that husband of yours."

"You're not wrong." They'd avoided talking about Sam during the last four days, an unspoken understanding between them. Juliet didn't want to get into a discussion about him now. She changed the subject. "Any word from Max?" She'd turned her own phone off as soon as she'd made it safely to Cai's place on Monday night. There was no reason to suspect Sam had the number, or even knew the phone existed, but she knew he'd do everything in his power to find her. And with the friends and contacts he'd built up in his world, he had a lot of power. Better to be safe than sorry.

"Not yet," Cai answered. "He said he'd be in that meeting most of the morning, and it's a phones-off situation. I suspect he'll let me know when he's on his way."

Juliet nodded, took another sip of water. Settled back into the couch some more.

Cai took the hint and handed Juliet the TV remote, before folding her legs back underneath her and pulling her laptop back onto her lap. "Put on something funny," she suggested.

Juliet did so and they enjoyed a comfortable companionship, laughing at a nineties sitcom on Netflix, Cai tapping away on her laptop at the same time. They were still there two hours later when Max arrived, laden with bags from both a local takeaway and bottle shop.

"Hey, hey, how're my girls?" He kicked off his shoes and held the food aloft, smiling at Juliet. "You still like Subway, right?"

She beamed back. "Sure. But wine? It's the middle of the day!" She exchanged a glance with Cai, who shrugged.

"That's for later," said Max. "Do I get a hug?"

"Of course." Juliet wrapped her arms around him, felt safe in the embrace of her friend. She hadn't seen Max for so long, but it was like they'd never been apart. How had she let this happen? How had she lost touch with the people she cared about most?

"Stop that," said Max, gently wiping away the tears Juliet hadn't even noticed on her face. Cai silently took the bags from him and he pulled Juliet in close. "You're safe now, kid. He can't hurt you anymore."

Juliet felt Max's phone vibrate in his pocket. She jumped on the chance to lighten the mood. "Ooh, someone's happy to see me."

He pushed her gently away and reached for the phone. "Ugh. Some random keeps calling me. I've been in a meeting all morning!" he yelled theatrically at the phone. "Don't you people know how busy I am!"

Juliet laughed. It was so good to see him.

"I'd better listen to these messages." He called to Cai, who was in the kitchen sorting out the food and putting the wine in the fridge. "You right with all that?"

"It's my house," she called back.

Max rolled his eyes at Juliet, then turned his attention to the phone. He didn't get to listen to the first message before the doorbell rang.

Juliet froze. The door to the little house was solid, so they couldn't see who was there. Max took her hand and led her silently into the front bedroom while Cai came through to answer the door. They'd planned for this, of course. Anyone comes knocking, Juliet was to hide and Cai to answer as normal.

Cai made eye contact with the two of them as she passed. Juliet backed into the bedroom and Max closed the door, then they heard Cai unlocking the front door. As soon as she opened it there was a loud crack as it was flung open and hit the wall behind.

"Who the hell…" Juliet heard Cai say, but there was another crash and Cai screamed.

Max grabbed Juliet and pushed her down behind the bed, but he wasn't fast enough. The door to the bedroom burst open, and Juliet's worst nightmare stood before them, gun in hand.

"Did you really think I wouldn't find you?"

54

Anik pulled up outside Max Reeves's place. It was the second in a row of neat townhouses in a suburb just on the outskirts of the city. It was lunchtime on a Friday, so they didn't expect to find Max at home, but if he'd been hiding Juliet here maybe Bonnie could get her to come to the door.

There was no response the first time she knocked.

"Juliet! Are you in there?" Bonnie identified herself. "It's important we talk to you. You're not in any trouble, you haven't done anything wrong. But you might be in danger."

She waited, nothing.

"Juliet, we think Sam is on his way. We need to get you somewhere safe."

Still nothing.

Bonnie banged again, while Anik tried to find a way around to the back of the row.

"Can I help you?"

Bonnie turned to find a woman in her mid- to late-sixties standing in the doorway of the townhouse next door. She held up her badge. "I'm looking for Max Reeves, or someone he might have had staying with him."

"Max will be at work now," the woman answered. "I don't know about any house guest."

Bonnie showed her a picture of Juliet. "You haven't seen this woman? She'd have short hair now. Really short. Possibly wearing a hat or some other head covering."

The neighbour looked closely, shook her head. "No, I haven't seen her around. Haven't seen anyone with Max for a while, actually. He's a nice young man. Brings my bins in for me every week, even though I tell him not to. I'm quite capable. Is he in trouble?"

"We just need to find him," said Bonnie. "Has anyone else been around looking for Max?" She found a picture of Sam Keller on her phone. "Have you seen this man?"

The woman studied the picture, another head shake. "Sorry. I'm not being much help, am I?"

Bonnie handed over one of her cards. "If you see Max, or either of the people in the photos, please call me immediately."

The woman took the card and held it in front of her with both hands. "I most certainly will, Detective Hunter. I did see a strange car this morning. Is that something that might help? Big black thing, not one of the usual cars parked around here."

"A BMW X5?"

"Oh, I don't know cars, dear, not really. Couldn't tell you a BMW from a Holden, to be honest. It was just big and black, had very dark windows. Looked out of place in this neighbourhood, that's why I noticed when I went out for my walk this morning."

It could be nothing, but Bonnie got a bad feeling. "What time was this?"

The woman thought for a moment. "I left the house just before eight. I know that because I listen to the news headlines on ABC radio at seven-forty-five, and there wasn't much of any interest being said this morning so I left for my walk not long after."

"And you saw the black car then?" According to Mars, Sam was still in Sydney at six am. He couldn't have made it down here in under two hours.

"No, it definitely wasn't here then. It was here when I returned, an hour later. Parked just over there." She pointed to a now vacant spot outside the house on the other side of hers, two doors down from Max's.

"Was there anyone inside the car?" Bonnie felt her heart beat faster. *He could have made it down here in three hours.*

"I'm sorry, dear. I didn't look that close. Like I said, it had very dark windows. I remember thinking I didn't recognise the car, and that I wouldn't like to drive something so big. Too hard to park. I like my little car, a Honda I think it is. My daughter bought it for me last year. But that's beside the point. I just remember seeing that big black thing when I returned from my walk, but then I went inside to feed Sook and didn't think any more about it."

Anik came back around the side of the row of townhouses. "Who's Sook?" he asked.

"My cat," the woman replied. "My granddaughter named him," she added by way of explanation.

"Did you see the car leave?" Bonnie asked. "Did you see Max this morning?"

"No on both counts, I'm afraid. My kitchen is in the back. Once I went through, I fed Sook, made myself some breakfast, and settled in to do the crossword. I didn't see anything else."

Bonnie tried pounding on Max's door and calling out once more, with no answer.

"I could see over the back fence," said Anik. "Place looks empty. No lights on inside, no movement. Maybe she's not here?"

Bonnie felt the eyes of the neighbour on them. She flicked her head toward the car and they retreated, thanking the neighbour for her help.

"Where else could she be?" Anik asked once they were safely out of earshot.

"Let's think," said Bonnie. "Max is her friend from high school. Her family said she hadn't spoken to him for a while, that there was some jealousy between him and Sam, have I got that right?"

"Yeah. Was Max an old boyfriend?"

"I don't think so. But male friend, boyfriend, it doesn't matter for someone as possessive as Sam. Even if there hadn't been anything between them, he'd have thought there was. I'm surprised Juliet came here, to be honest. She'd have to know it would be the first place Sam would look. And if that car this morning was him..."

"Maybe that's why she's not here," said Anik. "I mean, maybe she did know he'd come here."

Bonnie liked his thinking. "So, she got Max to help her hide somewhere else?"

"It's possible."

It was very possible. But it still left them needing to find Max right now, especially if Sam was following him. She took out her phone and called again, same result.

"Try sending a text," said Anik. "He might be screening his calls, but he'll read a text."

"Good idea." Bonnie cursed herself for not thinking of it sooner. "Can you find the names and numbers of Juliet's other school friends while I do that? Perhaps one of them has an idea where Max might be hiding Juliet."

It was Gwen Sneijder who finally gave them the information they were looking for.

"If she's anywhere, she'll be with Cai," Gwen said, after first protesting that Max wouldn't hide Jules without telling her and Tess.

"And who's Cai?"

"Max's girlfriend. Well, sort of. They have this on-again, off-again, casual style of thing going. I don't understand it, really—"

Bonnie cut her off. "Where does Cai live?"

"Ah, I think I've got it here somewhere. I sent a birthday parcel for Max to her address during lockdown because he holed up there with her for some of it. Yes, here you go." Gwen reeled off the address, which Anik punched into the car's GPS.

"Thanks." Bonnie buckled up as Anik took off.

It was a ten-minute drive from Max's to Cai's, and Bonnie spent the time on the phone. First to Nora, asking for as much information on Cai as the technical analyst could find. If Cai was hiding Juliet, Bonnie expected resistance when they fronted up on her doorstep and any inside knowledge Nora could provide would help. Then she called Max's office, asking again for the receptionist to intervene and call Max on her behalf. The woman sighed and informed Bonnie that PMC Consulting was an extremely busy workplace, and Bonnie had to counter with vague threats involving hindering a police investigation before the woman finally agreed to call Max.

Between calls Bonnie kept texting both Max and Juliet, with no response. She finally ran out of patience and shoved the bloody phone in her pocket before trying to calm herself with some deep breaths.

Sam doesn't know where she is. We'll get to her in time.

"That's Max's car," said Anik as he pulled into the driveway behind a red Volkswagen Tiguan. Bonnie was more interested in the black BMW X5 parked on the street out front.

"That's Sam's. Shit."

"Should I call for backup?" asked Anik.

"We're in Canberra," Bonnie replied as she checked her

weapon. "It'll be the Feds. Dammit. Get Cooper on the line, keep it open. He can call if necessary. Hopefully, it won't come to that."

Bonnie opened her car door but stayed seated, assessing the property. It was a free-standing house, small but neatly presented. Max's car in the driveway, another car under a carport farther in. Front door was closed, all the curtains at the front of the house were drawn. The suburb was quiet, most people probably still at work early on a Friday afternoon. This home would seem empty were it not for the cars.

"I'll take the side of the house," said Anik, earpiece in one ear so he could hear their boss. "Coop says be careful. Remember no-one's broken any laws."

Bonnie was about to say 'yet' but was interrupted by the sound of a gun shot from inside the house.

55

"Sam..."

"Shut up." He pointed the gun at her. "Just shut the fuck up and let me think."

Juliet did as she was told. All her planning, her preparation, months of saving, dreaming of a new life, a fresh start, it had all been ripped away seconds ago when her husband shot her best friend.

"He needs an ambulance," said Cai. They were in the living room, Max lying on the floor, Cai kneeling over him with both hands on his stomach trying to stem the flow of blood. Cai's head was bleeding, too, her right eye swelling up where Sam had struck her earlier. Juliet was standing next to them, two steps and yet a world apart.

"No," said Sam. "He needs to learn not to fuck with another man's wife."

"He didn't—" Juliet started before copping the back of Sam's left hand across her face. He was holding the gun in his right, but he'd always been adept at striking her with either. One of his many talents.

"This is your fault," he said, waving the gun over the scene on the floor. "Do you really think I'm that stupid? Of course, you would run to your boyfriend here. Staging that little scene, making it look like you'd been kidnapped by some serial killer." He sneered. "As if any self-respecting kidnapper is going to want you." He looked her up and down. "What the fuck did you do to your hair?" Leaning forward, he ripped the bandanna from her head, then laughed. "Jesus, Jules. You've gone all GI Jane." He held the bandanna out to her. "Here, put it back on. You look ridiculous."

Juliet took the bandanna and carefully tied it back around her head, locking eyes with Cai as she did so. She tried to convey how sorry she was, but she couldn't read Cai's expression. Didn't know if she could ever make up for bringing this monster to their doorstep. *Her* monster.

Cai's eyes slid from Juliet to Sam. "Listen, mate. You've got it wrong. Max is *my* partner. He and Juliet are just friends. That's all they've ever been, as I understand it."

"Is that right?" Sam cocked his head as he looked down on her. "What's your name, sweetheart?"

"Cai." Juliet noticed the woman's body tense ever so slightly.

"Well, Cai. Let me tell you a little something about your boyfriend here. He's had a thing for my wife for as long as he's known her. Isn't that right, Maxxy-boy?" Sam kicked Max's foot. Max, barely conscious now, didn't respond. "Yeah, that's right," Sam answered his own question. "So, Cai, I think you should be thanking me. Now you know the score, you can dump this sorry prick and find yourself a real man."

Sam went on, berating Max and telling Cai how lucky she was to find out the 'truth'. Juliet listened, waiting for her opening. This was how Sam worked. He needed to spew his verbal crap onto his audience – usually Juliet – before he'd calm down enough to be reasoned with. Well, not exactly reasoned with, more like pandered to. But Juliet knew she could talk him down. She'd had five years of practice. She just needed to wait until his anger had run its course.

Unfortunately, Max didn't have that kind of time. The puddle of blood beneath him grew, soaking into the timber floorboards. He coughed, and a trickle of blood escaped his mouth.

Think, Juliet. You know how to deal with Sam. Give him a distraction.

Max was still, too still. His eyes were fully closed now. "I'm pregnant," Juliet blurted, hating herself immediately for the betrayal to her unborn child. But Max and Cai needed help now.

"Juliet! No—"

"Shut up!" Sam interrupted Cai's protest by swinging the gun around and pointing it directly at her head. She raised her blood-stained hands, eyes saucer-wide.

"It's okay," Juliet said, her voice soft. *Stay calm.* She looked down at Max's wound, then back up at Cai. "Put your hands back."

Cai nodded and applied pressure again.

Juliet turned her focus back to Sam, who had resumed pointing the gun straight at her. "They've got nothing to do with this," she said. "Nothing to do with us. Let them go."

Sam ignored her. "You left with my baby?"

There was nothing helpful to say, so Juliet remained quiet. *Answer specific questions only, truthfully if possible.*

"How long have you known?"

"I don't know, not for sure. I mean, I haven't done a test. But I'm pretty sure." That was the truth. She hadn't done a test.

"How long?" Sam pressed.

"About five weeks."

"You're five weeks pregnant, or you've known for five weeks?"

"I've known for five weeks. I think I'm about thirteen weeks pregnant."

"My child," Sam said to himself. His eyes lit up, and for the briefest of moments Juliet thought she had him. Then it was gone.

"You were going to take my child away from me?"

Don't hesitate.

"No, Sam, I would never do that. I just needed a break. Time to think. It's a big deal, having a baby."

"But it's what we've been trying for," he said.

"I know, but..." *Get him to relax, focus on me. Keep Max and Cai out of this.* "Sam, do you think I could sit?"

He thought for a moment, then nodded. Juliet lowered herself to the lounge, slightly exaggerating the movement as if she had a visible baby bump. She made sure to position herself so that Sam's attention was on her, rather than the couple on the floor.

"I just got scared, Sam. I wasn't sure I'd be able to handle it. I'm not as strong as you."

He shrugged. "It's a baby, Jules. What's there to handle? It eats, sleeps, and shits. The first one's easy, you've got its food on tap." He pointed to her breasts, smiling at his cleverness. "We'll get the best damn baby crib and blankets and shit money can buy, so the second one shouldn't be an issue. And any woman can change a fucking nappy. Seriously, Jules. There's nothing to be scared about."

The irony of saying there was nothing to be scared about while waving a gun in her face was completely lost on him.

Agree whenever possible. "You're right." *Make it all about him.* "You always have a way of making me see sense, Sam."

Sam turned and sat on the couch beside her, shaking his head. "You're fucking useless without me, babe. What were you thinking?"

Juliet did her best to appear suitably chastised. A few more minutes of this and he might be calm enough to let them call an ambulance.

"I think it was the hormones," she replied. "They make you do really messed-up things. It was in a few of those baby books we read, remember?"

Sam had only flicked through the half-dozen books on pregnancy and parenthood he'd made her buy, but that didn't stop him professing to know all there was to know on the subject.

"Hormones are funny things," he agreed. He put an arm around her, his gun hand now resting on the couch on his other side. Letting his guard down.

Keep the focus on him, the protector.

Juliet cradled her belly, a pained look flashing across her face.

"Hey, what's wrong?" Sam asked.

"It's nothing. I can handle it."

"It doesn't look like nothing." Sam let go of the gun and turned to face her.

Juliet kept her voice as steady as she could, tried not to look at the gun. "Just morning sickness, I think. I've been sick a couple of times today already." It felt wrong, so wrong to be complaining of morning sickness while her best friend lay bleeding to death on the floor not two metres away. But it was the best chance they all had; the only way Juliet knew how to survive. Make herself small and helpless, make him feel like the hero, and he'll do anything to protect her.

Out of the corner of her eye, Juliet saw Cai slowly moving toward Sam's gun. *No! It's too soon, he's not there yet.* She couldn't convey any of this to Cai, though. Cai didn't understand. No-one understood.

Juliet didn't understand herself, if she was honest. Why?

Why was Sam like this? Why did he shower her with love one minute, and viciously hurt her the next? *You don't hurt the people you love.* Max had told her that once, years ago, not long after Sam and Juliet's wedding day. She hadn't been listening then. It hadn't seemed relevant.

Max saw it before she did. Saw what kind of man Sam was. He'd tried to warn her. She knew that now. Had known it for a long time, on some level. But Sam loved her. He could be kind, and gentle, and caring. He worked hard, they lived in a nice home, had nice things, went on nice holidays.

Nice. It was a word outsiders used. You have such a nice home! Your husband bought you that? Oh, isn't he nice?

No. He's not nice. He beats me. Berates me. Belittles me. Threatens me in that nice home in amongst all those nice things. Makes me sleep on the cold, tiled floor of that nice bathroom when I forget to pick up his dry cleaning.

Cai was inches from them now. She moved slowly, carefully, eyes darting between Sam and the gun, hand reaching forward. Sam was still focused on Juliet, one hand on her belly, the other on her forehead. Maybe this would work. Juliet locked eyes with her husband, willing him to keep looking at her for just a few more seconds. It was everything she could do to not look away, to not look at Cai's outstretched hand behind Sam's back, to not look at the alarming amount of blood coming out of Max on the floor. To just look at Sam, concentrate on him, even though he made her feel sick to her core.

Just a few more seconds.

"Police!"

The shout was accompanied by a loud banging on the door, and everything changed. Sam instinctively reached for the gun, his hand connecting with it at the same time as Cai's. For a nanosecond Juliet thought Cai had beaten him to it, but Sam wrenched it from her grasp and hit her with it in one smooth motion. She fell to the floor with a sickening thud.

When Sam turned back, Juliet knew she'd lost him again.

"Go to hell!" he shouted at the door.

56

"I'm not going anywhere, Sam," Bonnie shouted back through the door. Cooper, on the phone with Anik, had called for backup as soon as they'd heard the shot. Anik was now around the side of the house, assessing whether they could gain access from another door or window. Which left Bonnie at the front door trying to negotiate with a control freak with a gun.

"This has nothing to do with you," Sam called from the other side of the door. "It's between me and my wife."

"We heard a gunshot, Sam. Can't go away until we know everyone inside that house is okay. Is everyone okay, Sam?"

"Everyone that matters."

"That doesn't answer my question. Juliet, are you in there?"

"Max and Cai are hurt." A woman's voice, Bonnie assumed it was Juliet. "We need an amb—" she was cut off by what sounded like a slap.

"Shut up," Bonnie heard Sam say. "I'm in charge here."

"No, I am," said Bonnie. "There's an ambulance on the way, as well as a full contingent of Federal Police, Sam. I suggest you do the right thing here and give yourself up. No-one else needs to get hurt."

"Do the right thing? Are you fucking serious? My wife runs away, pretending to be kidnapped, and you lot accuse me of killing her. I have to come down here and find her myself, and now you think you're going to threaten me? All I'm doing is collecting what's mine. Now fuck off and leave me alone."

Bonnie couldn't help but remember the similar scene she'd found herself in a week ago. Why did so many men think they owned their wives? People are not possessions. A spouse is not someone to control and manipulate. Where was the love? Where was the respect?

"Tell me about Max and Cai," she said.

"They shouldn't have gotten involved," Sam replied. "It's their own fault."

"How are they hurt?"

No answer.

"Sam, you know I can't leave while they're in there hurt. Tell me what's going on."

"Max is shot." Juliet's voice, tentative. "He's lost a lot of blood, I don't think he's conscious."

"Okay," said Bonnie. "And Cai?"

"I'm all right," came a second female voice. "But Max needs help now."

"Help is on the way," Bonnie reassured them.

"Just shut up, all of you!" Sam was losing it. They didn't have much time.

Bonnie couldn't see into the house from this location. The front door was solid, and heavy curtains blocked out the front window. She had to get a better vantage point.

Anik returned from circling the house.

"Anything?" she whispered as he joined her on the front porch.

"There's a window on the side with a partial view of the living room. Can't see Max or Cai, but I got a glimpse of Sam and Juliet. He's got the gun trained on her. We have to be careful here, Bon."

"Tell me about it." She could hear sirens in the distance. "How long until the cavalry get here?"

Anik listened to his earphone for a second. "Two minutes for the ambulance, at least ten for the Feds."

"We need to get Max out of there. Show me this window."

It was an older house, and the sash window was open a fraction at the top which meant if she listened closely, Bonnie could not only see Sam and Juliet, she could hear them, too. Juliet was talking to Sam, trying to calm him down. It was a valiant effort, but Bonnie had been at too many scenes like this. Met too many men like Sam Keller. The time for reason had passed.

"What's the plan?' Anik whispered.

"Is there a back door?"

"Yes, but it's locked."

"Did you look for a key?"

Anik's eyebrows crept up his forehead. "A key? Like a hidden key? No. I'll go check."

As he did so, Bonnie returned to the front door. She didn't want to talk to them through the side window, didn't want Sam to know she could see in.

"Sam, the ambulance is almost here. Things will go a lot better for you if you let us come in so we can treat Max."

Bonnie heard muffled talking, Juliet again. Then Sam, stronger, louder. They seemed to be debating something, rather than arguing. Maybe she was getting through?

"It was self-defence," Sam yelled to Bonnie through the closed door. "He lunged at me, what was I supposed to do?"

Bonnie played along. "I'm sure it will all get sorted out, Sam.

But it'll be much worse if Max doesn't make it. We can't let that happen. *You* can't let that happen."

Anik caught Bonnie's attention from the driveway at the side of the house. He held a key aloft, his face a question.

Bonnie beckoned him over. "It's for the back door?" she whispered, examining the key. The branding on it was different to that on the front door lock. They'd only have one shot at this, so they had to get it right. If Sam heard them trying to get in the door and fumbling with the wrong key, things could get a lot worse than they already were.

"Yeah, looks like it." He pointed to the brand. "Same name on the back door lock. You want me to go in? Coop says it's your call."

Bonnie pointed to the earphone in his right ear. "You got the other one of those?"

He pulled the little white device out of his pocket and held it up. "Only one mic works at a time, though."

"So only one of us can talk, but we can both listen?" Bonnie clarified.

"Yeah."

She pointed to the one in his ear. "Give me the one with the mic."

They got themselves sorted and Bonnie tested the mic. "You there, Coop?"

"I'm here. What's your gut telling you, Bon?"

Bonnie didn't have a chance to answer before Sam called out again. "You still out there, Detective?"

"I'm here, Sam. How's Max?"

"He's, ah, he's not looking too good. How's that ambulance?"

The siren was louder now, and the ambulance turned into the street. Bonnie saw her chance. "The paramedics are here now, Sam. I'm going to go talk to them, and then I'll need you to unlock this door so I can come in and get Max and Cai. Is that something you can do for me?"

"Just you?"

"Yes, just me. All I want to do is get Max and Cai out of there so the paramedics can look after them. Then you and Juliet can sort yourselves out in peace." Bonnie prayed Juliet would understand.

The ambulance pulled up and killed its siren. Bonnie met them in the driveway and signalled for them to meet her at the back of the rig.

"We were told you've got a guy with a gun in there," the more senior of the two paramedics said as she joined Bonnie and Anik on the pavement behind the ambulance.

"Yeah," Bonnie replied. "There's two injured, one gunshot, not sure about the other. You're going to need a second unit."

"Already en route. Five minutes out."

"Good. Here's what I need right now." Bonnie outlined her plan as quickly as possible. After agreements and a few brief instructions one of them handed her a backboard and she was ready to go. Anik retreated to the back of the house.

"You sure about this?" asked Cooper in her ear. "You've got three innocent hostages in there."

"And I have to get them all out now," she whispered out the side of her mouth as she approached the front door again. "He's not going to play ball much longer. You just do your bit, Coop." She pulled her hair out of its ponytail and fanned it out so it covered the earpiece, then removed her service weapon from its holster and tucked it into the waistband at the small of her back. Her jacket should conceal it well enough; she'd just have to hope Sam didn't think to search her. "Sam?" she called to the still-closed door.

Bonnie heard the click of a deadlock, then the door slowly opened a crack. Juliet stood between Sam and the door.

Sam showed her the gun. "One wrong move and I'll end this, Detective."

Bonnie focused on Juliet's face. She saw fear, but suspected it was fear for her friends rather than herself. Underlying the fear was a look of resignation, the same look Bonnie had seen on the face of Rhonda Bessell a week ago.

No. Not happening. She'd be damned if she was going to lose another life to domestic violence. Not today, not on her watch.

She raised her hands as much as she could while still holding the backboard to show Sam she wasn't a threat. "Just here to get Max and Cai out to the ambulance." She tossed her head in the direction of the paramedics, who were waiting as instructed by their vehicle. "Can I come in now?"

Juliet opened the door wider and stepped aside. Bonnie slowly entered the house, carrying the backboard, hands still raised. She desperately wanted to take Juliet in her arms, tell her it was going to be okay, they were going to get her out. What this brave young woman had been through was enough. She didn't deserve to feel trapped for a second longer.

"He's going to be all right, isn't he?" Juliet asked as Bonnie made her way to Max and Cai. Max was lying on the floor, dark red streaks and puddles around him. Floorboards always made it look worse than carpet, because the blood tended to run rather than pool and soak in, but still. It was a lot of blood. Cai was half sitting, half kneeling beside him. She had the beginnings of a black eye and some nasty bruising to her face but appeared conscious and alert. That was good.

"The paramedics are just outside," Bonnie reassured her. "They'll do everything they can to help him."

"Well hurry up and get him the fuck out of here," said Sam. He still had Juliet in front of him, a firm grip on her shoulder with his left hand, gun in her back with his right.

"He's not conscious," said Bonnie, placing the backboard

beside Max. "I can't lift him onto this by myself. You're going to have to help me."

Sam shook his head. "You said you were coming in to get him out. Now get him out!"

"I can help," said Cai.

"Me too," said Juliet.

"No." Sam tightened his grip on Juliet's shoulder. "Just her."

Shit. Bonnie needed him to let go of her if the plan was going to work.

"Okay," she said to Cai. "Can you get his legs?"

Cai shuffled herself down to Max's feet and took hold of his ankles. "Like this?"

"That's it," said Bonnie. "Okay, let's try and lift him onto the board."

Cai picked up Max's legs, but Bonnie struggled with his top half. "He's too big," she said. "Please, Sam, we need help. Just let Juliet lift him in the middle. Five seconds, and it'll be done and Cai and I can carry him out of here."

Sam nodded reluctantly and let go of Juliet's shoulder. She crouched down next to Max and put her hands underneath his torso.

"Okay," said Bonnie. "This is it. I'll count us in. One, two—"

Anik was down the hall and in the living room before she got to three. Bonnie pulled her gun and pointed it steadily at Sam.

"Trust me, I'm a faster and better shot than you," she said.

For a brief moment she thought he was going to shoot. She stared him down, keeping one eye on his trigger finger, ready to act the moment she saw movement.

Anik closed the gap between himself and Sam. "Put it down, mate. It's over."

Sam sneered, looked down at his wife kneeling beside her best friend. "You're not worth it," he said, before handing the gun to Anik and putting his hands on his head.

Juliet stood as Anik cuffed Sam. She met his eyes.
"I'm worth far more than you'll ever know."

57

The smell of disinfectant and blue of the hospital walls took Juliet back to a time and place she didn't care to remember. She pushed thoughts of her broken arm – and the mess that followed – away as she hurried through the corridors.

"Juliet!" Cai called out from a small waiting room that Juliet would have rushed straight past were it not for Cai looking out for her.

"Any news?" Juliet asked.

"Hanging in there. He's in surgery. I'm working on the 'no news is good news' principle."

"He's tough," said Juliet with as much conviction as she could muster. "He'll pull through."

Cai nodded, resumed her seat on the couch. Juliet sat next to her so she wouldn't have to stare at the bruises darkening her new friend's face. Bruises Juliet should have, not Cai.

"How are you?" Cai asked.

"I'm so sorry," Juliet said. "I should never have come to—"

"Stop it," Cai interrupted. "You have nothing to apologise for. He did this. He did all of it, and he's been doing it to you for what... five years? Six?" Cai turned to face Juliet, took both hands in her own. "Promise me you'll stop apologising for that bastard, Juliet. Promise me you'll never apologise for him again."

Juliet nodded, fought back tears. This was the way real people behaved. People who cared for you and loved you. "I promise," she said, and she meant it.

She took in Cai's injuries again, this time with concern. "Have you had someone take a look at that? He... you were hit pretty hard. I'm worried about concussion."

A second ambulance had arrived at the house not long after Sam was arrested, but Cai had insisted on staying with Max. She'd ridden with him to the hospital, while Juliet had given the detectives a brief statement before getting a lift in with an ACT police officer.

"I'm fine. The paramedics checked me out once they handed Max over. I just need to rest for a few days, that's all."

"So, you do have concussion?"

"*Mild* concussion. Not a big deal."

"I'm sor—" Juliet stopped herself in time. Cai was right. She needed to stop apologising for Sam. "What do you think will happen to him?"

"Why don't we ask them?"

Juliet looked up to see Detectives Hunter and Jhaveri approaching the waiting room.

"How is Max?" Detective Hunter asked, her eyes full of concern.

"In surgery," Juliet answered.

"They said it could be a while," Cai added. "But they sounded hopeful."

"That's good news," the detective replied. "And how are the two of you?"

Cai reassured them she was fine, nothing that wouldn't heal. Juliet wasn't really sure yet how she felt, and said as much.

"That's quite normal," said Detective Hunter. "It's going to take time, Juliet. And help. You've been through a lot. You shouldn't deal with all of this on your own. I have some contacts I'd like to put you in touch with, if you'll let me."

Juliet didn't even have to think about it. She'd been alone for too long; she was happy to take all the help she could get. "Thank you, Detective Hunter."

"Please, call me Bonnie. And this here is Anik. I don't think you've been formally introduced."

"Thank you, Bonnie. Thank you, Anik. You both saved my life."

"You saved your life," said Anik. "We just cleaned up a little."

A layer of guilt sat heavily on her shoulders. "I'm sorry for all the trouble I caused. My disappearance. Wasting your time. I just... I didn't know what else to do."

Bonnie tilted her head toward the couches in the waiting room. "Do you mind if we sit? It's been a big day."

The four of them took seats; Juliet and Cai on one couch and Bonnie and Anik on the adjacent one so Bonnie was closest to Juliet. Bonnie leaned forward, elbows resting on her knees, hands clasped together.

"Juliet, I need you to understand something," she began. "I work with the Sex Crimes and Child Abuse Squad. That means I see a lot of cases of family violence. Unfortunately, I come across men like Sam all too frequently. Often, by the time I become involved, it's too late.

"Men like him do not change. No, that's not true. Men like him *can* change if they want to. There are a lot of programs, good programs, in place to help them. But they have to want to change. And in order to want to change, they have to recognise they have a problem."

Juliet shook her head. "Sam... I tried..."

"No." Bonnie was firm. "It's not up to you to try and change him. It's up to him. And from what I saw today, Sam was not one of the ones who wanted to make that happen. And men like that, they don't get better. They don't stop the abuse. They escalate."

Juliet knew what Bonnie was trying to say. Knew she had to admit it to herself. "He was going to kill me."

Bonnie nodded. She reached out and took Juliet's hands in hers. "It was only a matter of time. Juliet, you did the right thing. *How* you did it doesn't matter. You got away, and you survived. And you never have to apologise for that."

Juliet turned to her new friend on the couch next to her. "That's what Cai said."

"Damn straight," Cai agreed. "So, what's going to happen to him now?"

"Sam has been arrested for unlawful imprisonment and attempted murder," said Anik. "And that's just for starters on what he's done down here."

"Will I need to go to court?" Juliet asked.

"That will be a long way down the track, if ever," said Bonnie. "He'll be charged with some serious crimes for his actions today."

Juliet's thoughts turned to Max, lying on an operating table right now, fighting for his life. Sam would pay for that, as he should. She looked at Cai's injuries, the hurt he'd caused her, a woman he didn't even know. Cai would stand up to him in court. He'd pay for hurting her, too.

"You won't need to worry about him anymore," said Bonnie.

"No," said Juliet. "But I do need to worry about others like him. Others like me."

"That's not your job," said Cai.

"It should be somebody's. My face has already been all over the news, right?"

Bonnie nodded. "Technically you were a missing person, so

the media didn't protect your identity as they normally would have a victim of domestic abuse."

She said it as if she were sorry, but Juliet wasn't sorry. Maybe this was what she was meant to do. "Now's not the time, but can I come and see you one day soon, Bonnie?"

"Of course. But what…" Bonnie trailed off, and Juliet looked up to see two doctors in blue scrubs approach the waiting room.

Cai leapt to her feet. "Is he…"

The older of the surgeons nodded. "He's okay. He lost a lot of blood, but the bullet missed everything vital. We were able to repair the damage. My colleagues are just finishing up now. He should make a full recovery."

Bonnie's phone rang, and she and Anik stepped out while she took the call. The surgeon gave Cai a few more details on Max's expected recovery and when she could see him, then they left and Bonnie returned.

"Juliet, your family are on their way. They can't come to the hospital, COVID protocols. In fact, we should probably get you out of here as well. Essential personnel and one visitor per patient."

"I understand," said Juliet. She gave Cai a hug. "Say hi to Max for me."

"I will." Cai squeezed Juliet's arms and held eye contact for a moment longer. "Don't be a stranger. But perhaps a little less drama next time you visit, yeah?"

Juliet smiled properly for the first time in months. Maybe even years. "You bet."

58

B onnie heard the clatter of four sets of child footsteps race to the door before she even rang the bell.

"Bonnie!" Grace and Charlotte echoed from behind their brother as Michael pulled the door open. Patrick brought up the rear, wincing at the high-pitched shrieks of his sisters.

"Hello, Cooper Clan!" Bonnie gave them all hugs, lingering over nine-year-old Patrick. She pointed to his cochlear implant. "How's it going?"

He shrugged, signed his response. *Baby steps, Dad said.*

He's smart, your dad, Bonnie signed back.

Patrick smiled, took her by the hand, and led her through into the kitchen where his parents were busy laying out food. The rest of the kids had disappeared as fast as they'd appeared.

"You made it," said Liz, coming over to give Bonnie a hug. "Oh," she paused, arms in the air. "Are we hugging? I never know these days."

"Had my booster a couple of weeks ago. I think we're good." Bonnie accepted the warm embrace. "Besides, your kids have already been all up in here."

"Can't stop them," said Liz with a shrug.

"Don't want to," Cooper added, coming in for his own hug. "You good?"

Bonnie answered with a nod. It had been quite an interesting week since their confrontation with Sam Keller. Juliet had not shied away from the spotlight. After a long chat with both Bonnie and a liaison officer from one of Sydney's biggest women's shelters, she'd been adamant that she wanted to use her experience to help other women like herself. She'd already done one interview with a national current affairs program, and answered as many questions as she could without jeopardising the legal proceedings against Sam. There was obviously a long way to go, but judging by the way she'd conducted herself, Bonnie felt Juliet Keller – Juliet Wilson – was going to be a force in the fight against domestic abuse for a long time to come.

Bonnie looked around. The kids had resumed their game outside, taking advantage of the sunny winter's day. Anik was chasing the girls around the backyard, while Kate, Mars, and another man sat at the outdoor table deep in conversation. "Thanks for this. Good to get out of the house."

"Yeah," Cooper replied. "Thought it was time I started having the team over again. Speaking of the team—"

"Where's Deadpool?" Bonnie interrupted, not yet ready for what she was sure he'd been about to ask.

"I have no idea why they're okay with that nickname," said Cooper, shaking his head.

"Are you kidding?" said Anik, who'd chased the girls inside and now stopped to catch his breath. "They love it. I'm a genius."

Cooper bent to pick up one of the twins, giving her an exaggerated eye roll in the process. "What do you think, Gracie? Is Anik a genius?"

"What's a genius?" Grace asked.

"A very clever person," Michael answered. "Right, Dad?"

Cooper ruffled his son's hair. "Right. Like all of my kids. Geniuses, every one of you."

"I'll drink to that," said Bonnie as Liz handed her a glass of wine. They all stepped outside and the adults joined the others at the table while the kids started a game of something involving a ball and a convoluted series of moves in the garden.

"What are we drinking to?" asked Mars, raising his glass.

"A successful case," said Cooper. "Well done, team. Speaking of team…"

"Yeah, where are Nora and Zach?" asked Liz with a wink at Bonnie. "I haven't seen them for ages."

"They'll be here a little later," Cooper answered. "Why does everyone keep interrupting me?"

"Because you're trying to ask Bonnie to join Homicide, and she's not ready to give you an answer," said Anik. Everyone stared at him. "I told you. Genius. I don't know why you all keep doubting it." He smirked and swigged his beer.

The man Bonnie didn't know leaned forward and held out a hand to her. "I'm Harvey," he said as they shook.

"My other half," said Mars, slipping an arm around Harvey's waist.

"Bonnie. Great to meet you."

"So, I'll ask, then," said Harvey. "Why aren't you ready to join Homicide?" He was rewarded with a playful slap from Mars. "What? You all want her on the team, right?"

Bonnie had to admit, she was interested to hear the answers to that.

"Of course, we do," said Kate. "Well, I do. There was too much testosterone around the office before Bonnie came along." She turned to Mars. "No offence."

"Plenty taken," he replied with mock horror. "Yes, I would

like Detective Hunter to join Homicide, because I like nothing more than staking out a suspect's apartment all night and then backing up for work the next day as if I'd had a solid eight hours."

"That was you who made him do that?" asked Harvey.

"I didn't *make* him do anything," Bonnie countered, kicking Mars under the table. "He offered. And that was supposed to be between us."

"We don't keep Cooper out of the loop," said Mars, serious now. "On anything."

"Yeah," Kate agreed. "Homicide 101, dude. You're going to need to learn that one quickly."

"If you agree to join us," said Anik. "Which you haven't yet."

"*You* haven't answered Harvey's question yet," said Bonnie. "Do you want me on the team?"

Anik shrugged. "More the merrier, I say. And you weren't bad to work with. Only mildly annoying at times."

"Oh, only *mildly* annoying. I'd have to work on that, then." Bonnie sipped her wine, helped herself to the cheese platter in the middle of the table. She was aware all eyes were on her.

Liz came to her rescue. "Leave Bonnie alone, the lot of you. You won't get her to agree by pressuring her, I've told you that. She'll make her mind up in her own time. Won't you, Bonnie?"

Bonnie was actually wondering how much longer she could string this out. She'd already made her decision. Made it the moment she'd cuffed Sam Keller and handed him over to ACT Police. She was proud of her time with the Child Abuse and Sex Crimes Squad, but it had never felt like a team. As much as she loved working for Carmel Johnson, the rest of the squad had seemed like a procession of losers and idiots.

Some of that was her fault, of course. An old sergeant had once described Bonnie as 'diligent and thorough, but controlling and temperamental. Does not play well with others.' She couldn't argue with that. But some of the members of that squad...

Bonnie looked around the table. These were good people. People who worked well together. They worked hard, and they were good at what they did. And they were led by a guy who'd been to the brink and pulled himself back. A man Bonnie admired as much as a person as she did a police officer. The chance to work with a team like this was not an opportunity that would come along too often.

"I talked to Johnson yesterday," said Cooper. "Again. She's ready to sign off on making your move to Homicide permanent."

"Oh, for goodness sake," said Mars. "Put the man out of his misery or the rest of us'll never hear the end of it." He pointed the cheese knife at her in a mock-threatening manner. "You owe us, Bonnie."

"What for?"

"Unauthorised all-night stakeouts, for one."

"Freezing cold treks in the bush," Anik added.

"Making me partner with Mars," said Kate.

"Oh, well in that case..." Bonnie turned to Cooper. "All right, fine. I'll join Homicide on one condition."

He eyed her warily. "What's that?"

She raised her glass and circled it in the air in a salute to all of them. "We do this more often."

"Done," said Cooper. He leaned forward. "Seriously? You're in?"

Bonnie grinned. "I am. It's about time I was part of a real team."

"Finally," said Anik. "Can we light the barbie? I'm starving."

* * *

Thanks for reading Bonnie's story. If you'd like to see where it all began for Charlie Cooper, and find out what happened to his Homicide Squad, visit my website or your favourite store to check out the Detective Charlie Cooper Mysteries.

www.catherineleeauthor.com

AUTHOR'S NOTE

I realise MISSING is a difficult book to read in places, so I thank you for getting to this point. I can tell you it was also a very difficult book to write. Doing the research for this story was truly awful. I abandoned or almost abandoned this project many times.

I cannot imagine living in fear in the one place you're supposed to feel safe. Living in fear of the person who is supposed to love you the most. It's just unthinkable to me.

Writers write to make sense of things they don't understand. I will never understand people who bring harm to those they are supposed to love, but writing MISSING has been my little way of doing something. Saying something. I am in no way qualified to tell this story, but I hope I've done it justice in some small way. Thank you for reading.

ALSO BY CATHERINE LEE

The Detective Charlie Cooper Mysteries

Novels:

Dark Heart

Dark Past

Dark Secrets

Dark Chemistry

Dark Edges

Dark Country

Dark Justice

Novellas:

Dark City

Dark Paradise

The Detective Bonnie Hunter Thrillers

Missing

The Getaway Bay Cozy Mysteries

Arson at the Art Gallery

The Body in the Beach House

The Corpse at the Carnival

Death at the Dog Show

Evil at Echo Point

The Fatality at the Funeral

Printed in Great Britain
by Amazon